THE
BORDER
LINE

THE
BORDER
LINE

by

Walter S. Masterman

RAMBLE HOUSE

ISBN 13: 978-1-60543-416-2

ISBN 10: 1-60543-416-7

Cover Art: Gavin L. O'Keefe
Preparation: Fender Tucker

DANCING TUATARA PRESS #6

KILLER, DILLER, CHILLER, THRILLER— HERE TONIGHT
Walter S. Masterman

The book that you hold in your hands has a fairly quirky background even amidst the rest of *Ramble House's* publications, (most of which can be said to have pretty quirky backgrounds). When Fender, Gavin, and myself decided to launch *Dancing Tuatara Press*, one of the authors that I had under consideration to include in the program was Walter S. Masterman. However, Fender had already beaten me to the punch and issued several of Masterman's novels! As these titles did not include introductions, this introduction will not only discuss the title at hand, but also attempt to provide some overall context for Masterman's place in the annals of weird and detective fiction.

Now that we're used to not only seeing "horror" as a market category, but also "quiet horror", "splatterpunk", "supernatural romance", "weird menace", "SF horror", and as many other micro genres as one can imagine; it might be hard to visualize a time when all of the above were simply called "thrillers". The micro genres can be traced back to the U.S. pulps of the 1930s, where there was seemingly a pulp for every specialized interest imaginable. Even though this fragmentation was well underway, magazines such as the U.K.-based *Hutchinson's Mystery Magazine* and the U.S.-based *Weird Tales* served up a wide variety of fiction, wherein the reader was never quite sure what he was getting into until finishing the story!

This same attitude was reflecting by the British book publishers who targeted their wares to the lending libraries and several notable authors rose to the occasion, turning out a high volume to titles that ran the entire gamut as listed above. This group of authors included Edmund Snell, James Corbett, Ronald S.L. Harding, Arlton Eadie, and the present subject, Walter S. Masterman. Of this group, Masterman is likely the most familiar name to the modern reader, due in large part to being cited twice on Karl Edward Wagner's list of the thirty-nine best horror novels; once for "Supernatural Horror" with *The Yellow Mistletoe* and once under the category of "Science Fictional Horror" with *The Flying Beast*; (both titles available from *Ramble House*).

Perhaps no other author epitomized the eclectic nature of the British thriller better than did Masterman, beginning his career with the ingenious (if prosaic) mystery *The Wrong Letter*, which featured a laudatory introduction by no less a luminary than G.K. Chesterton, the author of the "Father Brown" mysteries; and quickly progressing to the rationalized supernatural horror of *The Green Toad* to the his first full-blown supernatural novel, *The Yellow Mistletoe.*

What was truly unique about Masterman's novels was the frequency with which he utilized a recurring main character in a wide variety of stories. Sir Arthur Sinclair of Scotland Yard is introduced in *The Wrong Letter*, and weaves his way through several additional novels ranging from the straightforward mysteries to his masterpieces of over-the-top mayhem like *The Flying Beast* and *The Yellow Mistletoe.*

To use a reference point from the realm of science fiction, Sir Arthur is Robert Heinlein's competent man cast in detective. Not only is he a master of ratiocination, but if the occasion warrants, also a man of action. If there's a criticism, it would be that as he character evolves, the more mundane sort of mystery doesn't seem to pose much of a problem; Sinclair needs the larger stage of globe-trotting adventure in order to really shine. It's in novels of the fantastic such as *The Yellow Mistletoe* (wherein Sinclair not only encounters a lost race, but winds up as their leader!) and the equally bizarre novel featuring a gothic mansion, super science, and a race of troglodytes (*The Flying Beast*) where both Sir Arthur and the author are at their best.

After his sojourn in Bulgaria, Sinclair returns in several more adventures, but he's not the only character of Masterman's to encounter the outré. We have Inspector Jackson dealing with the seemingly supernatural menace of *The Green Toad* (1929); and the present title featuring Inspector Dick Selden of Scotland Yard. While Selden is a much younger man than Sinclair, he displays the same gifts for detection and the vigor to deal with the multiple murders committed at Cold Stairs.

As many readers of Masterman know, his present day fame is due in large part to the inclusion of *The Flying Beast* and *The Yellow Mistletoe* on both the Wagner List and in *333*. For those not familiar with *333*, it is an early (1953) reference work compiled by Joseph Crawford, James Donahue, and Donald M. Grant, subtitled "A Bibliography of the Science Fantasy Novel". Of course, it covers three-hundred and thirty-three books; and despite over fifty years having elapsed since its publication, it remains remarkably useful even today. However, there are some curious omissions, among them being what is arguably one of Masterman's very best novels, *The Border Line*.

So how did this remarkable book get overlooked by these early scholars and by the very knowledgeable Mr. Wagner? I think we may well have the same situation here that I discussed in the case of Mark Hansom, (a contemporary of Masterman's, who has one selection on the Wagner list, and is omitted from *333* entirely). Many of the British thrillers were targeted to the lending libraries; a situation that had the advantage of reaching a wide audience, but also had some huge disadvantages for the modern collector. Standard procedure for new acquisitions included not only gluing card pockets and placing the library's stamp throughout, but also removing the dustjacket and discarding it. From that point on, the books were in for rough handling and many volumes were literally read to pieces. Thus, in the case of Masterman's 1930s titles, enthusiastic readers destroyed the majority of copies.

However, this doesn't account for the U.S. editions published by E.P. Dutton; we can only assume that with the plethora of domestic mysteries issued by this publisher, the U.K. reprints had comparatively small printings. However, when we look at scarcity in regards to Masterman's works, all of these titles that received simultaneous U.K./U.S. publication are still far more common than his last six novels, all of which were published only in British editions.

These last six books are impossibly rare; in twenty-odd years of collecting and researching Masterman, I have only seen one (*The Death Coins*) offered for sale. To my knowledge, only the British Library holds copies of the other titles, which is a shame, as in summary these titles sound very promising. Interestingly enough, after introducing a younger detective in the present book (Inspector Dick Selden), Masterman drops him and returns to using Sir Arthur Sinclair in his last six novels. For those of you who finish this volume wanting to see more of Inspector Selden, have just a bit of patience; Inspector Selden makes his return in the novel I'm currently working on. The book is a direct sequel to Richard E. Goddard's *The Whistling Ancestors*, but also links to Mark Hansom's *The Wizard of Berner's Abbey* and Clark Ashton Smith's "The Colossus of Ylourgne".

The Hooded Monster (Feb 1939)
The Curse of Cantire (Apr 1940):
The Death Coins (May 1940)
Back from the Grave (Nov 1940)
The Silver Leopard (Jul 1941)
The Man Without a Head (Mar 1942)

Their rarity and possibly that of the British edition of *The Border Line* (1937) has an explanation which goes far beyond the lending library scenario. In the case of the first five, we know that among the many targets destroyed in the Blitz, the warehouse district took a particularly hard pounding and this was the site where thousands upon thousands of new books awaiting shipment were stored. This would account for titles published through 1941 and for the unsold inventory of the earlier books. In the case of the 1942 novel *The Man Without a Head*, it was probably a victim of both wartime paper shortages and the public's diminished interest in the grim and grotesque amid the all-too-real horrors of war.

We can also promise that the search for these books continues and that when they eventually turn up, you can be assured that new editions will be issued under the *Dancing Tuatara Press* imprint. However, for the time being, I'm delighted to bring you this novel of murder, intrigue, and science gone horribly wrong. Enjoy!

John Pelan
All Hallows — 2009

THE
BORDER
LINE

PROLOGUE

The doctor stared moodily into the fire, where flickering blue flames started up like tongues and then disappeared in puffs of smoke. His massive head was cupped between his strong hands, and his elbows were firmly planted on his knees. Not a movement betrayed the fact that he was listening with painful intensity to the halting words of his young wife's confession.

Not a sign as she poured out her shameful tale. Standing with hands clasped behind her back like a schoolgirl before her mistress, panting now and then, as though the effort strained her heart.

It was a common enough story. He had been away for two years—such a long time—in New Guinea on a scientific expedition. For two long years she had received no letter as the party had been buried in the interior, and then they had been reported dead! It was harder for a young married woman in such circumstances than for a girl, she pleaded, though that was no excuse. . . .

All this came out in stilted sentences, while the blue tongues leapt and flickered, and the man sat like a stone image. Her voice trailed off into silence at last, and she waited. The bright autumn sunlight fell across her white face, seeming an insult; such a story belonged to the dark.

She waited for his verdict and sentence. She remembered his icy nature and iron will, which had only thawed with his overwhelming passion for her.

He had even neglected his scientific investigations for her during the brief year of marriage before he had gone off abroad.

He would never forgive; she was quite certain of that. He might kill her in some subtle scientific manner, perhaps with those poisonous snakes he had brought with him. She was prepared to face that, but her mind was tormented with worse possibilities than death. She recalled only too vividly the awful bleeding remnants that his assistant had carried from his laboratory and buried in the garden at night time. And what of the unborn child?

He raised his head slowly, like one of his snakes, and she saw the dull lifeless eyes, half covered by drooping eyelids. There was no trace of emotion, neither hate nor scorn or even humanity. And then he laughed, a dreadful harsh sound that sent a thrill of horror through the woman.

"The name of the man?" he rapped out.

She remained silent, and he waited a full minute.

"I understand; you will at least tell me this: Would he marry you if you were free?"

"I do not know—I don't think he would."

For one second there came into the man's eyes a look hard to describe, a gloating look of something like triumph, worse than hate or mere anger.

"The child, then," he said very slowly, "will legally be mine."

Her hands clutched her throat, and she reeled with sudden terror.

"Go to your bedroom. I will talk to you presently when I have thought the matter over."

She turned to the door, but the strain had been too great. She faced round, holding out her arms, imploring.

"What are you going to do?"

"I do not wish for any scene, please," he said, coldly polite. "This must of course be hushed up. There must be no scandal that would affect my work or position in the scientific world. I do not particularly care to be made a laughing stock among my friends. The absent husband and the faithful wife. Fortunately, as a doctor I can attend to you myself."

Something of the awful meaning underlying the words gripped her, and she crept from the room weak and trembling.

Later on, when the light had gone from the sky, and she lay in a dry fever on her bed, she heard him enter her room and close the door behind him. With a numb sense of dread she saw that he carried a bright metal case, which he laid on the table by her side.

He spoke in a dry hard voice. "This will give me the opportunity for which I have been waiting for years. I have given the servants a month's notice with pay, telling them that we are going on a holiday." Her beseeching eyes were on him, and his voice seemed to come from a long way off.

"I could not find a woman who would volunteer, and one who had been paid might indulge in blackmail. No harm will come to you, you may make your mind easy on that point. When the experiment is over, I shall return to my work abroad, and—watch results." He switched the reading light on above her bed, and tapped the metal case.

"I shall inject a certain serum that I have prepared into you. There will be no deleterious effects, in fact it will increase your vitality, and improve your health."

"But the child?" she whispered through bloodless lips.

"That is another matter. As far as I know it may produce a genius, a superman. On the other hand it may have queer results."

"No!" the woman shrieked. "I would rather kill myself."

"Do not be theatrical. There is no one in the house; and if you cry out it will do no good. If you make trouble, I shall have to give you a whiff of chloroform, and keep you under drugs until the experiment is over."

She saw him approach the bed, and turn down the bedclothes. He selected a place on her thigh where there were no nerve endings, and painted the spot with iodine. She felt no pain as the hypodermic syringe was pressed home and withdrawn.

"There, that will do," he said professionally. "I shall give you an injection each day. You *will* remain here, and either I or my native servant will remain with you, and bring you your meals. I have announced that you have gone away on a holiday, and will not be back until"—he paused and looked at her—"for some time."

He picked up his case without another word, and left her, and the Malay servant he had brought with him slipped silently into the room, and sat by the window, watching her with sombre eyes.

Every day the horrible process was repeated, and though her whole soul revolted against it, a strange sense of exhilaration, which she fought against with all her might, possessed her being.

Only once during those tortured weeks did he speak to her upon the subject.

"If ever you try to escape from me now, please remember that the results will be disastrous. I cannot tell what may happen with an incompleted experiment. You must go through it to the end."

She woke one night to find herself alone, and, in spite of his words, thoughts of escape came to her mind. She rose unsteadily and dressed. If only she could get away from this hateful place!

And then the door opened and the Malay came in, shaking with fear. In broken English he imparted his story. Her husband had been working in his laboratory, experimenting with the snake venom he had brought back with him, when a test tube had broken in his hand. He had severed his thumb as his only hope, and let the blood flow freely, but it had been too late. The poison had done its work, and when the Malay had come in answer to frantic ringing his master lay dead on the floor.

The servant only waited to tell his story, and then fled, fearing that he would be accused of murder.

Relief and horror struggled in the woman's mind. She hastily packed what few things she required, and the little money she had of her own. Then she removed all signs of her occupation of the room, and hurried from the house.

CHAPTER I

ℭHE HAUNℭED HOUSE

T HE BIG NOB AT THE B.B.C. was speaking.

"I don't like it, Hartley. We've tried these experiments before, you know; broadcasts from haunted houses. If nothing happens the public get annoyed, and I rather suspect that if anything remarkable did happen, the same public would declare it a fake, like our coconut shells for horses' hoofs."

He smiled a little bleakly at the eager face of the young man, and, adjusting his glasses, picked up the report he had been reading. Hartley's face fell; he had taken a lot of trouble over this scheme. "But, sir," he said, pleading, "this case is rather different. It has already been tested most thoroughly, by a committee of the Psychical Research Society, and there is abundant evidence that something is happening at Cold Stairs."

"So I observe from the report." Hartley went on rapidly, fearing his pet scheme would be turned down. "Sir John Harman, the owner, is the very last type of person to attempt a fraud. He's a jolly sort of country squire, not over-gifted with brains I should imagine. He's not the least disturbed by the manifestations, and simply laughs at any ghost theory. It was only because the people round there are very superstitious, and got to know of these rumours, that he wanted to scotch them.

"That's why he allowed the Committee of Three, as I call them, to investigate."

"So I see." The Big Nob glanced through the report. "They claim to have got results of sorts."

"I was down there, sir, with them," Hartley said in a graver tone than he had adopted. "There's something there, though what it is I can't make out."

"Probably one of the servants skylarking, or a loose joint in the water pipes."

"Everything was carefully tested," Hartley persisted. "There's only Mrs. James, an elderly respectable governess to Sir John's young niece, and her crippled son, a lad of about sixteen, and the small staff of servants. Sir John is seldom at the place except in the shooting season." The Big Nob smiled at Hartley's enthusiasm. "The people composing the Committee are all above reproach. Professor Johnson has a universal reputation, and though he may be a crank on Spiritualism, no one can deny his scientific attainments. Then Mrs. Seaton is a woman of means, and never takes any fees as a medium. She is quite sincere in her desire to get into touch with her late husband; that is why she became a member. The other, Stevens, is a hard-headed business man, and edits the *Weekly Aura.*"

"A formidable trio," the Big Nob said with a touch of irony.

"There was the children's evidence; but that we took with reserve. Still, they knew nothing about spooks. A year ago, Eric James came shrieking from his room, and fell down the stairs, injuring his back. He told his mother he had seen something awful that had alarmed him and was in a state of abject terror."

"Pork for supper," the Big One said scornfully.

"The girl was not frightened; she seems more level-headed, and almost took everything for granted."

The Big Nob moved restlessly in his chair.

"Children's testimony, my dear fellow."

"But our experiments, sir—I mean when I went with the Committee. We all heard someone moving about and a sound of crying. Every precaution was taken against fraud."

"And no explanation?"

"It wasn't a woman crying," Hartley said gravely, "but like a soul in hell."

"Here, steady, my boy; you're getting melodramatic."

Hartley hastily changed his tactics. "The Committee were not in the least upset; that's the trouble. They took it as a natural phenomenon and talked a lot of nonsense about 'presences' and beings that had been half released from their natural bodies and couldn't get back. They didn't even try to find a rational solution."

"Well," the Big Nob said, gathering the report together, "your Committee seems to have made out a *prima facie* case, but I'm not going to risk a fiasco like the song of the Nightingale, and one or two others. I quite realize that thousands of people are interested in Spiritualism. Send Professor Johnson along, and I'll have a talk. If I am sufficiently interested, we'll try it out, but only as an experiment, Hartley, remember. You can go there and make the necessary arrangements for a private trial. I'll have it switched through on the land lines, and listen. If there's really something in it, we might put it on the programme. That's all I can do for you at present."

Hartley thanked his chief; he knew exactly how far to go, and went out as the Big Nob pressed a bell for the next interview.

The young wireless engineer took his way to the strange den where he lived with his old Cambridge friend, Dick Selden. Both men had loathed the idea of a flat when they had set up house together, and lodgings were equally objectionable.

Selden had graduated through the Police College, and already made a name for himself in the Severinge case. Both were carefree, eager young men, with a saving gift of humour.

In their search for a suitable abode, they had come across an old dusty disused yard tucked away behind one of the most disreputable streets of Soho. Being a cul-de-sac, it was of little use to anyone, and they were able to secure it for a modest sum. One side was an old Mews, which was converted into a set of rooms communicating with each other, and the cobbled yard became a garden of shrubs and plants in tubs. The old rickety gate was replaced by a door, and their furniture, retained from their rooms at Cambridge, sufficed for all needs. Not a luxurious place, and never tidy, but a home. Mrs. Perks, an Irishwoman addicted to strong drink, and shoplifting, whom Selden had discovered singing loudly outside their door at twelve o'clock, came each day and looked after their needs, and up till the time of the conversation recorded above had proved trustworthy and honest while in the place.

Selden was sitting in their joint study, dining-room, and lounge combined when Jack returned from the B.B.C.

To anyone familiar with the old type of police officer his appearance would have given a shock. Slightly built and of middle height, he concealed an athletic body trained like a greyhound, and with strength of wrist and arm far above the average. Reddish tousled hair and blue-grey eyes did not suggest the relentless sleuth of fiction, and his bright smile hid a firm mouth.

In amateur theatricals and even in the sterner game of discovering criminals, he had sometimes assumed the costume of a woman with success. His chief at the Yard thought highly of him, and was watching his career with interest, as he was one of the first products of the new system of training, as intense and wide as that in any other profession.

He listened eagerly to Jack's report.

"I'm in this with you, mind. Unofficially, of course, but it sounds quite good."

"We agreed on that," Jack replied. "Who knows? There may be something in your line."

Dick grinned. "Everything is in my line. I have already attended spook meetings, and studied spiritualism in all its branches."

Jack grunted. "Is there anything at all that you haven't studied at your precious college?"

"A few things may have escaped our notice." The dancing eyes belied the conceit of the words.

"Brainy fellow, aren't you?—anyway, we are going to make a start now in earnest. Old Dogsbody is as obstinate as a mule, but I think I convinced him."

"Then the next thing is something to eat."

The old manor house of Cold Stairs might have been constructed especially for a Hollywood film. It was incredibly old, built of grey stone, and nearly covered with ivy and creepers that clung like withered shrouds round a dead man. It stood on the very edge of the great forest in that mysterious borderland between England and Wales over which for centuries bitter tribal warfare had been waged. Far below was the beautiful valley of the Wye, half hidden by trees.

The great forest was its background, impenetrable and secret, a monument to foresight gone wrong. An English Government had bought it in the time of the Napoleonic wars, for its oaks, wherefrom to build stout men-of-war, ships of the line, and frigates to fight the French. But iron and steel had long ago rendered oak obsolete. In grading penitence the forest had made partial reparation, yielding coal and iron, and deep mine shafts had been driven into the forest clearings.

The grim, dark woods and low, broad mullioned windows rendered Cold Stairs gloomy even on a sunny day, and it stood isolated, for the nearest village of Lydford lay five miles away, as though shunning closer proximity.

The scattered inhabitants of the district, descendants of charcoal burners or robbers, clung to their mouldering cottages, scratching a living somehow, as though afraid to dwell in the haunts of men, or had migrated to the mining centres for work.

Here was the very home of legend and ancient faiths, long ago crushed out from the town dweller by the inventions of modern times. Strange tales were whispered round firesides on winter nights, of things not human that haunted the forest depths, and of children who had strayed in the woods, and returned incurable idiots, babbling of dreadful things.

For centuries the Harmans had lived and died in the old place, in isolation and poverty, scraping a scanty living from the poor lands and meagre rents. The estate had gone from father to son in an unbroken line, for they had bred large families. But as in the days of the Patriarchs, they had been compelled to wander off into foreign lands to seek a bare living. Soldiers, sailors, adventurers, and pirates they had been, seeking fortunes that always eluded them.

John Harman, the last of the line, was no exception. Too poor as a younger son to follow a profession, he had accepted an invitation to go to Assam, tea-planting. He had enjoyed life as a young man of mettle to the full, but as a businessman had proved a complete failure. One after another his brothers had been killed—the war had taken toll of three—and he found himself the heir to the baronetcy.

And then a miracle had happened. Some enterprising engineer had discovered coal under the Harman estates; not a rich vein, but sufficient to save the impoverished property and turn poverty into comparative affluence. John heard the news in distant Assam, and hurried home at his father's urgent request.

But fate, which gives with one hand and takes with the other, dealt him a last blow, for his father died before he reached England, leaving a baby girl, the only survivor of his daughter's death.

So much for the family history; enough for the telling of this tale. John returned a baronet, master of Cold Stairs, and with an income of which he had only dreamed in his boyhood days.

He was not a man to allow the gloom of the old place to depress him. Electric light from his own plant replaced the old oil lamps, and wireless and a telephone were installed.

A governess, Mrs. James, was placed in charge of Sybil, his niece, and he retained the staff of servants. He had no intention of taking up his permanent residence at Cold Stairs, but spent most of his time in London, which was more to his taste, returning for the shooting and hunting.

Young Hartley, then at the beginning of his career as a wireless engineer, had installed the wireless, and it was a casual remark made by Sir John that fired the train which was to lead to such fatal consequences. Sir John had mentioned the queer noises in the house and the stories that were frequently being circulated among the forest dwellers, and had jokingly remarked that perhaps the wireless would put an end to the ghost. In an unguarded moment Hartley had repeated this to Professor Johnson, whom he had met in connection with a somewhat similar ghost story which the Professor had wished to have broadcast.

And so it came about that the Committee of Three had descended upon Cold Stairs, to Sir John's annoyance.

His easy-going nature was soon persuaded to acquiesce, and, once he had agreed, he threw himself into the scheme with enthusiasm. His position as a county magistrate enabled him to enlist the services of the police in a semi-official capacity, in order to ensure complete privacy and prevent fraud.

During the test there was to be the closest supervision, and already some rumours of what was to take place had leaked out, and strange men with cameras had been seen lurking in the neighbourhood.

It is necessary to go into some detail with regard to the precautions taken at Cold Stairs that night in mid-November, because the ghastly sequel was made more inexplicable thereby.

Hartley had fixed up a microphone in the so-called haunted room, a bedroom at the end of a long corridor. Selden had posed as his assistant, not wishing his identity to be known to the Committee.

An examination of a most searching character had been conducted by the two young men, and separately by the Committee.

The whole place from garret to cellar had been minutely examined for secret rooms or doors or other ancient devices. Then Selden went round and carefully sealed every window and the doors leading to the cellars and the back premises. He meant to render the place safe from outside interference. The servants had all been granted leave to go home, and had gladly availed themselves of the opportunity.

The upper floors had been entirely cleared of human inhabitants. Mrs. James, the governess, was to remain in her sitting-room on the ground floor, from which the children's play-room led out. In this room Sybil was to sleep on a camp bed. Beyond that was a small room that Eric had occupied ever since his accident, to avoid going upstairs. Both children were therefore under the immediate superintendence of Mrs. James, in case they became frightened in the night. The matter had been kept from them as far as possible, but naturally the strange happenings in the house had aroused their curiosity.

Selden, to whom every human being was a study, had made the acquaintance of the children on his arrival. Sybil was fifteen, but looked younger, with grave wide-open eyes, a mass of dark hair that had been allowed to grow, and the wild grace of a free thing of the countryside. And yet her colour was ivory white, instead of being burnt by the sun or browned by open air life. In her young life tragedy had filled a large part. The death of her father, by an accident when out hunting; the death of her mother, a strange unsolved mystery, and then her grandfather, of whom she was passionately fond. She had no girl friends of her age, and was driven into herself for companionship, with disastrous effects.

The boy, Mrs. James's child, was about sixteen, but had that queer waxen appearance that goes with tuberculosis, and light hair, almost curly. He spoke in a soft deliberate tone. Compelled to lie on his back since his spine had been injured, and be wheeled in a basket chair, the lad aroused Selden's pity.

The dining-room had been chosen as the scene of the experiment, where a loudspeaker and amplifier had been installed by Hartley, and a connection made with the telephone wires by the post-office, in order that the Big Nob might hear for himself in London.

An ample supply of food had been provided, and here the Committee met, with Hartley and Selden.

Sir John and Mrs. James joined them for a cold supper, after which Mrs. James retired to her room, and Sir John, who declared he would not take any part in the proceedings, went to keep her company.

Contrary to the usual custom observed among well-conducted ghosts, the manifestations had no fixed hour, nor did they happen every night. The investigators were prepared for a long vigil, and perhaps failure the first night.

At ten o'clock, Sergeant Perkins, a red-faced, stolid, local officer, reported that his men had taken up their stations round the house, which was closely watched on every side, while Perkins was to patrol the place. Already he had turned away some reporters with difficulty. One he had discovered up a tree, and another hiding in a coal shed at the back of the house.

The night was wild with a blustering wind and driven rain from the south-west, and the old house creaked and groaned. Perkins was refreshed and dismissed, and the party settled down to wait.

The hours crept on, as they smoked in silence, glancing from time to time at the loudspeaker that stood dumbly in the centre of the table. Occasionally one would rise noiselessly and replenish his glass at the buffet, and return to his seat.

The clock ticked loudly in the silence, and over all brooded a feeling of suspense; a hush that might preclude some startling sound from the loudspeaker.

Sir John was dozing in a large arm-chair before the fire in Mrs. James's room, while she sat opposite to him, mending clothes for the children. Several times she had risen and tiptoed through the connecting door, to find the children fast asleep in their rooms. Sir John woke with a start, and rubbed his neck, which had become stiff in the chair.

"What a fool I was not to have had a bed rigged up in my smoking-room," he said ruefully. "But I suppose with guests in the house that would hardly have done." He rose and stretched himself. "I'll go and have a word with them in the dining-room."

Mrs. James smiled faintly, knowing that he badly wanted a drink. He walked silently from the room, his old worn bedroom slippers making no sound. Only the melancholy soughing of the wind, broken now and then by heavy gusts, filled the silence.

In the dining-room Hartley became suddenly alert, and held up his hand. The others clustered round and every ear was strained for the slightest sound. A very faint noise came from the loudspeaker, an indistinct burr that conveyed no meaning, and then the sound of a muffled footfall, a curious halting dragging sound, back and forwards, a pause and then again, restless and uneasy.

Professor Johnson half rose as though he wished to investigate at once, but Hartley, who was only interested in his broadcast, motioned him back. Stevens brushed back his sleek black hair with a nervous gesture, and clutched the camera and flash-pan he had brought for a spirit photograph.

The sound stopped abruptly, like the turning off of a switch, and then in the thick silence came the sound of agonized weeping, hopeless and intolerable; the weeping of a man to whom even death has been denied. So might the Wandering Jew have wept in an agony of remorse.

At the dreadful sound a chill like an Arctic breath seemed to pass over the listeners, and Selden clenched his fists tightly. The others had heard it before, but to him it was new, and horrible. An unearthly shriek, a human cry of agony, rent the night; then a heavy thud, and silence. Only that dreadful sound seemed to echo through the house.

Selden was the first to recover. He recognized the human quality, and his professional instincts were instantly awake. He drew an automatic, and dashed open the door, heedless of Hartley's expostulation that he would ruin the broadcast, which was getting interesting.

A door opened into the hall, throwing a beam of light across the blackness, Mrs. James looked out, her face distorted with terror. "What was that?" she whispered shakily.

"Where is Sir John?" Selden asked sharply, a sudden foreboding coming to his alert mind.

"Isn't he with you? He left about ten minutes ago, saying he was going to the dining-room."

"I don't like this. Mrs. James, you had better go to the children. Professor," he added, as the latter came from the dining-room with Stevens, "Sir John is missing—come along."

"If he's been playing with us . . ." Professor Johnson muttered, as he followed Selden, who had bounded up the broad stairway, flashing his electric torch before him.

He proceeded more slowly along the corridor, turned the handle of the fatal room, and threw open the door. There was a sharp click, and the light came on, blinding them for a moment.

"What did you do that for?" Professor Johnson turned angrily to Selden. "We should have examined in the dark."

His voice trailed off into silence as he looked. The body of Sir John Harman was spread-eagled on the floor. The little group huddled at the doorway, gazing at the grim scene. Selden's voice broke the spell.

"Will you kindly remain where you are. This is a matter for me."

"Really," Stevens said sulkily. "I don't see what business it is of yours,"

"I'll tell you presently," Selden said. "I represent the official police at present, and must investigate. I don't want foot-marks." He cast a rapid glance round the room, and on the floor. The curtains were drawn and the iron-clamped shutters still fastened. Dust lay thickly over the carpet and the furniture was covered with dust sheets. Selden approached the body, noting the position, and then knelt down and placed his hand over the heart.

"He's dead," he said simply, looking up at the group by the door. "Before I examine further, Stevens, would you oblige me by taking a photograph of the body *in situ.*"

Stevens complied, only too anxious to be in the affair.

"Thank you," Selden said quietly, when two flashlight snaps had been taken. "Will you kindly return to the dining-room, and wait for me. Tell Hartley to 'phone his chief and merely say that the broadcast is over, nothing more at present."

The smiling quiet young man of a few minutes ago had suddenly become the man of action and authority, and they obeyed without a protest.

Selden gently turned the dead man over on his back and started at the sight. The face was swollen and purple, hardly recognizable, but in the wide, staring eyes was such a look of horror as Selden had never seen. It was as though the dying man had encountered something so appalling that the life had been struck from him at the very sight.

When Selden had completed his examination of the room, he returned to the dining-room, where the others were eagerly awaiting him.

Professor Johnson was striding up and down excitedly. He was a striking figure, well over six feet in height, and spare to leanness. He had a mass of greyish hair that stuck out in wild tufts from his head in a tangled mane. A large, powerful, fleshy nose protruded between deep-set sombre eyes which could flash like searchlights when his temper was roused. His habit of wearing a black cape, even when indoors, gave him the appearance of an ancient prophet or a brigand chief.

"It is quite evident," he was shouting when Selden entered, "there was something in the room not of this world, and that stupid fool Harman interfered with forces he did not understand, and has spoilt our investigations."

He came to rest at the fire-place, tucked his cloak under his arms, behind his back, and glared at Selden.

"Well?"

The latter ignored him. "Have you called up your chief?" he asked Hartley.

"I've been on to him, told him the test had been completed, and that I would bring up my report personally tomorrow."

"He suspects nothing?"

"Nothing of the truth," Hartley said grimly. "He's not the sort of man to give anything away over the 'phone, so I couldn't tell what he thought of the—show!"

"Good; I don't want anything said at present."

The Professor interrupted. "You will excuse me, young man. We are investigating this affair, which has now taken a sinister turn, but one capable of explanation by us, with our special knowledge. I would like to know exactly what status you have here. I fully understood that you were an assistant to Mr. Hartley."

"My friend Jack asked me to come down in that capacity," Selden said suavely, "but I am on the staff of the C.I.D. at Scotland Yard, and I take charge in that capacity, until I have consulted the local police and my own chief."

The Professor glared at the young man. "But I fail to see how you or any police officer would come into the matter—"

"Let's understand one another at once," Selden said with a touch of impatience. "There is no question of Sir John having died of fright, as you think. He was murdered."

At the ominous word, all eyes were fixed on the speaker.

"But I don't understand," Stevens remarked with an obvious effort. "I saw no marks of violence on him."

"I am stating a plain fact. He was strangled from behind. There are the marks on his throat."

"Then you will be able to obtain fingerprints," Jack suggested.

"In this case I am afraid not." There was something in his voice that made Jack look keenly at his friend, as though the young detective had chosen his words with great care.

He went on deliberately. "The marks round the throat were quite well defined, and pressed deeply into the flesh. They were made by no living hand." He looked challengingly at the Professor. "They are skeleton fingers, bony and jointed, and quite unmistakable in character."

"Good God!" Jack exclaimed, feeling a cold feeling down his spine.

There was a note of triumph in the Professor's deep voice.

"Then it is within our province after all." Selden sat down and lit his pipe. "Excuse me, these things are rather upsetting for the nerves. You haven't heard all. It is only right you should do so. As you observed, the whole floor is covered thickly in dust, so that marks show as clearly as though french chalk had been thrown down. The marks of Sir John's bedroom slippers show clearly. He entered the room, and stood still; the impression is deeper there.

There are no other marks of human feet, but the dust has a queer appearance, almost as though it had been beaten flat in places. There is a blurred mark where something sprang on the unfortunate baronet, and choked the life out of him."

"He was a strong man, and in good health," Stevens commented.

"There are no other marks of any sort, except those of myself, and Stevens when he took the photographs. My seals on the shutters are intact, and I have searched the room thoroughly, and locked it up. If you will assist me we will search the house, but first, Jack, would you mind fetching Sergeant Perkins from outside? I must work with the local police. I shall want statements from all of you, so you might write them now."

Hartley made a wry face—it was eerie work going into the dark, where something might be lurking that would spring on his back. Selden saw his face and laughed. He threw his automatic on the table.

"Take that, Jack, and shoot at sight, but don't hit one of the police."

Such is the force of authority that Selden had them all obeying his instructions, though the Professor was obviously very rebellious. Selden went with Jack to the front door, and let him out into the storm. Then he tapped at Mrs. James's door.

She was sitting quietly by the fire, showing no signs of fear, though inwardly terrified. Selden had summed her up as a woman of courage who could be relied upon, and told her briefly that Sir John had been murdered, omitting all details.

"I feared as much, when 1 heard that awful cry," she said calmly. "I went to see the children, but they were fast asleep. Come and see them, Mr. Selden."

She led the way into the next room, where Sybil was sleeping soundly, her head deep in the pillows.

Her dark hair almost covered her face, and the long lashes falling on her cheeks accentuated the whiteness of her skin. Her hands were clasping a box she hugged as though it were a doll.

"What has she got there?" Selden whispered.

Mrs. James smiled wanly. "She's a strange imaginative child. That's her wonderful box she will never part with, and scarcely ever lets it out of her sight. It's just a fancy of hers."

"What is in it?"

"Probably rubbish, but I expect to her each article has a magical character." She led the way into the further room, where Eric slept. Beside his bed stood the wicker bath-chair he used in the daytime.

They returned to the sitting-room. It's rather strange that neither of them heard that scream," Selden said.

"I'm very glad they did not. It might have frightened Eric badly," Mrs. James replied. "You know, of course, that was the cause of Eric's injury. He fell down the stairs after fancying he saw some frightful apparition."

"And what about Sybil?"

"That's the queer part that I can't understand, and it has worried me. Sybil is not in the least frightened, but seems to accept everything as a matter of course, and behaves as though she knew all about it."

Selden returned to the dining-room thoughtfully. And found Sergeant Perkins waiting for him. The sergeant rose at his entrance with the respect due to a C.I.D. officer The situation had already been explained to him by Hartley

"This is a bad business, sir," he said at once. "I am quite certain that no one got away from the house. My men were covering all sides and I went round all the time seeing that they were doing their work, for it's a bitter night to be out in."

He glanced at the dripping mackintosh he had taken off and placed by the fire.

"Before I 'phone the Yard, I want to have the house thoroughly searched. Perhaps you will all assist." Selden turned politely to Mrs. Seaton. "If you would go to Mrs. James and keep her company it would be a kindly action."

As Selden had expected, the search led to nothing but negative results. Every one of the seals was intact, and all windows shuttered and barred. There was no sign of human beings in the house beyond the ground floor.

Selden took Sergeant Perkins and Jack to the room of death, and unlocked the door.

"You will be in charge of the house, Perkins, and ought to see the room."

He had covered the body with a dust sheet, and neither of the others was anxious to see it uncovered.

"What a peculiar smell," Hartley said, scenting the air with disfavour.

"Damp, I expect," Perkins suggested. "This room wants air badly."

"I don't think we can do more here," Selden said hastily, and Jack saw by his friend's face that he did not wish to discuss the subject before the sergeant.

"You can take your men off as soon as you like now. Fetch a doctor as quickly as you can. He can do no good, but we must conform to regulations. For the present keep this entirely to yourself, we don't want a herd of pressmen round here. You had better have a drink before you go."

"Thank you, sir, I could do with one badly on a night like this," Perkins said gratefully.

The Professor and Stevens were waiting in the dining-room, having done their part in the search.

"Since you will not permit us to investigate further," the former said stiffly, "I shall get the sergeant to show me the way to the nearest hotel. But I warn you, Mr. Selden, I shall take the matter up with Scotland Yard, for I believe we can be of more use in discovering the truth about this affair than the official police. Mrs. Seaton has decided to stay with the governess."

"You must do what you think best," Selden said wearily. "Perkins, as you have finished your drink, take these two gentlemen with you, and look after them. Hartley and I will have no sleep tonight."

CHAPTER II

ᴛᴚᴇ ꙅᴇᴄᴏɴᴅ ᴍꙋʀᴅᴇʀ

S ELDEN WAS RIGHT IN HIS SURMISE as far as he was concerned, but Hartley curled himself up on the sofa in the dining-room, and was soon fast asleep.

He dreamt horribly of ghosts that chased him down long corridors, and fought violently when Selden shook him into wakefulness.

"Wake up, Jack, the dawn hath broken," Dick said, giving a last shake.

"Damn you—what do you want to wake a fellow for? What's happened?"

"Quite a lot," Dick observed cheerfully. "While you have been hogging it, I've been busy. The local medico arrived, and, after inspecting the departed, had the body removed to the village of Lydford, where he is not only a doctor, but Coroner and Medical Officer of Health. He could only say the man was dead, which we knew already, had a stiff whisky-and-soda, and asked if you were another corpse. Then he hopped it."

"Anything else exciting?"

"I 'phoned my chief, who told me to get in touch with the county police, and carry on."

"Bit up-stage, aren't you? Take care you don't come a cropper over this case, my bright lad."

"They know a good man at the Yard. Old Dodds said it was fortunate that I happened to be here."

"Pride goeth—" Jack stopped to yawn as Mrs. James came in, looking fresh and clean beside the jaded unwashed couple.

"I didn't know you were here," she apologized. "You know all the servants are away, so I'll get breakfast for you. Fortunately there is plenty to eat in the house. Mrs. Seaton is sleeping in my sitting-room."

"Mr. Hartley is very useful at household work; I'm sure he will help you. He's half asleep at present, but when he's put his head under the pump he'll wake up."

"You must be very tired, Mr. Selden," Mrs. James said sympathetically.

"Not a bit; you wouldn't believe the number of times I have had to be up all night over cases."

"His head swells when he gets tired," Jack called over his shoulder as he departed to find a bathroom.

"I wanted a word with you, Mrs. James," Selden said when the door was shut. "The police will be taking over the house this morning."

"I understand—you wondered where we could go," Mrs. James said quietly.

"You see, you must stay for the inquest, and we don't know anything about Sir John's affairs; at least I don't."

The woman flushed slightly. "I have no reason to suppose that he would leave me anything, but I am in charge of his niece at present. I don't expect that whoever is appointed guardian would continue to employ me with a crippled son."

"I don't think you ought to go far from here until something is settled," Selden said doubtfully.

"There is the lodge—that is empty and furnished. Sir John only dismissed the lodge-keeper a short time ago, as he thought it an unnecessary extravagance."

"Capital. That will be just the thing. If you can move down there, I am certain there will be no objection, and I don't think the children ought to remain here, even if that were possible. I suppose there's a family lawyer who will turn up when he hears the news." Selden was greatly relieved at getting rid of Mrs. James and the children from the house

When they were all sitting at breakfast, he took stock of Mrs. James in his usual way with everyone with whom he came into contact.

Seen in the daylight she looked older and greyer though her face was one that did not show signs of age readily. He judged that she had seen hard times and faced them bravely. Of her entire devotion to her invalid son there could be no doubt. She wheeled him into the dining-room, propped up with pillows, and waited on him with tender care.

Later on an old gardener was requisitioned to take their scanty baggage to the lodge in a barrow, and Selden and Hartley accompanied them. Sybil was carrying her wonderful box, and when Jack courteously offered to take it, she drew back in alarm. They walked together ahead of the others, and soon made friends. Jack had a simple, direct mind, and the touch of romanticism in the girl intrigued him.

Although fifteen and looking young for her age, in conversation she was grave and reserved, and even old-fashioned. There was no touch or suggestion of the modern blasé girl, and for this Hartley was thankful. As the last of the Harmans, she appeared to feel her position and showed a quiet dignity beyond her years.

They took possession of the cottage, and started to put the place in some sort of order. Mrs. James was not over-strong, and Selden guessed that she had not been accustomed to manual work. He would have offered his help, but understood instinctively that such an intrusion would have been unwelcome, Jack had no such scruples. He took off his coat, and got busy at once.

Selden walked to the door and saw Sergeant Perkins coming down the drive, signalling wildly to him, and went forward to meet him, with a foreboding of evil strongly in his mind.

"What is it, Perkins?"

"I'm glad to find you, sir," Perkins panted. "I was afraid you had gone; will you come at once!"

Selden glanced at the cottage behind him, and then went forward with the officer until they were well out of earshot.

"What is it, Perkins?" he said gravely.

"One of my men, sir, Calthorpe—who was on duty last night . . ." He was labouring under emotion, and the words came from him in gasps. "We thought he had gone home to Lydford; he's there." He pointed in the direction of the thick woods on the left of the drive.

Half-way back to the house, a green ride opened before them, grass-grown and narrow, a mere woodland path, delightful on warm summer days. Now, in November, the ground was strewn with fallen leaves and twigs. The sergeant paused, turning a tortured face to Selden.

"Calthorpe has been murdered. Up that path—one of my men found him, and is with him now."

Selden's face set hard. "Come on, lead the way."

He followed the sergeant, who made his way up the track, holding back the branches that straggled over the ride as though trying to bar the way.

"After you told me to dismiss my men, I ordered them to report to the bailiff's house which we had used as a temporary headquarters. I thought they could get dry there, and have something hot to drink before they went home."

"When did you miss this man?"

"When I went there. The others were waiting, and thought Calthorpe had probably gone home, but when I 'phoned the police station to report, I asked about him, as he lives next door, and found he had not returned. So we started to look for him, and have only just found him. The storm has left the drive very muddy, and Metcalf, one of my men, saw tracks leading up this pathway."

"I saw the tracks," Selden said shortly; "the man was running; the toes were deeply embedded, and the heel-marks did not even show."

"He must have seen something, and chased it," Perkins muttered. "There were no tracks coming back."

They turned a corner, and saw a policeman standing motionless under an old gnarled oak tree whose withered arms stretched out like the grasping limbs of some dead monster. On the ground was a huddled mass in blue uniform. A look of relief showed on the face of the constable at the sight of the two men. His vigil had not been a pleasant one.

"He's been strangled like the other one," Perkins said in a hoarse whisper, glancing round at the still woods. The second tragedy had shaken him badly, for murder was a new thing in these parts.

Selden knelt down and examined the body. The man was lying on his face, with legs and arms spread widely apart, but the head was twisted round, and the throat was exposed.

"You see, sir," Perkins exclaimed with a note of hysteria in his voice. "There are marks of teeth."

Selden stood up and faced the sergeant. "This won't do, Perkins. You are shaken up, I know, but don't for goodness' sake get wild ideas into your head. This is a plain, though rather gruesome, murder, you understand."

"Yes, sir." He swallowed hard, and drew himself up, as though trying to regain his poise.

On either side of the thorax of the dead man were deep indentations clearly marked and suggestive of something horrible.

"What's that?" The sergeant gripped Selden's arm in sudden fear. The branches were brushed aside, and Hartley came towards them, and the smile died from his face as the saw the group.

"I saw you dive into the woods from the lodge, and came after you. Good lord, another murder!"

Selden met Hartley's gaze with a steady frown. "This unfortunate officer," he said in a level voice, "evidently saw something, when on his way to the bailiff's house, and gave chase."

Hartley read a warning in his friend's eyes, and remained silent while Selden gave his orders. "Perkins, you had better go at once and fetch a stretcher, and 'phone for the doctor. Take Metcalf with you; my friend and I will wait here."

The two officers saluted and went off with evident relief.

"What's the idea, Dick?" Hartley remarked, coolly taking a cigarette from his case and lighting it. "I saw you frowning at me."

"I was afraid you would say something, Jack. These country policemen are badly frightened. I've no doubt they are brave enough in the ordinary way, but they, like all the people round here, are soaked in legend and grim stories, and I want to avoid anything bizarre creeping into this case. You understand; we don't want tales of monsters and devils being spread about."

"But how did this poor fellow get murdered up this path? You said he saw something or other."

"I said he saw something and chased it. That is not so."

Jack drew in his breath quickly. "How do you know that?"

"I have had a good training, but even common sense would have told me the story." Selden looked back down the ride that seemed a green tunnel, with the branches meeting overhead. "I saw the tracks, Jack; they are plain in this soft ground. The policeman Metcalf and Sergeant Perkins coming and going. These have naturally obliterated much, but the other tracks show as well. The running constable, flying for his life, and the pursuer following hard after him."

Jack shivered.

"There is no mistake about it. In places the traces of the thing that came after him have been superimposed over those of the running man. That is absolute proof. The constable was running for dear life, but a strong healthy man would not run away from a man in that way."

Hartley felt his blood run cold with horror.

"If that is so, why didn't he run straight down the road where he could get help?"

"We must not indulge in guessing," Dick said solemnly, "but I can almost see the wretched man flying down the drive from the house and turning his head as the awful thing gained on him. He saw the opening of this ride and hoped to elude his pursuer by dashing into it—remember it was dark. But he failed."

"And met his death here," Jack said harshly.

"Jack, you have good nerves—look at this."

He pointed to the throat of the dead man, and Hartley uttered a cry. "This is devilish!" He clapped both hands to his head.

"Come with me, Jack. I want to get certain marks rubbed out before the police come back. That is why I sent them off."

He led the way back down the ride, searching carefully, and paused. "There!"

Clear in the soft earth was the deep tread of the hunted man, rushing in urgent despair, and perhaps yelling for help. Overlapping, were other marks, at the sight of which Jack turned sick and faint. They were not even human, but the marks of a skeleton foot, and further off was another marked like a bird's tread in soft mud. Selden calmly slid his foot over them and stamped the place flat.

He followed the track, and here and there stopped and repeated the same process. Then he returned to Jack, who was leaning against a tree.

"The same creature that murdered Sir John," Jack gasped. "It must have got loose somehow."

Selden shrugged his shoulders angrily. "I'm not going to have my reason and training dragged into some supernatural explanation. It's the surroundings of the place, and those spiritualists. Everything is pointing that way, but I won't accept it."

Hartley watched his friend's stern set face, and understood that he was talking against himself; shaking off the dread sense of horror. He seemed to see that green tunnel stretching out before the doomed man, and to hear the dry wind of the Thing of Hell that gained on him with every stride.

The tread of feet interrupted his thoughts. Sergeant Perkins appeared looking more collected and spruce. "I've got a stretcher here, sir, and the doctor is on his way with the ambulance to the bailiff's house."

"Then fetch along the body, and be quick about it."

The men needed no hurrying, and picked up their pitiful burden, covering it with a sheet they had brought. Selden watched them marching down the drive, the gates of which had been closed and locked against intruders.

"Well, what's next?" Hartley asked with a forced smile.

"I suppose you will want to get back to London after you have dismantled your apparatus."

"I am not in a hurry, Dick. I had quite a long talk with my chief on the 'phone. He was awfully decent, and told us not to hurry, as the matter was interesting from our point of view, and he was keeping it to himself. He asked me to find out all I could . . ." Hartley paused, "that is, if I'm not intruding."

"I shall be glad of your help, old lad," Selden said seriously. "Look here, Jack, I'm going to be straight with you. This is the biggest case I've ever had to tackle, and there are many at the Yard who are infernally jealous of the small success I have had. My reputation hangs on this."

"Of course, I'll help, but I don't see how I can be of any assistance."

"That's where you are wrong." He laid his hand earnestly on his friend's shoulder. "Listen—this is not bally-hoo. You have a scientific training and brain, not muddled up with all kinds of junk like mine. I have a vivid imagination, which I suppose is useful for my work. Don't you realize I'm fighting for my reasoning faculties? I want to prove that there is some human agency at work here, and run the criminal to earth. But I haven't gone through my life without coming across the inexplicable, and I've read a goodish bit."

"I understand, Dick. Well, we've been pigging it together for some years now, and I'm game for anything. Besides," he grinned at his friend, "there may be something a bit dangerous, and I can be of service there, I'm fairly useful with my fists."

Selden silently shook hands in the way that men seal bargains.

"Then I'm going to explore this ride and see where it leads to. The murderer may have left some traces, or even be lurking in the woods. I don't mind telling you, Jack, I shall shoot at sight."

"That's the stuff to give 'em; lead on." Selden paused at the spot where the body had lain and remained deep in thought. He started when Jack suddenly put a hand on his arm.

"I say, old man, what about those tooth-marks on the neck? The footprints put the others out of my head."

"I know, Jack, that's what is puzzling me; in fact, everything is baffling here because it's so deucedly contradictory. They are merely marks, and haven't penetrated the skin to any depth. Now if there were some werewolf or fabulous monster at work, one would expect to find the throat torn out. Death was due to strangulation, but why those marks?"

"It may be some mad thing at large," Hartley suggested hopefully.

"Of course it may, Jack, but how in heaven's name could such a being exist here in the forest without being discovered, and how could he live? No—come along and let's find out all we can. Perhaps he has left some further traces."

They proceeded down this curious path cut through the forest, but no further indications appeared. It was as though the being had disappeared as suddenly and secretly as he had from the haunted room.

They were going up hill and the lane assumed a different aspect. Ferns grew knee-high, now blackened and withered for the most part, and strange grey rocks showed on the sides, some of such size that the lane took a turn round them. And then as they turned a corner the place opened up, like a picture of fairyland. A clearing had been made in the forest, in which an old grey stone cottage stood, with tiny windows and a thatched roof, having the absurd unreality of Tom Thumb's house in a pantomime. A small garden surrounded the place, and there was a pigsty at the back.

Blue smoke went up straight from the chimney, and disappeared in the clear blue sky. The blue and the deep green of the pine trees and the grass blended with the few red roses that still flowered about the open door, gave the impression of peaceful, contented life. A bright, clean, tiled kitchen showed through the open door, and clean white curtains adorned the small leaded windows.

The two men approached, almost expecting to see the three bears come out to greet them. An old woman was bending over the log fire, stirring a black pot, and turned her head expectantly at the sound of their footsteps on the stone flags. Then she straightened herself with an air of defiance.

Selden took off his hat. "Good morning," he said politely. "Forgive our intrusion. My friend and I are exploring the woods."

She regarded them sullenly. "My man'll be here shortly. He'll talk to you perhaps." It was not a promising beginning.

"My friend and I are feeling a bit thirsty, and seeing your cottage we thought perhaps we could get something to drink."

"Come in and welcome," the old woman said with the innate hospitality of the countrywoman. "You are not men from the newspapers?"

Selden laughed. "Oh no—far from it. I don't want to see them. No, no, we're just wandering round."

The old lady bustled out of the kitchen to the back, and they heard the welcome sound of liquid pouring into a jug. She returned with a tray on which was a great earthenware jug of foaming cider and two mugs, which she set on the table.

Hartley poured out, and lifted the mug with every sign of pleasure.

"Here's your very good health, Mrs.—" he said.

"Jenkins is my name. Morgan Jenkins is my man. He'll likely be back soon."

She returned to her stirring but sat on a stool sideways and kept the men in view.

"Charming cottage you've got. Have you been here long?"

Mrs. Jenkins seemed satisfied that these young men were harmless and answered frankly.

"Ay, all my life. It's a tidy place sure enough. I was born in this cottage, my father being a gardener at the Manor, and when Morgan came courting I was housemaid there, and he a footman. We've served the Harmans for generations."

"You have heard what happened last night?" Selden said quietly.

"Ay, a bad business." She shook her head. "Best not be talked of too much." In spite of the bright sunshine she shivered.

"Morgan's under gardener there. He told me this morning."

The sound of a heavy tread came from outside, and Morgan himself appeared, and stopped at the entrance. He was a powerfully built old man, with a mahogany face deeply wrinkled, with pale blue eyes and grey hair.

"Jenkins," the woman said at once, "these gentlemen have called round here about the murder." Her quick peasant's instinct had guessed the truth.

The old man sat down heavily.

"There's been another murder now, I've heard tell. A policeman this time."

"Mercy!" The old woman stared at her husband. "Not in the Manor?"

"No," he said slowly, "in the woods."

"The Lord preserve us," she muttered.

"Best say as little as possible," Morgan asserted, while his wife went for another mug for him.

"We mustn't interrupt your dinner," Selden remarked.

"That is no matter. I am not in a hurry. There's no more work to do, so Bailiff says, and maybe we shan't be wanted any more. Sir John was a good master to us," he sighed. "Ay, always kind and jolly-like, with a laugh for everyone."

Selden was looking round the place and his glance fell on a photograph of a soldier in khaki—faded now.

"That's our boy Jim," Mrs. Jenkins said as though glad to shift the conversation. "He's a proper lad. He is in the Engineers."

"A fine upstanding man as ever you did see," the old man added proudly. "I remember going down to Gloucester with him to see him off to India."

"It was quite a venture for Jenkins," the old woman put in. "He'd never been farther than Lydford in his life."

Selden realized in a flash the utter remoteness of these people, neither of whom had ever seen the sea!

"You ought to have a wireless set," Hartley said.

"Sir John did say he'd give us one, but we didn't care much for the idea. Seems like dealing with the devil."

"That's one for you, Jack. My friend here is a member of the staff at Broadcasting House, that's where they send out the news, and music, and so on."

The words evidently conveyed little to their minds. They merely blinked at the man who had these wonderful powers.

"That your only child?" Selden asked casually. He had been examining the photograph of the soldier son, and his eye had caught another photograph of a smiling country girl about fifteen years of age.

He wheeled quickly, hearing a stifled sob from the old woman.

"There, there, Mother," the old man patted her back. "The gentleman didn't mean to bring up the old matter."

"I'm sorry," Selden said in sympathy.

"It isn't your fault, sir," the old man said, "but the wife always takes on that way when our daughter Anne is mentioned."

The old woman's eyes flashed with fury. "Take on, is it? She was murdered, same as Squire was last night, and the policeman. Murdered I tell you." Her voice rose to a shriek, and placing her apron over her head, she hurried from the room.

"You must excuse her, sir, but the murder last night brought it all back to us, and she is upset."

"We had better go, hadn't we?" Jack suggested.

"No, sir, if it is Sir John's murder that you are interested in, as my wife says, I will tell you. It was two years ago as near as possible, and fresh now in our minds as ever. Our Anne was as fine a girl as you'd wish to see. She was afraid of no one, and like all the rest of us served at Cold Stairs. One night she came back home through the woods. She had been told not to come alone, and I always fetched her, but was kept that night at the Manor. No one knows what happened."

He paused as though the remembrance was too much for him.

"My wife was waiting up for her. She heard a bump and a scream at the door, and when she opened it there was Anne lying unconscious on the ground. When I came back she had recovered, but all she could say was that she had been chased through the woods by Something, but when we asked her what it was she went off screaming something awful. I ran out with my axe and searched around, but couldn't find anything. I went to the house, and Squire, he came with me, and the butler, but we couldn't find a trace, not even in daylight.

"Anne was a healthy girl and not given to fancies, and she was always about with young Miss Sybil; they were great friends, if I may say so, she being what she is."

Hartley looked up quickly.

"They were friends; that is interesting, eh, Dick?"

"Very," Dick said dryly, "but please go on."

"Of course Anne knew about the creature in the woods," Jenkins said in a matter-of-fact voice.

"What is that?" Selden asked.

"Well, sir, of course I've lived here all my life, and in these parts, especially in the forest, there have always been strange stories of people we don't like to talk about; not human, you understand.

"Some won't go out a'nights at all, and Tom, my boy, swears he saw an odd-looking thing go up the side of the wall of Cold Stairs one night, and through the window, though it were close shut. Right through the glass it went. But he only made a joke about it, being a soldier, and used to them queer things that happen in India."

"And your daughter died," Sinclair said softly.

The man appeared to hesitate. "Well, sir, that's my old woman's way of speaking—she always says that to strangers. As a matter of truth, she is in a home! Her reason never came back rightly."

"So when you heard of the death of Sir John," Selden remarked, "you weren't particularly surprised."

"I reckon it was a mistake sending down them people to investigate and that new-fangled wireless business. It upset things."

"What exactly do you mean by that?"

The old man glanced cautiously round the cottage. "It don't do to talk too much, and I do think if they'd left things alone Squire would have been alive now."

The old woman crept silently back into the room, and set about getting her husband's dinner. The two men rose to go.

"I am so sorry to have interrupted your meal," Selden said.

"It is no matter," Jenkins assured them.

They insisted on paying for their cider, and took leave of the old couple. As they trudged along the track that led directly to Cold Stairs, Hartley glanced at his companion. "What do you make of that?" he asked with a forced laugh.

"Damn it; at every step one takes one is up against this spook business. The whole countryside here is full of it. If only they would take a practical view things would be easier."

"Of course this is a lot of hoky-poky," Hartley said guardedly.

"One expects this sort of thing in remote countries but hardly in England," Selden said fretfully. "I suppose some hobbledehoy chased the girl, and she already full of thoughts of hobgoblins, imagined impossible things. I expect she was weak-minded in any case. Then the soldier on leave had probably been celebrating in the 'local' and saw some creepers waving in the wind. That's how the stories grow."

Hartley stopped to light a cigarette and carefully stamped on the match.

"Dick, old lad, aren't you trying to convince yourself? It's unlike you to get peevish like this."

"I suppose I am; that's where you can help quite a lot, with your practical common sense. Let's treat this as a human problem. We shall get a true perspective when we get away from this depressing atmosphere. These people see a rock with a lichen growing on it like the hair of a dead man, and take it for an earthborn creature of the old legends. Every tree becomes a being with stretching arms about to clutch, as in the Erl King."

They emerged at the back of Cold Stairs, bare and grim. On the left was the walled garden, but immediately behind the house the tall trees almost came to the walls. The stabling and outhouses, where the electric plant had been installed, were apart from the house itself. Selden's car still stood beside the front door of the deserted premises.

"While we are here, you may as well fetch away your gear," Dick remarked, gazing thoughtfully at the grim close-shut windows. As in most ancient houses the shutters, of great thickness, were inside the windows, and this gave a ghastly appearance, making the small diamond panes look like dead eyes.

Jack made a face. "I'd rather have you to hold my hand. I can't say I like the place."

"Come on then," Selden laughed. "Who's afraid of the Big Bad Wolf?" He unlocked the front door and entered the place.

"No one has a right to keep children in a house like this," Jack exclaimed indignantly. "They ought to be in a modern flat with every convenience."

"You have no sense of romance; that comes of being an engineer."

Together they removed the loud-speaker and wires from the dining-room, and proceeded up the stairs, Jack rolling the wire as he went. At the door of the haunted room Selden paused, and Jack saw his hand go to his pocket. "Going to shoot at sight?" he laughed jerkily.

"Certainly; the murderer is either in this house or in the woods and I'm taking no risks."

Even at the moment it flashed into Jack's brain that Selden, who was as brave as a man could be, was still stubbornly forcing his mind to a rational explanation, and refusing to consider any other.

"Get your mike down, and let's get away," Dick said, when he had switched on the light.

Hartley got to work, while Selden crawled on the floor like a great cat, examining the dusty carpet.

"I've got it all now," Jack said, winding up the wires.

Dick got up and dusted his knees. "I can't make it out, Jack."

"What's the trouble now?"

"There is something all wrong here. There were queer marks like skeleton hands on Sir John's throat, but not a footmark of the same gruesome kind. In fact, there are no traces of—the assailant. In the wood it was the reverse. The feet were those of a skeleton, but there were no such marks on the throat of the constable. I don't like it; there ought to be a lead there, but I can't follow it. And both men were above the average in strength."

"I don't like the air in here, anyway," Jack observed. "I noticed it before."

"I know you did, and swivelled you off before the sergeant. It made me think a bit before I could locate it."

Jack moved towards the door. "It's not exactly a bad smell like drains or a dead rat, or even damp."

Selden closed and locked the door before he spoke. "It's not a bad smell in the ordinary sense, Jack, it's an evil smell."

"Here, steady on, Dick. You will be suggesting brimstone and treacle soon."

"No! It's musk, and there's something else—frankincense, unless I'm mistaken."

"Good lord! The stuff they use for mummies, do you mean?"

"Hardly." Dick gave a mirthless laugh. "You are thinking of myrrh and aloes."

"How the devil did it get here, anyway?"

"It may be a smell to hide a smell," Dick said thoughtfully.

"Here, easy on—you make me all jittery."

Jack breathed a sigh of relief when they emerged into the open air.

"Where do we go now—I feel mighty peckish."

"We'll run down to the village and get some food. I must see the doctor in any case, and make my position right with the county police."

The doctor was standing in front of the bailiff's house as they passed, and Dick stopped the car. He was talking to Sergeant Perkins, and Jack saw a good-looking, middle-aged man, with a grey moustache and alert features, who greeted them with a large geniality.

"Glad to see you, Selden. I'd like a talk. You fellows had lunch? No, I thought as much. Come along and have some with me. Perkins, jump in, and I'll give you a lift. The others can follow my car."

CHAPTER III

ᴄꞚꞒ ꝺoᴄꞒoꞅ ꞂꝐꞒꝲꞂꞂ

D R. HUGHES WAS A BACHELOR, with a scattered practice, which would not have made a living for him, but, holding several public positions, he was able to indulge in golf and hunting in the season in his leisure hours. He was a shrewd, well-read man, fond of a good table and congenial company, and kept a well-stocked library of selected books.

He made the two young men at home at once, and with studied courtesy refrained from any mention of the double tragedy until they had finished lunch and retired to his comfortable library.

He was frankly puzzled by Selden's youthful appearance. The mop of red hair, and face almost feminine in its delicacy, ill accorded with his ideas of a C.I.D. officer, and yet, even in this remote place, he had heard his name mentioned as one of the brightest of the new school of detectives.

During luncheon he had discussed wireless with Hartley, who was transparently a keen and energetic engineer. Selden had remained strangely silent.

"And now," the doctor opened, when cigars had been lighted, and they were comfortably settled down for a talk. If the doctor had been quietly studying Selden, the latter had in his usual methodical way summed up the doctor, and assessed his mental qualities. "I would like to discuss the questions of these murders and I am sure you are also anxious for any information that I can give you. It will help me also in my capacity as coroner for the district."

"I was here by mere accident," Selden answered lightly, "and am really only holding a watching brief, until I have got into touch with the county police. My chief instructed me to remain here for the present."

"Quite so. You will both understand that Sir John Harman was a great personal friend of mine, and I feel his death keenly."

Hartley, listening to the two, felt as though he were watching a fencing bout in which each of the contestants was seeking for an opening.

"I suppose, Doctor," Selden said in his suave voice, "Perkins has given you an account of the whole sad business."

"A very trite account," Hughes smiled. "Of course we three are intelligent beings, and can dismiss the supernatural explanation that has already gained currency round here. You will have difficulty in getting any reliable information in these parts."

"I have already found that out; but from a purely medical view, Doctor, what do you make of it?"

Dr. Hughes rose, and threw away his half-finished cigar, a significant gesture to Selden's quick mind. It spoke of nervous irritation not shown outwardly.

"A less imaginative person than Harman I've never known," the doctor said, "or a more fearless man in the hunting field. I can't imagine him making any enemies, and he certainly never died of fright."

He stared straight at Selden, as though issuing a challenge.

"He was strangled from behind," the latter said quietly.

"That is so; I came to that conclusion without much difficulty."

"You saw the marks on his throat?"

"Of course." The doctor's fingers clenched tightly. "A human hand, but what fingers! The man must have been a giant, and Harman was a strong man."

"It won't do, Doctor! If we are going to discuss this matter, let's be frank."

For a moment the doctor showed signs of anger, then he laughed. "Very well, let's face it then. The marks were apparently those of a skeleton hand. I wondered whether you had noticed them."

"And the constable?" Selden persisted.

"There was no such appearance on his throat, but surely the man was either an escaped lunatic . . ." He paused and filled his pipe from a jar on the table.

"You think it was a man?"

"Damn it, man"—the doctor gave a short, hard laugh—"you are not suggesting a woman, are you?"

"Did you notice anything peculiar about the constable's throat?"

"The man was strangled."

"Doctor, I don't think it is much good our continuing to discuss this. For some purpose of your own, you are suppressing the truth."

It was some moments before the doctor replied; he filled the gap by lighting his pipe from the fire with a spill.

"I beg your pardon, Selden," he said at last. "You are quite correct. I underestimated your intelligence. As a doctor, I did not want to appear as panicky as these people round here."

Selden bowed slightly, and a little ironically.

"You are quite right," the doctor went on. "The marks on Calthorpe were made by teeth. I have seen similar marks in my younger days made by a puma or another of the carnivora."

"You mean the size of the canine teeth."

"You are observant, Selden. I've never seen such canines in a human jaw." The doctor's sang-froid had gone, and he paced the floor with quick, nervous strides. "I had hoped to keep this to myself. It will give rise to the wildest stories in the forest."

"I see no purpose in making it public. But, as a doctor, can't you tell me more?"

"You are the very devil, Selden. I believe you know already. The marks were made after death, not before, and were not the cause."

"I thought as much, but wasn't certain."

There was a feeling of strain in the air, and Hartley was almost butting in with some commonplace remark when Selden spoke.

"You mustn't take this amiss from a much younger man, Doctor, but you know more than you will tell."

"You are quite wrong; I know nothing more about these two murders than I have told you."

It was a battle of looks, and the doctor's eyes dropped first. Selden went on relentlessly. "Perhaps I have expressed myself badly. You know no more of the actual murder, but you are trying to convince yourself that it is an ordinary murder. I am referring to Sir John, of course. At the back of your mind there is a doubt, because you know this country, and suspect, am I not right?"

"I am afraid I made rather a bloomer, Selden," the doctor laughed. "One so associates detectives with grave-looking, solemn men with hooked noses and beetle brows—you know the sort of film detective—that I could not treat you seriously. You are quite right."

Dick smiled. "Then we can now get ahead. You were here when Anne Jenkins was taken ill?"

The doctor bit hard on his pipe. "I was. The poor girl was badly scared, and it affected her reason, never very strong. She is in the county mental institution. It was a dreadful case." The doctor seemed to be labouring under strong emotion, and beads of perspiration stood on his forehead.

"I had her here in this very room. They sent for me, but I could do nothing at the cottage, and brought her to my house with her mother. She was struggling and screaming, and raving about things that I don't suppose have been more than whispered in this country for centuries. . . . I'm pretty tough, but I had to give her a hypodermic injection."

"Morphine?" Selden asked sharply.

"Yes, and atropine; her heart was giving out. Perhaps it would have been better if it had."

"And that boy, Eric James—he too was frightened by something, and fell down the stairs."

"Damn it, Selden, why all these questions? What are you leading up to?"

"You know perfectly well, Doctor," Selden said grimly.

"Very well then," the doctor said in a calmer voice. "Since you will have it, I'll show you something I thought never to let the human eye see."

He walked to his desk and unlocked a drawer with a quick, nervous gesture. He returned to the fireplace with two photographs in his hand. "I am a bit of an amateur photographer and am especially keen on snaps of bird life. Eric James used frequently to come with me, before he met with his accident, and sometimes asked me for the loan of my camera. I used to develop the negatives for him. They were just ordinary snapshots of his mother and Sybil and woodland scenes. One day he brought the camera back, and I developed the films. Most of them were shots in the woods, rather pretty, for the boy has an artist's eye for sunlight effects. One, however, was not pretty."

He handed one of the photographs to Selden. It showed a very ancient oak tree, with the sunlight coming through the branches.

Selden stared in surprise at it, and then looked up and saw the doctor's face.

"Here is the other. Apparently it is precisely the same scene."

Selden took the print gingerly, and his eyes became riveted on it with a sense of creeping horror. There was the same tree, and the sunlight effect, but against the trunk was a dim, filmy form, immense and amorphous. The outline of skeleton ribs and a grinning skull, through which the tree could be seen, showed clearly.

The grisly shape, wraith-like and unreal, was marked out like a spectral form on some ghost pictures of the films.

"You must remember," the doctor said in a passionless voice, "the boy saw nothing. I questioned him closely without his knowing my object. He let out that he felt somehow frightened, and ran away. He said he had a cold feeling, but soon recovered. Further, no one but myself has had access to this film. I bought the spool myself at the local chemist's shop, and Eric gave me the camera when he had finished. I developed them the same evening, and had to tell him that the last two had been spoilt. I destroyed the negatives, but kept these two prints."

Jack Hartley had been examining the picture. "If the Committee got hold of that, they would make whoopee," he said.

"I do not propose to allow anyone to see it," Hughes said coldly. "I trust that you two will keep this entirely to yourselves. You forced my hand, Selden, by your persistent questions."

He carefully replaced the photographs in the drawer and locked it.

"And you have no explanation to offer?" Selden asked.

"None whatever. Come, let's have a drink—this talk is unhealthy."

The doctor clearly was not going to say anything more, and Selden knew when to stop asking questions. He picked up his glass thoughtfully.

"I am much obliged for your confidences, which Jack and I will of course respect. This is a strange sort of problem to be thrust on a youngster like me, just beginning his career.

"I should think the sooner Mrs. James and the children left this place the better. I wonder you didn't suggest it, Doctor."

Hughes did not take offence at the remark, as Selden had expected, but answered almost sadly:

"That was one of the few matters on which Harman and I did not see eye to eye. Quite apart from what we have been talking about, Cold Stairs is not a place in which to bring up young children. The boy, in my opinion, should go for proper treatment; and boarding-school and healthy companionship would do that girl good. She's getting morbid here."

"Is there any chance of the boy recovering?" Hartley asked.

"I don't know, I can't say," the doctor snapped impatiently. It seemed as though he did not care to discuss the case, which Selden inferred was too much for a local practitioner of sporting proclivities.

"We mustn't keep you," Selden said. "I shall, of course, return for the inquest, but must go to town to consult my chief and get instructions. We shall hope to see you again, and many thanks for your hospitality."

The doctor came to the front door with them. "There is one thing, Selden," he said diffidently, "I ought to have told you. It's a small point perhaps, but I don't want you to think I am one of those neurotic persons who draws imaginative inferences from trivial things. The boy Eric had taken one of Sir John's dogs with him when he took that photograph. He told me, and again I have to emphasize that he was quite frank about it, not seeing anything significant, but merely puzzled."

Seldon waited as the doctor boggled over his words.

"The dog, a retriever, interrupted him by nozzling under his arm, and was growling and 'pointing', its tail straight out, and, if the boy can be relied on, the hair on its back was quite stiff. It seemed frightened at something. He noticed when he came back, the dog followed closely at his heel, but appeared quite normal as they got away from the place. I give you that for what it is worth. The boy may have imagined it, but taken with the film you saw . . ."

"You have given me a most valuable piece of information," Selden said gravely. Then he added slowly: "When we get to know each other better, Doctor, perhaps you will be able to tell me the whole of what you know. No! Please don't get angry. I am much obliged for what you have told me."

He held out his hand before the doctor could collect his thoughts, and followed Hartley to the car.

CHAPTER IV

SIR JOHN HARMAN'S WILL

N IGHT HAD FALLEN IN LONDON before the two men arrived. The lights, the neon signs, and the roar of traffic
had a soothing effect on their nerves after the grim experience in the forest country. Here was modern England, prosaic
and machine-driven. The daily scramble to work, the formal needs
of food and house-room, and the continual dread of unemploy-
ment, kept minds fully occupied.

Sensation they got at the pictures; news and potted knowledge
from the wireless, or from the hurried glance at the daily papers,
while standing in a crowded carriage in their rush to business. A
commonplace murder was dwarfed by the glorious orgies of blood
at the pictures, and the fragmentary accounts of the murders at
Cold Stairs passed almost unheeded.

Jack took his way to Broadcasting House, to make his report.
He had received explicit instructions from Selden as to the line he
was to take. The Big Nob sent for him at once, and Jack found him
in a more genial mood than usual.

"It's just as well," he said when he had heard Jack's colourless
report, "that I did not put this on the official programme. From
what you tell me, Sir John Harman heard someone in the house,
and went to investigate. I suppose he frightened the intruder, who
was either skylarking or a lunatic, and in the struggle met his
death."

"That seems the most probable explanation," Hartley agreed.
"The constable, I suppose, nearly caught the criminal, who turned
on him. Well, I expect the police will catch him all right. He can't
very well get away."

A watery smile crossed the face of the Big Nob. "It was a pity,
too, for even I was getting quite thrilled listening to it here. You'll
have to attend the inquest, of course; you'd better take a week's
leave. I shall be interested to hear the result."

Hartley found himself curtly dismissed without further discussion. Meanwhile Selden had gone straight to the Yard. His chief, Chief Inspector Dodds, had already smoothed over any difficulty there might have been with the county police, and had arranged for Selden to return to take up the case.

He had great confidence in his young officer, and was watching his career with interest.

"What's your next move, Selden?" he asked when he had heard the whole story, without the unusual episodes, which Selden kept to himself.

"Tomorrow morning I'm going to call on the family lawyers. I want to find out what will Sir John made and all I can about the family."

"That's quite sound: you know their names?"

Selden smiled. "I asked Mrs. James. These lawyers for some extraordinary reason wrap their names up in mystery. One goes to a firm called Hopkins, Hopkins, Trythe and Swaile and find a Mr. Richardson who tells you that all these gentlemen have been in their graves years ago, and that a Mr. Jopkins is now head of the firm, but he is in South America, and Mr. Pooson will see you."

The Chief Inspector agreed with a smile.

"Here," Selden went on plaintively, "Mrs. James says the firm of lawyers are Sandilands, Hoskings and Bright, and the real man is the old clerk. She remembers him coming to see Sir John once."

"I wish you luck. Keep in touch with me, and there is an Inspector Lloyd from the Gloucestershire Constabulary going to Lydford either today or tomorrow. He need not interfere with your work."

Selden thanked his chief, for whom he had an intense loyalty and admiration.

"I'll do my best, sir, but this is a tough nut to crack. As a matter of fact, there is an element of something outside the ordinary run of detective work."

"I knew that," the chief said quietly. "Professor Johnson has been here."

"I am rather glad of that, sir." Selden's face cleared, "I rather hesitated to tell you everything or you might have put a more level-headed detective on the job."

"My boy"—the chief put his hand lightly on Selden's shoulder—"I have lived long enough in this world to know that there have been many cases both here and abroad which have never been solved by ordinary police methods. Don't be afraid of what you can't explain by logic. But take care. I trust you; and what I am going to say is between us two. Don't neglect the aspect of this case that may appear to you inexplicable. You may have to face dangers that an automatic or human courage will not solve. I think you should see Professor Johnson. He is not a crank, but a fine scientist."

Selden went out somewhat sobered by these grave words, quite unusual with his chief. On one point he felt relieved. The dangerous equilibrium he had fairly maintained in his mind, between the natural and supernatural, was evidently appreciated by even so practical a man as Chief Inspector Dodds.

On the following day he took his way to Bedford Row to see the lawyers, where a pleasant surprise awaited him. The small boy messenger ushered him into the presence of an old friend and Cambridge colleague, Ned O'Connor.

He was a large-limbed giant of a man, a great oarsman, but not over-fond of work, with a mop of dark hair and merry blue eyes that betrayed his country of origin.

His presence formed a striking contrast with the gloomy room, the walls of which were covered with shelves containing iron deed boxes, with the names of members of the "nobility and gentry" prominently painted in white, for lawyers are as expert in window-dressing as any Bond Street milliner.

"Come in then and sit ye down, Dick! It's glad I am to see yez, lad." He held out a huge hand and shook Selden's heartily. "I wondered what you were doing in the sleuth line, and it's not hard to guess what brings you here."

"What in heaven's name are you doing here, Ned?" Selden smiled and wrung his crushed hand.

"Sure, 'tis no mystery at all. My father, God rest his soul, was senior partner in this firm, a very old business concerned with management of family estates and the like. When I managed to get a pass degree in Law, as you remember, he took me into his office, and when he died I became the head of the business. Of course, Sandilands, Hoskings and Bright died before the flood."

"It must be a very easy business to run," Selden said with quiet irony.

O'Connor eyed him suspiciously. "I'll not conceal from you, Dick, that I have the benefit of having a chief clerk who knows as much as an encyclopaedia, and he's a great help to me, but I'm neglecting me duties." He pushed a box of fine cigars across the enormous desk.

"It's a fortunate thing, Ned, finding you here. I came, as you guessed, about the Cold Stairs murders, and especially to find out about the will of the late baronet."

"You've come just in time then, for I was going down there to-day. It's a strange business, me boy. Anything I can tell you I'll be pleased to do. I'll get my chief clerk."

He touched a bell on his desk, and the man himself appeared like a jack-in-the-box from the next room. The place was dark, and for the moment Selden had the impression that a skeleton had entered, clothed from head to foot in black. It was some trick of the half-light on the thin cadaverous face and hollow cheekbones. The man was very tall, and the skin clung like parchment to his skull-like face.

"You rang, sir," the man said in a creaking voice in keeping with his appearance.

"This is an old college friend of mine, Mr. Selden, now of Scotland Yard. This is Mr. Coffin, my head clerk."

Selden held out his hand with a queer feeling that he would grasp bony fingers, but the hand, though thin and long, was of flesh and blood.

"Just fetch the box containing the papers relating to the Cold Stairs estates," O'Connor said majestically.

"I have them here, sir. When Simmons told me who had come, I guessed you would want them."

"Good." O'Connor gave a glance at Selden as though to say, "I told you so."

"Here is the will of the late baronet," Coffin said, producing the document. "It was executed in your father's time, Mr. Edward, and as far as we are aware has not been revoked. It is, if I may say so, a somewhat strange document."

O'Connor took the will and was unfolding it. Coffin cleared his throat. "You will excuse me, sir, but it is hardly professional to show a will to a stranger before it has been 'read'."

"That's all right. Mr. Selden is in charge of the murder and represents Scotland Yard. But you know what's in it, and can save us wading through the clauses." He tossed it back to Coffin.

"The will was perfectly correctly drawn up and properly witnessed," Coffin said in a dry, cold voice. "Sir John leaves certain small legacies to servants and dependents on the estate and, after succession duties have been paid, the whole of the remainder goes to the son of an old friend of his, a certain Dr. Gilkie, whom he knew in Assam."

Selden stared bleakly at the solemn clerk. "Do you mean he left nothing to his niece, Sybil, his own sister's child?"

"He left a life annuity to her, but the baronetcy lapses, as there is no male heir. We have not been able to trace any descendant in the direct line."

O'Connor broke in. "But who is this Gilkie to whom the money is left?"

"That is rather a mystery, sir," Coffin said impassively. "The wording is strange. He gave no actual Christian name. I recall that your father commented upon it at the time, but Sir John would say no more than that he left his property to 'the son of my old friend, Dr. Gilkie', and no address or means of tracing him were given."

"It's the maddest thing I've ever heard," O'Connor said indignantly, and Selden guessed that he was not best pleased at being found so ignorant of the whole question.

"We had better advertise for him in the usual way," Coffin suggested.

"I think you ought to have informed me of all this before," O'Connor said severely.

"I am sorry, sir, but no one anticipated an early decease of the baronet, and there are so many cases in our hands," he added tactfully.

"All right, Coffin—you had better lock up the box, and we can go thoroughly into the whole matter later on."

"I have already been through all the relative documents; they are all in order, sir. Sir John left quite a considerable sum."

"Never mind that now." Coffin retired without a word more. "This is a nice kettle of fish," O'Connor growled. "We shall have to take out letters of administration, as I believe our firm have been made executors, and then hunt about for this fellow, who may be dead for all we know."

"If he knows the terms of the will, he'll turn up fast enough when he hears of Sir John's death," Selden commented.

"I shall have to go to Cold Stairs, and examine Sir John's papers, and take that skull and cross-bones with me."

"He's a cheery soul to have about the place," Dick laughed.

"Ach! He fairly gives me the creeps at times, but he's been here for hundreds of years."

"That's a long tune."

"It's only a figure of speech, but he was here with my grandfather, and that's going back some time. Between ourselves, if he wasn't here, Dick, I should have to work!"

"That would be dreadful."

Ned O'Connor did not seem to notice the irony. "It's lucky old Coffin has just come back from leave. First time he's taken a holiday for years; he's so keen on his work."

Dick pricked up his ears. "It doesn't look as though his holiday had done him much good."

"Oh, nothing changes his appearance, like Cleopatra. He only returned yesterday."

"That was lucky for you."

"It was, my boy; you see, I had a competition at my golf club, and I couldn't resist it. Old Coffin had the place to himself, and I found him here this morning. I believe he generally comes here about six o'clock, and sometimes stays all night. He's a devil for work."

"I suppose the other clerks, and the boy who admitted me," Selden spoke casually, "would work automatically when you are away, as long as the chief clerk is here."

Ned uttered a hearty laugh. "Bless your heart, Dick, I've only got one other clerk, and a typist. This show works itself. It's not like Criminal Law. But it's a fairly paying concern, as most of our clients make us executors of their wills."

"So your absence would not be particularly noticed." Selden came back to his point.

"I doubt if anyone would know I was away, unless there were callers, and then Coffin would see them, and spin some yarn. He slips in and out with his own key, and goes into his den. I never see him unless I ring for him." O'Connor glanced at the clock. "It's dry work talking, Dick; will you be after taking a little liquid refreshment with me? I have a convenient club round the corner where they don't worry much about the licensing hours."

"Ned! I'm ashamed of you—a lawyer."

"Sure, and if you lived in this atmosphere, Dick, my boy, you'd acquire a thirst, and of course we can talk business at the club."

"Or golf," Dick remarked, smiling at the genial giant, as he heaved himself up from his chair.

CHAPTER V

Ħ SCIENTIFIC DISCUSSION

T HE COMMITTEE OF THREE, as Selden had christened them, were assembled in Stevens's flat, waiting for the arrival of the young detective. On the ground floor of the building were the offices of the *Weekly Aura,* but the editor had established himself at the very top, where he commanded a view of Broadcasting House and the back of Queen's Hall. In this calm atmosphere matters appertaining to Spiritualism were discussed without the noise and bustle of the streets. In summer a roof garden with palms in pots and trailing plants on trellis work enhanced the idea of splendid isolation, but now, in November, curtains were closely drawn and a bright fire burned in the hearth.

Selden had received their request for an interview when he returned from seeing his friend O'Connor, and knew that a difficult task awaited him. He was broad-minded and always open to learn, but the way in which these people fairly gloated over the two murders, as though they had been done for their especial benefit, put his back up.

The Professor was elated because the experiment, as he called it, had been conducted under the supervision of the B.B.C. "We are always 'suspect'," he told Selden, "because our arrangements are necessarily surrounded by a certain amount of secrecy."

Selden accepted the challenge at once. "You think that here you have some psychic influence at work. In plain language, that the murders were committed by some being not of this world; the devil himself, perhaps."

"We do not put it in that way," Professor Johnson said patiently, as though speaking to a child. "It does not necessarily follow that a being on another plane has intervened. It is more likely some earth-bound soul, unable to obtain release from this plane. Such cases have been known."

"The marks were tangible enough," Selden remarked, annoyed at the smug complacency of the man.

"That is, of course, quite natural," the Professor said. "If such a being materializes, he possesses in enhanced form the attributes of a living man."

Mrs. Seaton, herself a well-known medium, chimed in. "Many cases have been known, and have been correlated by us, but of course the ignorant public refuses to accept any evidence that is not direct, and commonplace."

"There is, for example," the Professor went on, before Selden could even reply, "the question, little studied by doctors unfortunately, of suggestion. There have been plenty of examples in history, the stigmata of St. Francis of Assisi, for example."

"One could hardly call that more than a legend," Selden answered. He gazed at the smug faces of the three persons, and realized the impossibility of argument, but they were all people of influence, and might interfere with his work. He laughed quietly.

"I am afraid I am like Daniel in the den of lions! Of course, you hold your opinions, and in fairness I am bound to admit that the affair at Cold Stairs presents some unusual features."

"Believe me, Selden," the Professor declared earnestly, "there have been hundreds of cases, which we have tabulated with the same care as you people at Scotland Yard have done with crimes. The difficulty of our work as pioneers has been that the public are incredulous. Proof! Proof! they always demand. 'Unless I see, I will not believe' is their slogan."

His sombre eyes shot fire, and his voice had the power and timbre of a prophet.

"There was a case in Transylvania some little time ago. A man was killed in a similar manner, and the peasants had no doubt about it, but the police merely saw a case of robbery and murder, but no one was caught, and nothing had been taken."

Stevens had taken a bulky volume from a shelf, and was turning the pages. "The Lamarc case in the Ardennes. He was found in a wood without a mark on him to show how he died, and no trace of poison. It was brought in as death from exposure."

"Why not? I expect the police were right."

"The police were wrong, Mr. Selden," Mrs. Seaton said quietly. "I was there at the time and saw the body. No man who died of exposure would show on his face such signs of absolute horror as he did."

"Undiscovered crime is common enough, unfortunately," Selden remarked.

"Exactly," the Professor boomed, "and there you have laid your finger on the crucial spot. You police merely shrug your shoulders and say: 'Undiscovered crime', because you will not penetrate into that land of mystery that lies behind material matters and yet is all about us."

"Vampires, werewolves, naturals, and so on," Selden laughed ironically. "I thought the motor-car and vacuum cleaner had got rid of all that."

The Professor was as patient as though instructing a boy.

"Because there is much trickery and fraud, the truth is hidden. Cold Stairs is situated on that mysterious border country, soaked in legend, and still retaining perhaps secrets that have been lost in the world of machinery. The very woods hold cromlechs and barrows where hecatombs of warriors are buried with their chiefs, slain in border warfare as successive waves advanced westwards. Men call these beliefs superstitions. Can you dismiss Stonehenge or the pyramids as mere myths? There are mysterious powers and dark secrets that have been lost but are now being re-discovered."

Selden shrugged his shoulders. "If you take that line I have no answer."

"Listen for a moment, Selden. I hope I shan't bore you. I will be as short as I can. I am a qualified doctor, though I have never practised. I took my degree many years ago in Natural Science at Cambridge. If I took that examination now, and gave the answers I did at my Tripos, in chemistry, for example, I should be conveyed very courteously to the nearest asylum. I am speaking metaphorically, of course."

Selden nodded, and the Professor went on.

"That is clear. Now conversely. If I had given my answers in that Tripos with the knowledge we now possess I should be treated in the same way."

"I agree with all that, of course," Selden said with a grin.

"Now follow a step farther. Science, which some born idiots claim to be fixed, immutable, is more in a state of flux than invention or Religion or Philosophy. Yet the scientists in Astronomy and medical knowledge lay down the law as though it were that of the Medes and Persians."

The Professor was evidently wound up on his favourite topic, and Selden settled himself in his chair to listen. He had made it an axiom that one can always gain knowledge from any fellow mortal who reveals his mind, whether a man of learning or a fish salesman.

"Very well then. Science has progressed, undoubtedly and very greatly in the centuries, but, like Architecture, Painting, and Music, the progress has not been in one straight line, but in waves, like a temperature chart, with its risings and fallings. We cannot build Gothic cathedrals like Chartres or Rouen. We can imitate, but the effect is ghastly. We now build concrete atrocities like Thames House or the Shell Mex horror. We cannot paint like Michael Angelo or Murillo or the first Renaissance artists. For Beethoven and Mozart we have jazz and the crooner. I will not elaborate.

"Now in Science the same holds good. In the middle ages the alchemists, at whom we moderns have mocked for years, were searching among other things for the transmutation of base metal into gold—and that is now within the sphere of practical knowledge, and undoubtedly is theoretically proven. They were searching for the Elixir Vitae, which should prolong life, and that is what all our modern scientists are doing; Voronoff and his glands, vitamins, and gland extracts.

"The so-called witches or 'wise women' gathered herbs and vegetable products and other ingredients and stewed them in a cauldron, making remedies and preventatives for diseases—even for the plague. They were burnt for their pains, though their remedies were undoubtedly efficacious. The nineteenth century laughed uproariously at their ignorance. But mark this, Selden, they were doing, without knowing it, and through knowledge handed down by word of mouth from mother to daughter in some dark secret place, precisely what our chemists are doing now, though they were acting synthetically and now we work analytically—they were practising organic chemistry without knowing it, making strychnine, quinine, belladonna and others of the alcoloids familiar to us now.

"Half our industries now are based on the fact that organic materials can be changed in constitution by chemical means. Trinitrotoluol, cordite, ordinary alcohol, petrol from coal, artificial silk, the aniline dyes, and a hundred more. They are all around us, these mysteries of organic chemistry, a very land of miracles, and the ordinary citizen accepts them as commonplace when he buys a shirt made of wood or a cough mixture extracted from coal."

"Excellent, Professor," Selden commented. "You speak like Socrates."

"Bear with me for a moment and I have finished. Why were these secrets lost—why was not the line of progress straight? I will tell you. As the infidelity of the Renaissance destroyed the faith that built the Gothic churches, so the greed and avarice of that accursed age gave the alchemists and so-called witches the opportunity of revenge for the persecutions of the past, and a chance of making fortunes. They committed the unpardonable sin; they called good evil and evil good. Instead of healing they gave poisons, and practised on the foolishness of the age with love philtres which were nothing but aphrodisiacs. They became rich and powerful and dreaded, like the Church and, like the Church also, they lost their faith. So their knowledge was lost in a welter of fraud and necromancy."

"I quite agree, but what bearing has all this on your case?"

"Is it too much to apply the analogy to the Spirit world? Knowledge of this too was lost; stamped out by persecutions and burnings at first and then by the wave of materialism that came with invention as though the steam engine and wireless were the work of man's hand, and not as much a revelation of God as the Bible itself.

"So, all around us is this mysterious world into which we are only now dimly penetrating. But we are coming back, Selden; slowly and painfully, and with much fraud mixed with genuine truth, like the tares and the wheat. But we are advancing onward, as in every other branch of science."

The Professor finished on a note of triumph, and then his lifted hands fell.

"I must apologize, Selden, for my enthusiasm," he said in a different tone. "This will not interest an unbeliever like you."

Stevens stroked his sleek black hair, and spoke like a director at a Board meeting.

"We are not all men with the great imagination of the Professor. I, for one, am a practical business man, and my work is chiefly to collect and classify information and as far as possible to discard all fraudulent or doubtful cases, but you can't dismiss the whole matter as the imagination of lunatics.

"Let us come, then, to the actual case with which we are dealing, and stick to facts. Sir John Harman was not a complex character, nor was he a man of imagination from what I hear. He was completely devoid of nerves. I believe he spoke quite genuinely when he told Mrs. James he was going for a drink. When in the hall he must either have heard or seen something that made him go on the spur of the moment to investigate. We can dismiss the practical joke theory. He probably thought he could catch the person red-handed, if trickery was being employed."

The Professor interrupted, demonstrating with his lean fingers to accentuate his words.

"To a room which had been searched, in a house in which every exit had been sealed, and where no living being could have penetrated."

"You have me there," Selden said with his unaffected, boyish laugh.

"Then, when your police have finished their investigations," Mrs. Seaton said silkily, "perhaps you could obtain permission for us to investigate on the spot."

"I shouldn't think you will have much chance. The lawyers will take over the property and will either sell it or pull it down, I should imagine."

The Professor sighed. "That sort of thing always seems to happen when we have a really good case. Here, for example, if the stupid police—I beg your pardon, I am not referring to you, Selden—have concluded their investigations, there may quite likely be another murder, for this earth-bound creature, tethered to this plane, and driven mad by its inability to escape, will be tied still more forcibly, and all its freakish passions will be evoked."

Selden felt that he had strayed into a madhouse, and was listening to the ravings of the inmates, but his keen sense of humour came to his rescue.

"I had some idea," he said solemnly, "of getting a parson to exorcise the spirit with bell, book, and candle."

"That might be of some service," Mrs. Seaton said, to his astonishment. "It has been efficacious in several cases."

"What do you propose to do if you get permission?"

"The first thing, I think," the Professor said slowly, "would be to hold a séance in the room in which the first murder took place. We should require some articles belonging to the late Sir John."

"But will there not be danger for you?" Selden said, falling in with their mood.

"We shall draw a magic circle, into which the earth-bound may not penetrate, and call upon it to appear."

"Splendid! I would like to be there."

"The very presence of an unbeliever might prevent any manifestations taking place."

Selden laughed. "Heads you win; tails I lose. Your earth-bound has a pretty taste in the gruesome."

"That is because you don't understand," Mrs. Seaton said patiently. "He may be a suicide, or possibly a murderer, who could not altogether escape at his passing, and is bound to earth."

"On the other hand," Stevens broke in, "he may be a true earth-born, belonging to the forgotten race that has lived on in remote places, that is neither human nor really living, but may change and pass."

"Vampire stuff," Selden scoffed.

"There has, I know, been a lot of nonsense written about vampires. It is doubtful whether such ever existed. Legends have collected round them, especially in Transylvania, but it is merely a way of hinting at something that the peasant can't understand or explain by natural means."

"I am going down to Cold Stairs tomorrow," Mrs. Seaton said with an air of finality. "A woman can sometimes find out more than a man, and I shall carry out my researches in my own way. You need not be alarmed, Mr. Selden, I shan't interfere with you."

"We can have no objections to that," Selden said gallantly.

"Then we are agreed at least on this, Selden," the Professor said. "We each work in our own way, and follow the light that is in us." He laid his hand on the young man's shoulder in a kindly fashion. "Who knows whether the two paths will not meet."

Selden started in spite of himself—the conversation had sunk into his mind, for these people were not frauds, even if they might be fanatics. "Parallel lines don't meet," he said doggedly.

"That's where you are wrong, my boy. You should study Einstein."

A sudden thought that had been lurking at the back of Selden's mind flashed up. "By the way, Professor, I wanted to ask you something. Did you ever hear of a certain Dr. Gilkie?"

The expression on Professor Johnson's fine face became hard and bitter. "That man! Yes, I knew him. I will be fair to his memory, though he and I differed on everything. He was a brilliant scientist, but an infidel in every sense of the word. He believed in nothing but pure science which he claimed was the basis of all life. His theory was that every action, thought, and passion of a human being was merely a matter of the arrangement of molecules, and the quantities of certain salts in the ductless glands. He was especially opposed to our researches, which he attacked bitterly, saying that life ended with death, completely and absolutely, as a tree rots away and dies."

"That is very interesting," Selden said eagerly.

"He held that the relative distribution of carbohydrates made the difference between a genius and a devil. Of course, he didn't believe in a soul."

"You would hardly have got on well together," Selden laughed.

"We could have agreed to differ on theory," the Professor said solemnly. "We are all entitled to our opinions. He did a lot of pioneer work. He foresaw much of the work on ductless glands that is much studied now, and the effects of anti-toxins and cultures. But it was his character that revolted me. He was utterly ruthless, and would have sacrificed his own kith and kin for the cause of science, I believe."

The Professor was greatly moved, and Selden could picture the fight that must have been waged between two such incompatible natures.

"He is dead, I suppose?"

"It was a sad end to a brilliant man, but only Nemesis. He cut his finger with a test tube when experimenting with snake venom, and died almost immediately. When they found him in his laboratory, he had cut his thumb off in an attempt to stop the poison spreading, but it had been too late."

"He had a son, I believe?"

"He had no son!" the Professor said firmly. "He had been away on an expedition for two years in Assam and New Guinea."

"But surely you must be mistaken?"

"It is a matter I do not wish to discuss. He died twenty-six years ago now, and I have no wish to rake up old scandals. His wife disappeared. She is probably dead by this time. I hope so, at any rate."

"Why?" Selden persisted. "Was there anything bad about her?"

The Professor's face assumed a hard, grim look. "I happen to know what Gilkie did; it is a thing I prefer not to discuss. You will be wise to forget the very name."

He refused to say another word, and Selden took his leave. He walked back to the mews deep in thought. Certain facts were becoming clear. Sir John had been in Assam as a young man, and had left all his money to "the son of Dr. Gilkie", whose very Christian name he appeared not to know, nor his residence.

Was this strange will some sort of reparation for a wrong done? The solution seemed to rest with the finding of this son, now about twenty-six years old, if he still lived. The balance seemed to be swinging over to a natural and material explanation. It was, at any rate, a relief from the talk to which he had been listening.

CHAPTER VI

Che Secret of the Woods

THE DOUBLE INQUEST which had been held in the Memorial Hall at Lydford had just concluded. Jack Hartley hurried away, and drove to the lodge, as he had promised Mrs. James to let her know the result. He found her alone in the small sitting-room, busy with household duties.

"It's all over, Mrs. James. Dr. Hughes hurried the proceedings, and the obvious verdict in both cases of murder by persons unknown was returned. It was the only possible verdict, and leaves the police with a free hand."

"So that they are no nearer to a solution?" Mrs. James said gravely.

"In my opinion," Jack said, seating himself on the table, "they never will be, but my friend Selden is hot stuff. By the way, I have some news for you. A lawyer came down from London, with his clerk, who looks as though he had been dug out of a cemetery for the occasion. O'Connor is an old Cambridge colleague of Dick Selden and myself, and a rattling good fellow—you'll like him." He looked round the room cautiously. "Where are the children?"

"Eric is in his chair, sitting in the sunlight, as it's rather stuffy in here. Sybil is with him, I expect. Why do you ask?"

"I'm glad they are out of the way. I want to talk to you. Dick Selden and the lawyer have gone up to the house on business, so I promised to inform you. It appears Sir John made a will leaving nearly all his property to the son of an old friend of his, a certain Dr. Gilkie, and no one knows who he is or where he is to be found."

"I have heard Sir John speak of his old friend, Dr. Gilkie, but of course I know nothing of the will, or about his private affairs."

"He has left Sybil an annuity for life. Seems rather shabby, but I suppose it's better than nothing. It will pay for her education and so on. She will become a ward in Chancery, O'Connor says, but I hope you will get the guardianship."

"I should be very sorry to part with Sybil," Mrs. James said with feeling. "She is a strange girl, and I think I understand her better than anyone else."

"She is a very pretty child," Jack said enthusiastically.

Mrs. James looked quickly at him. "She is hardly such a child as you think, Mr. Hartley. She is nearly sixteen."

Hartley laughed. "I thought her about ten. She—"

"I know what you are going to say. Sir John, for some reason I never could understand, although kindness itself on all other matters, would insist on having Sybil dressed as a mere doll, and treated her as such. She has never been to school."

"So that really there is little difference in age between your son and Sybil," Jack said in a puzzled manner.

"They are like brother and sister, and Sybil is very good to him. He would miss her if she were taken away from me."

"It's awful cheek of me, Mrs. James," Jack said nervously. "But oughtn't your boy to have expert treatment? I mean a country doctor like Hughes can hardly be an expert."

Something like scorn showed in Mrs. James's face, "Dr. Hughes! I would never ask his advice. He's all right for influenza and maternity cases among the people in the Forest and Sir John's tenants, but not for a case like this. Sir John was most generous in this matter. He paid for a specialist, and I have taken Eric to London. They say that in time he may get right. He should go to a proper place for treatment."

"I quite understand," Jack said sympathetically.

The door opened and Sybil came in, and then stopped as she saw Hartley.

"Good morning," he said with sudden change of manner after what he had been told. The child was indeed a strange figure for her age. Her clothes came just below her knees, and her dark hair was in ringlets and tied with a bow. In this place of grim secrets, even such a small matter as this was significant.

She greeted Jack in an open, friendly way, and now that he had learned her age he understood the collected manner in which she spoke.

"I am going to see Mrs. Jenkins, Auntie," she said. "I must say good-bye to her."

"I don't think you should go there alone, dear, after what has happened."

"You are going away, then, Mrs. James?" Jack said.

"There is nothing to keep us here now. We can't stay on in this lodge."

"But hadn't you better see Mr. O'Connor first? He will want to know where you are going."

"Of course, that will be necessary, but this place is not good for the children."

It was on the tip of Jack's tongue to say that she could not take Sybil away now, without consent from the executor, but he felt that it was none of his business. He slipped off the table, and took one of those queer resolutions that was to affect the lives of all of them.

"I have nothing to do until Mr. Selden comes back. I'll come with you if you like, Sybil."

"I should be very grateful," Mrs. James said.

Sybil eyed him gravely. "I'll show you the woods."

The day was warm for the time of year, but there was a crisp feeling that presaged frost, and the leaves dropped steadily from the trees.

They set off up the drive, and rather to Jack's astonishment Sybil turned off into the green ride in which the constable had been murdered. Perhaps, he thought, the girl did not know. She showed no signs of fear as she took the path, with Jack following.

Even when they passed the spot where the body had been discovered and Jack was able to walk beside her, she showed no special interest, but chatted on about the woods and the various trees with a knowledge that was almost uncanny.

They emerged into the clearing and saw old Mrs. Jenkins sitting in her doorway, peeling apples and crooning over her work. She was very still and witch-like. At their approach she looked up and gave a smile of welcome to Sybil.

"Good morning, my dear." Sybil ran to her and the old woman folded her in her arms. Jack's instinct told him that the bitter memory of her lost daughter called forth all her motherly affection for this motherless child.

"I am glad to see you, sir," she addressed him, holding Sybil close to her side. "It's no place for her to be wandering alone. She's too fond of the woods, to my thinking."

"I've come to say good-bye, Mrs. Jenkins. We are going away." Sybil spoke in her soft, level voice.

"I shall miss you, my lamb, but it's glad I am to hear it." A look of great relief came to her wrinkled old face. "That gloomy house is no place for a young girl like you. You'll meet others of your age and take your station in life as you should, my dear."

They made a pretty picture in the sunlight, with the background of the picturesque cottage. The hungry, gripping woods all round the clearing seemed waiting to devour it, and close in again as soon as the human beings who had dared the solitude of the forest had gone. Hartley, engaged in the most modern of all inventions, one that brought the world within a second's reach from Pole to Pole, could hardly realize that here in England was a spot as wild and unfrequented as in the jungles of the Congo, where primitive needs were satisfied in primitive manner.

If old Jenkins and his wife died or left the cottage, in a few years the roof would fall in, and the forest encroach on a weedy patch, and then only a skeleton of grey stone covered with green grass would remain.

"We shall miss you, my dear," the old dame said wistfully. "I suppose some strangers will take Cold Stairs, or perhaps they will make it into an hotel, and I've know a Harman there since I was born. Well-a-day. I don't know what will happen to Jenkins and me. We're getting old."

Sybil flushed, and something of the pride of race came to her indignant eyes. "They would not dare. But you need not worry, Mrs. Jenkins, you shall never leave your cottage or want for anything. I will see to that."

"Thank you, my dear." The old crone was nearly crying.

"Jenkins would like to see you, just to say good-bye like."

"Of course I shall see him. I'll show Mr. Hartley the woods and come back . . . Would you like to have a walk?"

"I should be delighted. I've lived all my life up in London, and this is all new to me."

They took their way deeper into the still forest.

"I suppose there are many cottages scattered about here?" he asked lightly.

"There were many years ago," she said, fixing her grave eyes on him. "They were charcoal burners', but most of the cottages are in ruins and overgrown with creepers."

"You know the forest very well," he said, wondering at her fearlessness and old-fashioned manner of talking.

They entered a sort of green tunnel where a brook, now dry, had run. The dead leaves formed a mushy carpet under their feet, deadening all sound. Everything was very still and silent. On each side of the sunken way trees stood dark and upright, and the dried dead branches of the undergrowth filled the gaps. No flowers bloomed here, and the sunlight could hardly penetrate. All was faded, dead. They might have been alone in the world.

"You are not afraid of the forest?"

"I? I love it," she said with an intensity strange in so young a girl.

"I shouldn't care to come here by night," he laughed.

"Why not? You are not afraid?"

"No," he replied doubtfully, "but I should get completely lost."

And then the world seemed to split in two, and for a moment he doubted the sanity of the girl walking quietly at his side. Quite naturally she remarked:

"They are harmless as long as you don't disturb them and don't show fear. Poor Anne got frightened and tried to run away. She would have been all right but for that."

Jack remained tongue-tied, his mind in a whirl. Was this child talking gibberish, or was he going to hear something that would throw light on the dark mystery of the woods?

They had left the dry bed of the woodland stream, and came to an open space, and the scene was strangely familiar to him. A sense of unreality stole over him. The sombre silence of the place, as though the trees were listening, and the dappled sunlight making a patchwork of gold on the ground; he had seen it all before. And then, with a feeling of misgiving, he realized that this was the place in which the boy Eric had taken the photograph that Dr. Hughes had shown them.

There could be no mistake; here was the vast tree against which that shade of evil had been projected on the film of the camera. He moistened his dry lips.

"They?" he asked, almost in a whisper. "Who are they?"

"The people of the woods, of course," she answered readily.

"There hardly seem any people here."

"Of course they are not human, you know," she said with perfect frankness.

"The sooner you get away from these woods the better," Jack muttered to himself. He would not ask further; the imagination of the child had evidently become too strong for her growing intellect.

Sybil led the way to a great green mound that rose in the forest like some ancient barrow of long dead warriors. Trees grew on the summit, and the sides were covered with encroaching shrubs. He heard Sybil speaking: "It used to be a house, with gardens and flower-beds, but it got burnt down, and was never rebuilt."

Sybil took his hand, and he felt hers was cool and smooth in his, which had gone damp. She led him round the mound, and pushed some bushes to one side, showing the stone uprights and lintel of what had once been the entrance to a farmhouse.

Within was a queer chamber, quite shapeless, and formed of half-burnt beams on which the marks of the fire were still visible, which had remained locked together like a tent roof. The place was half-filled with debris and provided with a dim green light, like the tanks of an aquarium, which filtered through the green boughs round the entrance.

There was a smoke-blackened old fire-place in the wall, and Jack guessed this to have been the ancient kitchen. "This is where I used to come to meet him," the girl said softly, as though speaking in a church.

"What in the world are you talking about?" he exclaimed almost angrily. "Meet whom?"

"I never saw him. I was blindfolded," she said.

"Look here, you are talking an awful lot of rot, Sybil," Jack began, and then suddenly remembered that Selden had asked his help, and perhaps he was on the verge of discovering something of importance.

"You think I am lying." Her hand was quickly withdrawn from his, and the grey eyes flashed. "I'm sorry I brought you here."

"I beg your pardon," he said humbly, "but I suppose I'm not used to these things. As I told you, I am a Londoner, and an electrical engineer." He felt the explanation was rather weak. "Tell me about this man."

"Man!" she said scornfully—"he is the god of the wood."

Jack kept a tight hold on his reeling senses. "Of course," he agreed.

"He used to call me and I came," she said indignantly, still smarting at his words.

"And what happened when you came?"

"I mustn't tell you," she said stubbornly. "They are secret rites."

"Very well then, I won't ask. But how did he call you? I don't understand."

She was quite open in her answers. "I used to hear him call me at night—always in the summer—and of course I got up at once and came here."

"That's clear," he said, falling in with her mood. "But how did you get out of the house without anyone hearing you?"

"I slept by myself, you see; I have always since I was a child. And I went through the window. It's not a real window, you know, it's a fairy window and was always open when he called. That was the sign."

Here was something tangible at last, embellished with the child's wild fancies.

"But how did you get down?"

She seemed puzzled for a moment and then smiled.

"I see what you mean. By the rings, of course. I went straight down with my nighty on as Mrs. James always took my clothes away at night to brush and fold up."

"You weren't afraid?"

"Not a bit—I loved the woods by moonlight, but after Anne was frightened I was a little scared."

A sudden suspicion crossed Jack's mind like a shadow crossing the sun. "Did she know all about this that you have been telling me?"

"Oh yes. She brought me the first time and showed me everything. But Mrs. Jenkins doesn't know. You won't say anything to her, will you, Mr. Hartley?"

"Certainly not," he replied stoutly. "We must get back though."

She led the way, reluctantly, he thought, and spoke over her shoulder. "I haven't been here since Eric was frightened."

"But weren't you scared too, didn't you see anything that night?" Jack felt he was hot on the trail of something.

"No . . ." she said doubtfully. "I don't think I should have been frightened. Eric screamed and fell down the stairs."

"Don't think I am asking too many questions. Do you think that what Eric fancied he saw was the god of the woods?" He found himself slipping into a way of talking as though he accepted her story. He was afraid she would be offended again and he would learn no more.

"Oh no!" she exclaimed indignantly. "He would never come to the house. That was the Evil Spirit. I knew it was there and told the god of the woods about him. He said no harm would come to me."

It seemed gibberish to Jack, but he listened as she prattled on with weird impossible stories. The Evil Spirit of Cold Stairs was apparently well known to the creature of the woods, and had to obey him, and there were others, attendants and splendid beings who joined in the ceremonies.

The woodland opened out and the cottage came into view. Jack was glad to see it there. After the experience he had gone through he would hardly have been surprised to see it walk off on four stumpy legs into the forest, and little old men with long white beards sedately keeping pace.

Old Jenkins was back and having his tea. He looked suspiciously at Hartley, having no use for strangers who came "nosing around".

"I hear you are going, Miss Sybil," he said, rising as they entered. "I can't say I'm sorry, though we'll miss your sweet face. These woods aren't healthy for young girls like you, axing your pardon."

"I hope to come back again sometime," she replied, taking his hard hand in hers. "I shouldn't like to think I shall never come again. That would be dreadful."

"We don't know what's going to happen at present," Hartley said as the old man looked bewildered. "The family lawyer is down here settling things up, about Sir John's will and so on. Meanwhile, Mrs. James is going to London with the children."

Her good-byes over, Sybil waved her hand to the old couple and made for the short cut to Cold Stairs.

The back of the house was covered in creepers that encircled the long low windows, with small diamond panes set in leaded frames. The leaves of the Virginia creeper showed splashes of red like blood where a few leaves still retained their hold.

"That is my bedroom window," Sybil remarked. She pointed to a window on the first floor, now closed and shuttered.

"Where are the rings you were telling me about?"

The girl walked straight to the wall, and thrust her hand among the creepers. "Here." She took Hartley's hand and placed it on an old iron ring, flattened out, and driven into the wall. It was very old and dirty.

"We had better get back," he said. "I expect Mr. Selden will be waiting for me, and Mrs. James will be anxious about you."

As they went down the drive a thought came to Hartley's mind. "Do you mind telling me one thing?"

"Certainly; I feel I can trust you. I always either trust or hate people at once."

"What do you keep in that mysterious box of yours?"

Her manner at once became secretive. "I can't tell you that; I don't know myself. He gave it to me to keep for him."

"Then it's of no use asking," he said with a smile. "Hello! What's all this?"

They had turned the corner of the drive, and saw a group of people in front of the lodge. Mrs. James came forward quickly to them. Her face was flushed, and she was trembling. Jack saw Dick and O'Connor and some strangers clustered round the door.

CHAPTER VII

ᴄꞪꞸ BOMBꞩꞪꞸꞭꞭ

SELDEN AND O'CONNOR had gone to Cold Stairs, little knowing what a bombshell was about to burst.

The detective unlocked the front door, and a wave of musty air was emitted.

"Phew! What a state a place gets into when it's been locked up for a few days," O'Connor said, holding his handkerchief to his face.

"We'll have the whole place open, now the inquest is over," Selden said, leading the way to Sir John's study.

He unfastened the shutters and threw open the windows. A large desk stood in the centre of the room, and a safe had been let into one side of the wall. Both had been sealed up by the police, who had taken possession when Selden went to London. The two men settled down to examine the contents, with a strange feeling that at any moment they might come across some document that would throw some light on the mystery.

Receipts, old bills, and a mass of correspondence were piled untidily in the drawers. Yellow faded notices of meetings and requests for subscriptions were mixed up with correspondence going back to Sir John's father's time. Selden glanced rapidly through them, and flung them impatiently on the floor.

"There's a week's work here."

"I'll get old Coffin to go through them," O'Connor said; "sure it's no job for the likes of us. He'll gloat over this junk. Let's try the safe; I know the combination."

They had just begun to examine the contents, which seemed in the same state of confusion as those in the desk, when a woman's voice, harsh and ill-tempered, came through the open window.

O'Connor went to the front door, not wishing strangers inside. A large stout woman dressed entirely in black stood at the entrance, and a gaunt ill-favoured lad of about eighteen was peering

over her shoulder. He too was clothed in an obviously new black
suit.

"I am afraid you can't come in here," O'Connor said politely.

"Ho! Can't I, young man, and who are you, may I ask?"

"My name is O'Connor, and I am the family lawyer to the late
Sir John Harman."

The woman's face assumed a more genial expression. "Then
you're the very man I want."

She brushed past O'Connor, and came into the library without
ceremony.

Selden rose from the desk. "Good morning, madam," he said,
guessing that the woman would not come without some sort of
warrant.

There was an air of suppressed triumph about her, as though
she had something up her sleeve. "And are you another lawyer?"

With his habitual caution Selden replied, "I am assisting my
friend, Mr. O'Connor, with these papers."

The woman sat down heavily with a sigh of relief, while the
youth wandered round the room, examining everything in an irri-
tating manner.

"I have come to claim my rights," she said, opening a large
black handbag. An ominous silence greeted her words, and Dick
and Ned exchanged a rapid glance. "I am Lady Harman, the lawful
wife of the late Sir John Harman," she exclaimed dramatically,
and grinned at the two men. "What's more, my son Bill is the new
baronet; Sir William Harman, bless him."

"You have, of course, all the necessary proofs?" O'Connor
managed to exclaim.

"Proofs! Do you think I'm a fool, young man? A lantern-jawed
guy I saw at the hotel in Lydford told me you would be here. Sir
John married me all right, but the dirty dog would never give me
my right place; I suppose he was ashamed of me and Bill. I wasn't
class enough for his friends."

She fumbled in the bag and produced some documents tied
with black ribbon.

"I've got my marriage lines here, and the birth certificate for
Bill."

"May I see them?" O'Connor asked, holding out his hand.

"You may, but I'll keep my hands on them if you don't mind."

"Sure and that's a wise precaution," O'Connor said with a
merry laugh, though he felt in no laughing mood at this unex-

pected turn of events. "My firm has had charge of the Harman estates for many years."

"Then I may employ you, though you are over-young for a responsible lawyer."

She laid the documents flat on the desk before Ned, and held the corners tightly. O'Connor saw at a glance the familiar marriage form at a Registrar's office in London, properly signed and witnessed, but Selden's keen eyes saw more. The name was plain "John Harman" and the occupation was given as "Tea Planter".

"You married Sir John while his father was alive," he asserted quietly.

"Of course I did," she answered fiercely. "That doesn't make any difference."

"None whatever. Undoubtedly you are the widow of the late baronet."

"I've got something else that's of more importance," the woman declared. "This is his last Will and Testament, and all in order."

O'Connor gave a start, and a frown crossed his face. He took the document which Lady Harman, as she had become, allowed him to handle. With growing apprehension he read, *"I wish to revoke all former wills that I have made previous to this date etc."* and he saw that the date was recent, only three years ago. The document seemed to be in order, and had been properly drafted by a lawyer. A feeling of anger came to him that Sir John should have done this behind his back, and caused this confusion.

"You see," the woman said in a patronizing tone, "I have the use of all the income, and any money at the bank at the time of my husband's death, until William is twenty-one, when he comes in for the whole estate. Then I get an allowance."

She cast her eye on the sloping-shouldered youth, who grinned sheepishly.

O'Connor examined the will with care, and then remarked:

"I notice that in the event of your son's death, without issue, the whole of the property goes to Sybil, Sir John's niece."

"You can make your mind easy about that; Sir William will marry all right when he is old enough. There are many who would be proud to be called Lady Harman."

"This appears to be in order, but the will must be proved."

"Since your firm has done the work before, and knows the ropes, I'll employ you. But don't you start charging me too much; I've got a good eye to business."

O'Connor's face grew red, and his Irish temper rose, but Selden intervened before he could speak.

"You couldn't do better, Lady Harman," he said heartily. "My friend is the soul of honour, and highly respected in the profession."

O'Connor met a warning look from Dick, and swallowed his pride.

"Then we can call that settled," Lady Harman said, evidently glad to get someone to shoulder the responsibility.

"If I am to act for you," O'Connor said stiffly, "I would be glad to know why this was kept a complete secret even from my firm."

"You may well ask! I was young and pretty once." The stout face positively simpered. "John Harman was on leave from somewhere in the East, I never could remember names, and he was a gay young spark in those days. I was in a tobacco kiosk at Wembley, and quite a child. He made love to me; well, Mr. O'Connor, you are young yourself, and things will happen. Before he went back he married me, and used to send me an allowance. Believe me, young men," she turned to the two with a bland air, "I didn't even know that his father was a baronet. I wasn't after any title, but his father died and then he told me. He used to come to London every week, but kept on putting me off when I suggested coming here to live. But at last I got sick of it. Bill was in hospital with scarlet fever, and I came down here, three years ago."

"You've been here before then," Selden remarked, keenly interested now.

"I have, young man." A look almost of fear grew in her eyes. "I wanted to see the place where my son would one day be master. I don't mind telling you there was a first-class row. I had wired to John and he met me at the station, and tried to make me go back. I told him straight I wasn't going to put up any more with hiding in a London flat, and at last we came to an agreement."

"You mean the will," Selden said.

"You're sharp, young man. I insisted on coming here, as a friend, you understand, just to see the place, and found a stuck-up governess with a son and John's niece. But I only stayed two days."

She paused for breath, and then said abruptly, "Bill, just go outside and have a look at the gardens."

"Why should I, Ma? I want to hear."

"You do what I tell you, or I'll box your ears," she exclaimed with sudden forgetfulness of the boy's new dignity.

The lad slunk out of the room, muttering to himself.

"I have never told Bill," the woman went on in a hoarse whisper. "This place isn't healthy; I don't mean the drains are wrong, but there's something here that's not nice to know, and that's a fact. I saw it and heard it, and I'm not a nervous woman. It's my belief that this house is haunted, and from what I read about my poor husband's death, I think I'm right."

"So you went back?" Selden asked, as the woman was going to elaborate on her theories.

"We came to an arrangement," she said pompously. "John made a will in my favour as you've seen, and I agreed, on my part, to stay in London, and keep quiet about my marriage. I didn't particularly care to live here."

"You will probably want to sell the place?" Selden asked.

"Don't you run away too fast, young man. It would take more than a bogey to keep me out of the family house, for Bill's sake, now he's a baronet. Once we have it cleaned up and redecorated throughout, and a lot of these trees cut down, you won't know the place."

Selden smiled at her notion of exorcizing a ghost, but remained silent.

"Meanwhile, Mr. O'Connor," she said aggressively, "I know from what John told me he had a good fat sum lying in the bank, and I shall want some of that on account. If you can't do it, I'll go to another lawyer."

Again O'Connor flushed with annoyance, but Dick squeezed his arm, and he muttered that it could be arranged when the documents had been examined.

"Very well then," Lady Harman said with an air of finality. "Now we'll have a drink. In the dining-room I think."

She led the way, followed by Selden and the lawyer. Bill had forestalled them. They found him drinking a stiff whisky-and-soda, and smoking a cigar. The good lady helped herself to gin. "Easy on with that whisky, Bill," she remarked, as the boy started on a second.

"Shut up, Ma. I'm a baronet now—Sir William. You can drop that 'Bill' business."

As the gin percolated into the good woman's brain, she became more affable. "I'll make a new place of this." She glanced round the old dining-room. "We'll have a nice bright paper instead of this dingy wood panelling. And modern grates put in."

Selden looked at the beautiful old linenfold oak panelling, and strolled to the window in disgust. A young man straight from the tropics, caught by a pretty face. The inevitable consequences, and the unfortunate sense of honour of an ancient race. That had brought about the disinheritance of Sybil from her birthright, and the Harmans were now represented by this scraggy vulgar youth and his impossible mother.

He turned back, and found O'Connor discussing certain legal matters with Lady Harman, whose face was now flushed and smiling.

"The will leaves everything to you and your son unconditionally," Ned was saying.

"You bet your life: I saw to that. But I'm not greedy, like some people. I shall treat the servants and the peasants handsome, and that child Sybil; she must be growing up now. I must do something for her."

"It would be an act of ... kindness," O'Connor said. He had almost said "justice".

"You leave it to me. I don't mind her staying here, she'd be company for Sir William; but I can't stand that governess woman, I shall give her the sack. And I couldn't stand a cripple about the place."

"I don't think we can do anything more here," Selden interrupted. "I'll take you in my car, if you like. Just let me lock up."

He wanted to get them away from the place, and put an end to this, but by bad luck, as they came to the lodge, Mrs. James emerged, wheeling Eric in his chair, and he was forced to stop the car.

"Good afternoon, Mrs. James," Lady Harman said with odious patronage, "and how are your son and Sybil?"

She got out of the car and held out her flabby hand.

Mrs. James stared at the woman in surprise. "Good afternoon, Mrs. Thomas," she said frigidly.

"Not so much of your Mrs. Thomas," Lady Harman said. "I came down before *incognito*. I have been having an interview with my lawyer."

Like most women of her nature she wanted to keep her news back for effect.

O'Connor cut her short. "This is Lady Harman, widow of Sir John Harman."

Mrs. James started, and her hand clutched the rail of Eric's chair. Eric half raised himself on his elbows with an effort and stared fixedly at the woman.

"You needn't gape at me, boy." She pulled Bill forward. "This is the new baronet, Sir William Harman. We may be able to do something for you later on."

"I was thinking of Sybil," the boy said in his soft voice.

"Sybil will become a ward in Chancery," O'Connor hastened to say. "The question of guardianship will be fixed by the Court."

"Well, I am sure I shall be happy to look after my husband's niece."

The blow was a shrewd one, and Mrs. James paled, but she had too much sense to argue. "I suppose," she said meekly, "there will be no objection to my looking after her until something is settled, and until you have moved in here, Lady Harman?"

"I shall have no objection to that," Lady Harman said loftily, "provided that I know where you are, and I shall make a small allowance to you while you continue to act as her governess."

It was at this precise moment that Jack and Sybil came in sight, and Mrs. James went forward to break the news in a hurried whisper. She knew Sybil's spirit. and feared a scene.

"So this is Sybil—come here, child. My word, she has grown. But what clothes! We must alter all that. Do you remember me, my dear? I expect I shall send you to a boarding-school."

Sybil listened gravely to the gush of words. She held her hand out stiffly to avoid the kiss she feared was coming.

The situation had become impossible, and Ned's eyes twinkled as he saw how Dick handled it. The lout Bill was wiping his mouth with the back of his hand, preparatory to saluting his new-found relative, and Dick promptly offered him a cigarette. Then he seized Lady Harman's hand vigorously.

"I am very pleased to have met you," he said. "I congratulate you and your son, though it is a sad occasion. I am afraid I must get off myself, but I expect you would like to have a look round. Here are the keys."

He had the party broken up as neatly as a policeman separates a crowd round an accident or a street fight.

Mrs. James, with a slight bow, wheeled the chair round and went into the lodge, followed by Sybil, and O'Connor had to conduct the woman and her imp of a boy to see the scene of the constable's murder, which they both demanded to inspect, like the chamber of horrors.

"What a woman," Jack said, when the two friends were alone.

"I couldn't have stood much more of her. Why, Jack, what's the matter?" With his uncanny instinct Dick saw that something had upset Hartley beyond the mere shock of finding Lady Harman.

"Dick, I want to speak to you privately."

"Jump in then, and we'll go and have a spot of food. I've had no time for lunch."

When they were seated in the coffee-room at the "Horse and Groom" at Lydford, and food had been served, Jack turned to Dick.

"I've heard such a fantastic story from Sybil that I almost doubt her sanity."

He recounted faithfully all that had taken place, and Selden's face grew very grave.

"That girl is certainly not mad, Jack; and you can take that from me. But she is lucky to have escaped."

"You think there is something beyond imagination?" Jack spoke with a note of relief.

"You poor mutt," Dick said with a laugh. "You are a mechanic, and are in daily contact with one of the mysteries of the universe, wireless. You play about with valves and heterodynes and other gadgets, but you really know nothing about the force you are dealing with. Supposing you were trying to explain wireless to a race of intelligent savages, don't you think they would either call you a first-class liar or deem you mad? Sybil has a vivid imagination, but she is no liar. She has faithfully recounted to you what she has seen, or fancied she has seen. The facts are straight enough; it's the explanation we want. As soon as you have finished that cheese, and drunk a glass of port, as a gentleman should do with such excellent cheese, we'll go straight up to Cold Stairs and investigate."

Jack looked in astonishment at his friend. He had never seen such a look on his face before.

"It's a race, Jack—a desperate race," he said solemnly. "Can I unravel this in time, or will there be further catastrophe?" Not another word would he say until they had arrived back at the gloomy old house.

"I shall have to do a little housebreaking," Dick said, and then stopped as he saw the front door was slightly open. "Hello! What does this mean? I hope O'Connor hasn't brought her ladyship and the imp back."

There was no one in the ground-floor rooms, and Dick ascended the massive staircase, followed, rather unwillingly, by
Jack. On the landing he paused, listening. "There's someone in the
house, Jack," he whispered.

A faint sound came to them, and Hartley's pulse quickened as
he saw they were going straight to the chamber of death. Dick
drew his automatic and turned the handle, flinging the door wide
open. The room was flooded in daylight, and the shutters had been
turned back. For a moment they thought the room was empty, and
then Jack gave a suppressed cry, and clutched at Dick's arm. A tall
thin figure was standing by the bed, motionless and staring at
them. To Jack the figure appeared like Death himself, but Dick
instantly recovered, and slipped his automatic into his pocket.

"Why, Mr. Coffin, this is a surprise!"

The clerk came forward, with as much of a smile as he was capable of screwing into his face.

"Mr. O'Connor sent me here to go through all the papers, Mr.
Selden. I am making a rough inventory of the place."

"Of course, that's all right. Dirty work here, isn't it?"

"It is uncommonly dusty, but interesting, especially in this
room, where I understand the murder actually took place."

Selden laughed easily, as he saw Jack backing hastily from the
room. "We won't interrupt you," he said, and followed.

"Lord! He gave me a fright—who is he?" Jack said when they
had closed the door.

"That amiable-looking gentleman is Ned's chief clerk, bearing
the appropriate name of Coffin. But we didn't come to gaze on his
cheery face. I want Sybil's room. Now let me think. I went all over
the house and ought to remember."

"She showed me the window from the outside," Jack observed.

"I remember now—I seldom forget the plan of a house. It's
along the corridor at the end, next to Eric's room, and Mrs. James
slept on the other side of that."

He led the way without hesitation, and opened a door. The
room was still closely shuttered, and he switched on the light,
showing a clean bright room, such as a young girl would take a
pride in. He carefully unhasped the shutters, and turned them back
into their sockets in the thickness of the wall, and then gazed
thoughtfully at the window.

"The seal is intact," Jack said, intensely keen on this strange
adventure.

"I wonder," Dick said half to himself, "what Sybil meant by fairy windows."

"Moonshine, I expect."

"You have no imagination, Jack. We have to accept her story, with the embellishments due to a child's imagination, but it's not false. If the window was merely open in the ordinary way, she would scarcely have used that curious expression."

He carefully cut the tapes of the seal, and threw the windows open letting in a breath of fresh air.

Jack watched the keen alert face of his friend, contrasting it with the usually smiling boyish countenance of everyday life.

"Hello! I've got it, Jack."

Dick closed the window and hasped it. "Now observe, my wireless friend. I found this because I was looking for it." His delicate fingers moved round the edge of the leaden frame in which the panes were held, and found a small stud, which he pressed. The heavy frame remained in its place, but the window flew open.

"Clever! I should never have guessed it if Sybil hadn't told you in so many words. You see, there is an inner window inside the frame, with a hinge of its own. If this was thrown right back, it would give the exact appearance the girl described, she'd feel like Alice when she walked through the looking-glass."

He leant out and felt among the thick creepers. "She was right, I can feel the first of the 'rings' as she called them, though they are more like staples. We are getting warm, as children say in hunt the thimble."

He closed the inner window with a click. "We'll keep this little discovery to ourselves," he chuckled. "We know at any rate of one method of entrance to the house without our seals being broken." He burst out laughing. "Jack, do you observe how your Committee of Three played into the hands of someone by moving the children downstairs and leaving this room empty?"

"You think the murderer came in by this means?"

"I think nothing at present. I only said it is a method of access. At any rate, Doubting Thomas, you will grant that there was some truth in Sybil's story."

"I am awfully glad," Jack said; and then, seeing a merry smile on Dick's face, hastily added, "Have you seen enough here?"

"Quite. We'll go."

They drove down the drive in silence till they reached the lodge. "I promised to see Mrs. James," Jack said nervously.

"Oh, Jack! She's old enough to be your mother."

"Don't be an ass, Dick."

"I should be sorry to lose you, but of course if you are contemplating matrimony," Dick said as Jack sprang out of the car, "I shall have to see the local police. I'll go back by train and leave you the car."

"Thanks very much," Jack said warmly, as he made for the lodge door.

Dick watched him for a moment, and then walked through the iron gates and strode off to the village. "Jack's a fool," he said to himself. "He's going to take that family away before Lady Harman can stop him, and there'll be the devil to pay." He shrugged his shoulders and walked steadily on.

Mrs. James opened the door a few inches, and then, seeing who the visitor was, welcomed him in. The small lodge sitting-room was littered with clothes and two suit-cases half packed were standing on the floor. Mrs. James closed and locked the door and faced him with blazing eyes.

"Impertinent wench!" she cried passionately. "I wonder I kept my head at all and could be even civil."

"I quite agree with you. She's impossible."

"It was only for Sybil's sake I kept my temper. She shan't have the child."

"You've met her before?"

"Yes, Mr. Hartley, and I half guessed the truth then. She couldn't hide her air of proprietorship, and the familiar way she talked to Sir John—only I thought then she was his cast-off mistress."

"You realize that the old will is now valueless. Everything goes to her, and Sybil doesn't get an allowance."

"I don't care. I have a little money of my own, enough to manage."

"Then the thing to do," Hartley said cheerily, "is to clear out. Do a bunk. I see you are packing. Where are the children?"

"In the bedroom. I wanted to get them out of the way: this room's too small for packing."

"I'll help. I have the car and will run you up to town. I say, this is rather a joke. You know possession is nine-tenths of the law. Besides, these legal matters take ages."

At the back of Jack's mind was not the urgency of getting away from this virago, but of removing Sybil from these woods and her queer imaginings.

"That is very good of you, Mr. Hartley."

"I'll run Eric's chair to the station first and send it by rail. I can carry him."

"He can manage that little bit all right," Mrs. James said. "He can walk a little, but I am afraid to let him."

When Jack returned from his errand he found Mrs. James and the children waiting, and he noticed that Sybil was hugging her mysterious box tightly. She took her seat by his side sedately, and Mrs. James, having piled cushions in the back, helped Eric into his place and covered him with rugs.

"Mr. Selden and I live together, but he won't be back tonight," Jack said. "We'll drive there, and then make arrangements for lodgings for you."

CHAPTER VIII

ⱭꞆ ⱢꝨDfoꞂD

HERE WAS ONLY ONE INN at Lydford, the "Horse and Groom", where the inquest had been held. Here Selden had taken up his temporary quarters. A small crowd of villagers hung round the door discussing what to them was a great event.

A glance into the coffee-room showed Selden a trio composed of Lady Harman and her son with O'Connor, looking very bored, in deep conversation. He hastily shut the door, and turned into the saloon bar, from which a small select smoking-room opened.

Inside this a solitary man was sitting, smoking quietly, with a very small tankard of beer in front of him. Mr. Coffin was waiting for his chief, as they were travelling back together.

Selden nodded to the man, and touched a bell on the table. "Will you have one with me?" he asked pleasantly.

"Thank you, sir," the other replied gloomily, taking his pipe from his mouth.

"You've had a busy time at Cold Stairs?" Selden said when the waiter had taken his order.

"Very, sir, but it will take a long time to clear up the mess there. It is the most untidy house I have ever seen."

"This is a very unexpected turn of affairs to you, and my friend Mr. O'Connor," Selden remarked when Coffin had taken a solemn draught from his tankard.

"Very, sir. It has of course altered things considerably."

Selden for once felt at a loss; it was like talking to an automaton.

"I suppose you hadn't the slightest idea of the existence of this Lady Harman."

"None, sir," Coffin replied laconically.

"I understand from my friend that you did come down here to see Sir John, so you know the place?"

The answer surprised Selden.

"I have been here many times, sir, when old Sir James Harman was alive, and before Mr. Edward joined the firm. His father sent me when they discovered the coal in the forest, and we carried out the negotiations for royalties and so on."

"That's very interesting; I expect if the truth were known the Harmans owe a great deal to your handling of the matter."

A very faint colour came to Coffin's dead white face, and the dull eyes showed a look of pleasure for a fleeting moment.

Selden had touched the right spot: Coffin's grievance that his own work had never been recognized in a suitable manner.

"Can I persuade you to have another bitter—unless you would prefer something else, sir?"

Selden hated bitter, but he was too intent on his inquiry to say so, and consented graciously.

"And please drop the 'sir', Mr. Coffin. If you had been given a chance, you would have been in a far better position than I, and you are an older man. Please call me Selden."

Coffin actually smiled. "Certainly, if you wish it." He gave the order, and relit his pipe.

"You don't mind these questions? You know, of course, I am investigating these cases, and any assistance and advice will be most useful."

"If I can help you I shall be only too pleased."

So far, good; Selden had got him where he wanted him, and prayed that Lady Harman would delay O'Connor as long as possible.

"I suppose you heard a lot of rumours about all kinds of ghosts and so on when you came," he said casually.

"Not until Sir John came into the property, after his father died. Then I did, but you will understand my visits were purely business ones. I came down about that will, which is now a dead letter."

"Ah! That's interesting, because there's something fishy about that, don't you think?"

Coffin had seldom been treated with this respect, and his usual reserve was broken down.

"Mr. Edward's father was alive then, but very ill, and when Sir John wired to him to come down at once on an important matter he sent me to find out what he wanted. The baronet was very upset about something. He told me he wished to make a will now that there was something to leave. I got the particulars, and was, I must say, surprised at the wording, as he was leaving practically everything to this son of his old friend Dr. Gilkie. I even went so far as to offer a mild protest, reminding him that the property had been in the hands of his family for a very long time, and that it was a serious matter to alienate it to a complete stranger."

"What did he say to that?"

"He flared up, and said some rather nasty things about impertinent clerks. I am used to that, Selden." There was a bitter note in Coffin's voice. "You see," Coffin leant forward and spoke in a more confidential manner, "it was rather a strange position, but I did not care to explain matters to him after what he had said. The property is entail, and had there been a son he could only have left the royalties on the coal mines and his personal money. If that will had stood, and not been revoked, there would have been a pretty lawsuit when this woman and her son turned up."

The eyes of the two men met for the fraction of a second, and Coffin picked up his tankard hurriedly.

"I understand, Mr. Coffin," Selden said slowly.

"We had no idea of the existence of a wife and son when this first will was drawn."

"This conversation is absolutely confidential, Mr. Coffin; I hope you understand that. I am very glad of your help, because you can see farther than most men. You mean that if there had not been a second will, and the former had stood, young William would have claimed what was entail, as the son and heir, while this Gilkie would have had the rest."

"That is the position," Coffin said stiffly, seeming to withdraw himself into his shell like a hermit crab.

"That complicates matters; I thought I saw light for a moment. If there had been no son the entail would have been automatically cut."

"You evidently know something of law," Coffin said, with a smile. "It is entail on the male side, and Miss Sybil would not have inherited."

"Exactly—that's my point. In other words, if this Gilkie by some chance had become aware that the will made in his favour was null and void, he would— to put it very mildly—be extremely annoyed."

"Who would not be, Selden?"

"Well, that's interesting, but doesn't bear directly on these crimes. You say that before then there had been no haunting business."

"I didn't say that," Coffin said. "I said there had not been in the time of Sir John's father."

"Mr. Coffin, let's be frank. Have you any ideas about this business yourself?"

"About the murders—none whatever," Coffin said sharply. "With regard to the will, I believe for some reason Sir John was forced into making that first will. Shall I tell you what my impression was? Don't think me fanciful, Selden. All the time that Sir John was talking to me, he would not keep still a moment, and his eyes were wandering about the room, as though he saw something I could not. I had a queer feeling that something was listening or watching, to see that he did what he had been told to do."

A flush appeared on the high cheek-bones of Coffin's face, and his reserve seemed suddenly to give way.

"I don't know why I am telling you all this," he said in a sudden burst of confidence. "Mr. Baines, Miss Sybil's father, was killed in the hunting-field. No one was close at the time. His horse had not refused a fence but had suddenly shied at something, and threw him. A pure accident."

"Yes; I heard of that," Selden said seriously.

Coffin swallowed hard, and took a pull out of his tankard. "Mrs. Baines was found dead in the woods, from heart disease. There was no suggestion of foul play; the doctor knew she had a weak heart. Rather foolishly she was carrying a comparatively heavy box she had found."

Selden pricked up his ears. "Is that the one Sybil always carries?"

"I don't know, I am sure. I didn't know she did; but it was empty, and very old. She may have kept it in memory of her mother."

"And then Sir John was murdered," Selden remarked quietly.

Coffin laid a bony finger on Selden's arm. "They were narrowing down one by one," he said in a sepulchral voice.

In spite of himself Selden felt a shudder pass through him.

"Hello! There you are. I have been looking for you, Coffin."

O'Connor entered, bringing a breath of fresh air to the sinister conversation. "Well, Dick, and you're having a quiet drink with my clerk, while I, bad luck to it, have been listening to that dreadful woman, with never a drop to quench me thirst. That's the worst of being a lawyer."

He ordered two double whiskeys in spite of Selden's protest, and another tankard for Coffin.

"We haven't much time to catch the train," he observed; "that woman and her son are travelling by the same one, but we must dodge them somehow. Are you coming, Dick?"

"I'm staying here for a day or two. My chief thought it best."

"And Jack?"

"He's taken my car and made a break for London. I shouldn't be surprised if he has taken Mrs. James with him, and the children."

"Here; that won't do, you know, eh—Coffin?" O'Connor said uneasily.

"I hardly think we can interfere at this stage," the clerk replied in a tone completely different from the one in which he had spoken to Selden. "You see, sir, nothing has yet been actually proved about Lady Harman, and until one will is indubitably valid, we have no authority to act. If Mr. Selden knows where they are, and can produce them when called upon to do so, I should imagine that would be sufficient—"

"Oh, you're too long-winded for me. All right then, we'll put the responsibility on to you, Dick, me boy."

Selden watched them go rather wistfully. He was young enough to feel solitude. With middle years come self-sufficiency and a capacity for concentration within one's own cosmos. It seemed as though his friends had deserted him, leaving him to the company of the stolid Perkins. He almost made up his mind to visit the doctor, but pride kept him away.

With a feeling of impatience he walked into the coffee-room, determined to have some food and then write up his notes, especially with reference to the conversation with the saturnine Coffin.

A woman was sitting alone, reading a book, and evidently waiting for dinner, which was long in coming, for the events of the day had taxed the resources of the inn, and lunches had cleaned out the larder.

She glanced round at his entrance, and then smiled. Selden was pleased to see Mrs. Seaton, and shook hands warmly.

"Come and join me, Mr. Selden," she said. "You knew I was coming down here?"

"Of course, but I had forgotten it in the confusion of all that has happened today."

Mrs. Seaton was what Selden described to himself as a "clean-looking woman". About forty, and passably good-looking, she gave the impression that she never had a hair out of place, nor wore any garment that was not in harmony with her general appearance. She also had a manner suggestive of quiet capacity and mental balance. She put him at his ease at once.

"You will probably think I am interfering in this case, Mr. Selden," she remarked when tardy and half warm soup had appeared.

"Not at all; any help is very valuable."

"I am neither a wild fanatic in these matters, like my friend Professor Johnson, nor am I taking an interest in psychological research merely for a living, like Mr. Stevens. My husband was killed in a motor accident, and I attended meetings in a sincere endeavour to get into touch with him, if such a thing were possible."

"And have you done so?"

"Up till now, I have not, but I have become so interested in the study of the subject that I have kept on. Besides"—she gave rather a sad smile—"there is nothing much for me to do. I have no children, and enough to live upon. I do not believe in women taking jobs when they can live without."'

"You are interested in this problem?"

"Very." She addressed herself to the meal, as though waiting for the detective.

"May I ask you a very leading question?" Selden said, and Mrs. Seaton nodded assent.

"Do you think there is something supernatural behind these murders?"

"That all depends upon what you mean by supernatural," she answered guardedly.

"Let me put it bluntly. I am a detective, as you know, and am after a criminal. You have no such interest I take it, but are trying to investigate the psychic side, if I may put it that way."

"You are wrong, Mr. Selden." Mrs. Seaton smiled at him. "I am here for one reason only; one you would not guess, but I am going to tell you. I am very anxious about that girl Sybil."

Selden started. Coming so straight upon Coffin's last remark that the line was narrowing, and on Jack's tale, it was almost uncanny.

"What exactly do you mean? Do you consider her in danger?"

"In very grave danger; though hardly the sort that comes in your sphere of investigation. Mr. Selden, you sent me into Mrs. James's room on the night of the murder. Of course it was the right thing to do, as the poor woman was greatly upset; but had you any other motive?"

Selden laughed. "I suppose I wanted partly to get you out of the way. It was a man's job."

"May I have a cigarette?" Mrs. Seaton said quietly, but her eyes were on Selden, as though in disapproval. "We will leave it at that then," she remarked, lighting up as she spoke.

Selden was quick enough to grasp the fact that she did not believe him.

"Mrs. James," Mrs. Seaton proceeded in a level voice, "told me a good deal about her life at Cold Stairs, and of the children. You remember Sybil has a sort of mysterious Pandora's box she was hugging like a doll?"

"I saw it," Selden said quietly.

"Mrs. James seemed to think it unhealthy for a girl with such a vivid imagination. While we were talking that night, we heard a noise in Sybil's room, and of course went in. The box had fallen from her bed to the floor, without waking her, luckily. To the surprise of both of us, it was not locked, and we looked inside."

"And what did it contain?" Selden asked gravely.

"Nothing but rubbish. A few withered flowers, and bits of stick, and odds and ends of ribbon and material that looked as though they had come from a Christmas party. Nothing else. Johanna Southcott over again!"

"Yes, but she was mad as a hatter."

"That is not the point. What I don't like is that Sybil probably imagines these things are of enormous importance. There is something behind this."

"There is something enormously important behind it. I am glad you told me. What did you do with the box?"

"We carefully closed it, and brought it into the sitting-room. Mrs. James made me lie down after that."

"What happened to the precious box?" Selden asked in a seemingly casual voice.

"When I woke, Mrs. James had gone to get breakfast, and the box was gone. Sybil had taken it."

"What inference do you draw from that?"

Mrs. Seaton laughed merrily.

"Really, Mr. Selden, if your chief at Scotland Yard heard you talking to me about a girl's box he would wonder whether you were the right man for this job. Only, I had a quiet talk with Sybil, while we were waiting for breakfast, and she has had strange experiences, though she was very reticent."

"Perhaps it's just a child's imagination?"

"Sybil is not a child; not mentally, and I can tell imagination from fact. I have a more open mind than you. That is what I am going to investigate in my own way."

"You think there is something outside the ordinary run of murders here?"

Mrs. Seaton laid her cigarette down deliberately and faced Selden. "I not only think, I know. But take care, it may turn out to be something utterly different from what you think. No," she added, as Selden started to speak. "I am not saying anything more at present. Perhaps when we meet again I shall have some startling news for you."

"I sincerely hope so," Selden replied.

CHAPTER IX

DEATH IS AT WORK

L ADY HARMAN WAS FEELING the joys that come to a self-centred snobbish woman with the acquisition of riches and a title. The obsequious manner of waiters and the floor stewards at the London hotel, and the softly spoken, "My Lady", were like rare and refreshing fruit. She was proudly conscious of the envious glances cast at her by less fortunate females, very largely imagined on her part. O'Connor had been able to get a liberal advance from the bank pending the granting of probate.

Among the many idiotic absurdities on which lawyers thrive is the anomaly that while probate cannot be granted until succession duties are paid, nothing of the property may be sold or touched until probate is granted!

Already Lady Harman had driven in an enormous hired car of an expensive make to several of the great stores that stock everything from grand pianos to sardines, and had spent several entrancing days with managers of departments, ordering at pleasure for Cold Stairs. The said managers being men of tact and precision, guessing her atrocious lack of taste, had led her gently into the paths of right choosing and judgment. Even her announcement that all the old oak panelling must be covered up, and bright warm papers substituted, had been received without flinching.

She was in an affable mood when she drove to the dingy offices of Sandilands, Hosking and Bright. She refused to sit down in O'Connor's office until the boy who had shown her in had carefully brushed the chair. Then she brought herself to anchor, a picture of stout contentment, with a sound that might be vulgarly called a grunt.

"My William's quite the young gentleman," she announced. "He's about seeing London. I want him to have his fling before he settles down, and he must have a 'tooter'. Now he's a baronet he must take his proper place, and he's got to have education. After a couple of years he'll go to Oxford."

O'Connor smiled broadly. "That would, of course, be the best course."

She flicked an imaginary speck of dust from her black silk dress.

"When the place has been done up to my satisfaction, and the Court has granted me the custody of that girl, she will come to live with me, and she'll be company for William."

"And Mrs. James?" O'Connor asked a little anxiously.

"I can't stand that woman, Mr. O'Connor; and I couldn't bear a cripple about the place." She paused, and then said: "I suppose that nice young man who was helping you down at Cold Stairs would not come as 'tooter'? I liked the look of him, but I can't remember names."

Selden had strictly cautioned O'Connor that on no account was he to reveal the fact that he was a detective to anyone, and replied evasively, "I don't know, I am sure, Lady Harman. I could ask him."

"I would be obliged if you would, and if his references and qualifications are satisfactory, I might employ him."

The merry look in O'Connor's eye escaped her.

She meant to have her money's worth out of the lawyer, and discussed in great detail her plans for the renovation of Cold Stairs, and what she called "opening it out". She had already planned house-parties, and liberal hospitality, thinking, as so many of the new rich have done, that she would be immediately received into county society, and become a centre of attraction. O'Connor stifled a yawn, as she rose at last to go, and the small office boy conducted her to her limousine with great ceremony. As soon as the door was shut, Selden emerged from an inner office, to which he had fled at her approach. The two men burst into a hearty laugh.

"Golly! What a woman," Dick remarked. O'Conner took a cigar—he never smoked with women clients in the room.

"Sure, I couldn't have stood much more of her. It's money well earned to deal with the likes of her. She's going to try to make that brat of a son of hers into a gentleman with the aid of a 'tooter', as she calls it. God help him!"

"So I heard," Selden replied—"and suggested me for the job."

"I could hardly help laughing at her, but I didn't give you away, Dick, my boy."

"I am glad you didn't," Selden said seriously. "It may be that I shall take the job."

"Whatever for?"

"Ned," Selden said without replying to the question, "I doubt the wisdom of Lady Harman and her son going back to Cold Stairs, until we have cleared up this mystery."

"You think there may be danger to them; surely that's a bit far-fetched?"

"The local police have come to a standstill in their investigations. My chief is getting very annoyed. Wherever the police turn for evidence they are met with stories of bogeys and horrible things seen by night. Perkins says he can't get a word of truth out of them."

O'Connor laughed. "Bless your soul, where I come from in Ireland, even the wireless and the pictures haven't scotched the banshee and the leprechaun. I can picture your stolid county policeman taking down statements, and being told of hobgoblins that prance outside their cottages when the moon is full."

"I don't like it," Selden commented. "It looks at present as though the police will drop it for want of any shred of evidence. Of course they will carry on, but only half-heartedly."

"And you?" O'Connor knew perfectly well that Selden was not the man to let difficulties baffle him.

"I shall carry on, but I wish you, as Lady Harman's lawyer, could persuade her to sell the place, or better still, pull it down."

"You heard her! Nothing on earth would stop her going there and trying to become the great lady. When she finds she is gently snubbed by everyone, she may become reasonable. Perhaps she would go for a voyage round the world."

Selden did not respond to the lawyer's sense of humour.

"That may be too late. There may be another murder."

"Here, steady on!"

"I want your help, Ned. The will which Sir John made, and which you showed me in this office, is now revoked."

"Of course."

"But before this woman turned up, you had inserted an advertisement for the son of Dr. Gilkie to come to your office. I saw it in *The Times.*"

"Perhaps it was a little hasty, but we didn't dream of this development."

"You don't quite follow my meaning. Has he done so?"

"No, we've heard nothing; but, then, he may be abroad, or he may be dead. We can't tell anything; it's all so vague."

"Well, follow it up, Ned. The man is about twenty-six years old now, and may be in Assam. He may see the advertisement or someone may tell him, *before* he gets the news of the other will. If so he will cable or write."

"I see your point, but suppose he doesn't?"

"Then I shall draw my own conclusions," Selden said very gravely.

"I'm hanged if I can see what you're after," O'Connor said in a puzzled manner.

"I never theorize. It puts one off one's stride, but I can at least put two and two together. This son of Gilkie's was evidently known to Sir John when he made his will. That is obvious. He wouldn't leave his money to someone he thought was dead."

"That's clear. But his wife was alive then?"

"Exactly, and he was desperately keen on keeping her existence hidden."

"Oh, I should think that was mere snobbery."

"I wonder! Sir John was an honest, decent sort of fellow, and one would think the type who would acknowledge her and his own boy."

"What are you hinting at, Dick?" O'Connor wheeled his swing chair round and faced the detective.

"I mean this, Ned. If Sir John had been *compelled* to make that first will, and then later on, from a sense of justice perhaps, or to keep his wife away, had made the second, it would have been only after his death that the marriage would have been known. He was an easy-going man, and may have taken the safe course."

"It's a blacker business than I thought," O'Connor said soberly. "You are suggesting blackmail."

"I'm suggesting nothing," Dick said crossly. "I may be totally wrong, but I can see no rhyme or reason in Sir John going to another lawyer, and getting a new will drafted, when he could have come to you and torn up the former one quite easily. Surely it's not too much to suppose that he had some very cogent reason. Now you understand my wish to keep Lady Harman and her precious son away from Cold Stairs."

O'Connor gave an uneasy laugh. "I wish you hadn't told me this, you'll give me sleepless nights."

"This man Gilkie has now been done out of what he will consider his lawful rights."

"You are not suggesting that he was the murderer."

"He may have had at his disposal forces of which we are in ig-norance."

"Oh lord! I thought you were a detective."

"Ned," Selden said, with a queer expression on his mobile face, "you remember, when you went to see who was at the door at Cold Stairs, we had opened the safe. There was a sheet of paper there, in a cover. It's hard to describe. If you can imagine a man finding a book to which he took an unreasonable hatred, and tear-ing the contents out savagely, leaving the boards alone . . . that was how it seemed to me. It gave me an unpleasant feeling."

O'Connor watched his friend keenly. He knew Selden was not given to allowing his intellect to be overruled by his imagination.

"One sheet was left, Ned, but it taught me much. On it was written: *To the son of Dr. Gilkie. To be read after my death, from John Harman, with bitter regrets.*"

O'Connor remained silent; there was an intensity in Selden's voice that stifled comment.

"If that book hadn't been torn to pieces, Ned, we might now be in possession of the secret of these murders."

Selden paced the floor restlessly. "Perhaps, for my peace of mind, it is better that I did not read that diary, as I rather suspect it was. It might have told a tale that would have shaken one's mental balance. One other thing I found in that safe that may have some bearing on the problem; certainly it's curious. It's a very old book on folklore, such as one sees on second-hand bookstalls. You know the sort of stuff. It's called *The Ritual of the Woods.*"

"The sort of book you would find in a house like that," O'Connor exclaimed contemptuously.

"I agree," Selden said slowly, "but there was more in it than that. On the fly leaf, in faded ink, was written 'from A. Johnson to W. A. Gilkie' and a date nearly thirty years ago."

"Well, I don't see much in that!"

"It's queer."

With an obvious effort Selden shook off the ugly thoughts that had crowded to his mind.

"I'm sorry, Ned, to inflict my difficulties on you. Let's treat this as a practical problem, without trimmings." He laughed, but Ned saw perspiration standing on Dick's forehead, and understood the mental conflict that was going on between the trained scientific detective and the man of vision, who saw beyond the material facts of the case.

"I must go and see Jack," Selden said in a calmer voice. "He brought Mrs. James and the two children up to town, and seems to be taking an uncommon interest in them. Well! An interlude of a more jolly nature will be a relief. Of course he can't hide them away."

O'Connor went to the door with Selden, and laid his hand on the other's arm. "Dick, old friend, you are worrying more over this case than you will tell me. I don't want to force your confidence, but if I can do anything to help, I'll do it. You know that."

Dick turned to him and wrung his hand. "I know, Ned; you're a brick. It seems ridiculous that I, as a trained detective, should behave like a stupid woman. I may come on you for help before we are through with this."

Jack had brought Mrs. James and the two children to London, and had found lodgings for them in a quiet square not far from the Mews that he and Selden occupied. Mrs. James seemed delighted with the change, as though a burden had been lifted from her. But Sybil showed a strange restlessness which hurt Mrs. James, as she attributed it to the girl's desire to remain at Cold Stairs, instead of coming to London, and to her company, rather than that of Lady Harman. Hartley, who knew the inner secrets, understood that she was yearning for the deep cool woods, and those mysteries which were so much a part of her life. The noise and bustle of London was strange and bewildering to her.

Eric seemed to take things quietly. He had a singularly placid nature, Hartley thought, and was not easily disturbed. All day he lay about on a sofa reading, as Mrs. James was afraid to take him into the crowded streets. They were discussing plans for the future when Selden came in.

Their rooms were on the ground floor for Eric's sake, and a bright front sitting-room looked out on the square.

"Well, how are things going?" Selden inquired.

"We were talking about the question of proper treatment for Eric," Jack explained. "Mrs. James has got into touch with a German doctor who is very clever at such cases as his. The difficulty is that Eric can't go alone, and if his mother goes with him it means leaving Sybil here."

"I suppose I couldn't take her with us, Mr. Selden?" Mrs. James asked.

"You know I've gone as far as I dared in letting Jack bring her away. I can't let you all bolt to Germany."

Mrs. James sighed. "I really don't know what to do for the best."

"You will excuse me," Eric interrupted. "My mother is taking Sybil to the pictures. If they get in before one o'clock they only pay one shilling."

"If you are sure you don't mind," Mrs. James said.

"I shall be quite happy with my books. I get quite a lot here, Mr. Selden." The boy gave a weary smile.

"I am afraid I must get back to Broadcasting House," Jack declared, looking at his watch. "Coming my way, Dick?"

"As a matter of fact I am; I promised to see the Committee of Three. Lady Harman won't let them go to Cold Stairs, and they are annoyed."

Hartley snorted. "Committee of Three—the Three Impostors, I call them. I wish they'd never come to Cold Stairs."

"Then, Mr. Selden," Eric said softly, "we should not have met you, and Mr. Hartley would not have met Sybil."

The words were spoken so innocently that Jack could take no exception, but he turned the colour of a beetroot.

"Come on, Dick, I shall be late." He led the way to the door, and Dick followed, laughing.

"I envy you your clean, wholesome job," he said when they were in the street. "You are taking part in the biggest thing on earth, and I am dabbling with sordid crime."

"I must say I'd rather have my work, especially now that television has become a practical proposition."

"Jack," Selden said suddenly, "if only we had had a television set in that room!"

"Perhaps it's just as well for our sanity that we hadn't," Hartley said soberly. "I had thought of it, but I did not like to suggest it to the chief."

In Great Portland Street they separated, Hartley going to Broadcasting House, while Selden went to see the Three Impostors, as Hartley had now christened them.

As they stood for a moment on the pavement, Hartley suddenly blurted out: "I say, old man, I wanted to ask you something. If Mrs. James takes her boy to Germany, do you think we could put Sybil up? Our housekeeper would look after her and so on, only—"

"Only you are very interested in her. Take heed, Jack, my boy, girls grow up very quickly, you know."

"I knew you'd pull my leg, but I am interested in the sense that if she goes back to Cold Stairs I think she'll go crackers."

"I am rather inclined to agree with you. Jack, I want to ask you one thing. You know that mysterious box that Sybil treats as a sort of totem, and hugs like a doll. Has she still got it?"

Jack's eyes opened wide in wonder at the question. "Whatever has that to do with the affair?"

"I just wanted to know," Dick said lightly.

"As a matter of fact that is rather curious. As you know, they are in lodgings, and not over comfortable. Sybil, of course, goes out much more than she did at Cold Stairs, and one day found the landlady examining her box, and was so upset about it that I offered to have it put in a safe deposit. She seemed greatly relieved, and we went round together to Chancery Lane, and placed it there."

"Good," Selden commented.

"Only she made a curious reservation that rather puzzled me. She made me promise that if ever she went back to Cold Stairs I would get it out for her."

"I'm glad you told me that," Dick said earnestly. "I'm not trying to swank, but little things that appear trivial to you are to my mind of considerable interest. Get right out of your head any notion that Sybil is mad or even neurotic. She has a steady, well-balanced brain; and, you remember, some things she told you we have verified."

"But surely this box is rather ridiculous?"

"On the contrary, it has supplied me with a possible line of thought that may be vital. In the language of sleuths, it is a clue."

"Then what about my plan of keeping Sybil?"

"You might suggest it to Mrs. James, and in view of what you have just told me I think Sybil might be useful. I must, of course, consult Ned O'Connor. It won't be for long I should imagine, and if the Court gives Lady Harman the guardianship of the child, as seems almost certain, Mrs. James can do nothing; she has no claim whatever on Sybil."

"That means she will return to Cold Stairs," Jack said unsteadily.

"Undoubtedly." Dick looked keenly at his friend. "She will return there if Lady Harman goes back."

"But she's only up in town buying things and spending money."

"I am doing my best to induce her to get rid of the place. It's a matter of her pride against her fears, and I am very much afraid that pride will win."

They parted company, and Selden took his way to Stevens's house.

The Professor was out when Selden arrived. He had gone to meet Mrs. Seaton at Paddington. Stevens explained that a letter had been received from her that morning that had puzzled them both. In it Mrs. Seaton had stated that she had information of the utmost importance, which she dared not communicate by a letter, but that she was returning at once, and requested Professor Johnson to meet her.

Selden did not particularly care for a *tête-à-tête* with Stevens, whom he had already summed up as a toad and sycophant, and departed, promising to return later.

It was nearly four o'clock when he returned, to find the Professor in a towering rage, and pacing the floor like a hungry cat. He had been to Paddington, but could see no trace of Mrs. Seaton, and she had neither turned up nor wired.

"It's absurd!" he exclaimed. "If she has been detained she ought to have let us know. Clare is a level-headed woman, and would never have made that statement unless she had something of the gravest interest to tell us. I am convinced we are on the eve of some revelation that will clear up the so-called mystery."

"Perhaps she went too deep and could not escape," Stevens said, with a look of fear on his dark olive face.

"I'll call up my chief," Selden said abruptly. "He can find out from Lydford whether Mrs. Seaton left there."

He was put through at once, and heard Dodds speaking.

"That you, Selden? Where on earth have you been all day? I've called up every place I could think of."

"What is it?" Selden replied, with a sinking feeling in the pit of his stomach.

"Haven't you heard? A murder; a certain Mrs. Seaton."

"At Cold Stairs?" Selden asked, gripping himself tightly.

"No! In London. But the devil of the thing is that she had just returned from Lydford; that's what is upsetting. Come round at once, and I'll give you details."

Selden replaced the receiver and faced the two men, who had remained silent at the words "Cold Stairs".

"What is it?" Stevens whispered, laying a trembling hand on Selden's arm.

"Mrs. Seaton was murdered in London this afternoon—that is all I know at present."

"Good God!" Stevens fell back into his chair and covered his face with his hands.

"Poor Clare," the Professor said. "And she had information which we may never know now."

The callous tone annoyed Selden. "It may be that very information caused her death," he said.

"If I had only met her, this would never have occurred," the Professor muttered.

Stevens looked up fiercely. "How did you come to miss her?"

"In the crowd, I suppose; there were a great number of people there on the platform, and I am rather lost in a mass of people, being short-sighted and unpractical."

"I suppose you waited about for some time?" Selden asked soothingly, as he saw Stevens was becoming excited.

"Yes; I went up and down the train, and as the crowd thinned I had another look. Then I came here, as I thought she would taxi to this place at once."

"I must go. But one more question, Professor: I suppose you had no idea as to the nature of the information that Mrs. Seaton said she had obtained?"

The Professor hesitated. "Nothing direct, but we have discussed this affair in all its details many times, and I know the lines on which she was proceeding. Pardon me if I say no more than that. We shall endeavour to get into communication with Clare as soon as possible, now that she has passed on, but there may be delays, as it is very confusing at first on the other side."

"I suppose it is," Selden observed. The Professor's apparently callous manner might be due to the sure faith these people had in the continuity of life.

CHAPTER X

CHE MURDER IN
CARDIGAN STREET

I'M GLAD TO SEE YOU, SELDEN," Chief Inspector Dodds remarked as the young detective entered.

"I taxied straight here, sir, but I have not been wasting my time, as a matter of fact."

"Very good, Selden, just read through that statement by P.C. Jones. It's very clear and concise."

> On Saturday, November 23rd, I proceeded along Cardigan Street, W.C.2, to make my point with Sgt. Wilkins at 2.35 p.m. There was a thick fog at the time, and the street was entirely empty. When passing the back of the warehouse of Messrs. Stiggins & Smart, Pickle Merchants, I saw a well-dressed woman lying on the path, and proceeded to examine her. She was dead, but the body was still warm. As far as I could ascertain the woman had been strangled. There were no finger-marks. While I was carrying out my examination, Sgt. Wilkins came up, and also examined the body. From documents in her possession, the name of the victim was Clara Seaton of 490 Paradise Mansions, Maida Vale. A suit-case was on the path, and the head was resting on this. No handbag could be found. I fetched an ambulance and we drove to Bow Street Station.
>
> *(Sgd.) P. Jones.*

"That's all quite clear," Selden said, handing the document back. Chief Inspector Dodds went on:

"I have myself been to see the body and discussed the matter with the Divisional Surgeon. I want you to remember this, Selden, Cardigan Street is a narrow road almost entirely taken up with warehouses and high blocks of offices. There is not a shop, a public house, nor a private one in the road, and this is Saturday afternoon, and foggy. Every place was shut up and the street was deserted. An ideal spot for a murder."

"Or for dumping an inconvenient corpse," Selden commented.

"Exactly, we must not lose sight of that. I have confirmed Jones's report. The woman's clothes were all clearly marked, and there are no finger-prints, but the doctor says she was undoubtedly strangled from behind. It reminds one of the old garotters."

"Was the suit-case touched?"

"Unless it had been carefully repacked, no. Everything appears to be quite as it had been packed and there was money and four good silver brushes there."

"We can eliminate robbery," Selden declared. "The woman had been down to Lydford to investigate for the Committee of Three, about whom I have told you. She arrived at Paddington, I believe, at 1.38."

Dodds looked up quickly. "You know that?"

"She was due to arrive there, and it certainly looks as though she did. She was to have gone straight to Stevens's flat at the back of Langham Place. Can you find out whether she had lunch on the express?"

"I'll do so at once, and ask our plain-clothes man at Paddington to come to Bow Street and see the body in the mortuary. He watches the arrival of all the main-line trains."

"Cardigan Street," Selden went on, "is right out of the line to Langham Place."

"You think she drove there? There are difficulties, Selden. You are either suggesting two men at work, the driver and the murderer, or that the driver stopped the car, got down and killed his victim. If she took a taxi, the driver must have been in collusion, and if a private car, she must have expected it to meet her. Then it was someone she knew."

"There is another possibility," Selden said gravely. "If someone met her at the station, and they hired a taxi, she was murdered in the car, and the murderer slipped out. It would be easy in the fog. He might have given Cardigan Street as a destination, and when the driver got there and found the corpse he dumped it, afraid to be mixed up with the affair."

Chief Inspector Dodds was watching his young assistant with a careful scrutiny. "Selden," he said gently, "I have read all your reports of the Lydford murders. What you have just put forward as a possible theory is not what is at the back of your mind."

"Candidly, no, sir," Selden said with a faint smile.

"You think this murder was done by the same hand as the other two?"

"The method is similar. And I can tell you this, sir, Mrs. Seaton had written to say she had information of the utmost value and was returning to London to communicate it to Professor Johnson and Stevens."

"Why in heaven's name didn't she go to the police, like a sensible woman?" Dodds growled.

Selden spoke deliberately. "Perhaps her information was of such a nature that she knew the police would not believe her and would think her mad."

The Chief Inspector swore expressively. "We don't want to introduce this supernatural business. It is a tangible murder all right. Besides," he added, "you are supposing that the person must have followed Mrs. Seaton in the same train. It's too absurd."

"You mean that possibly the appearance of such a person might cause comment in a respectable express train," Selden said, his clear gaze on his chief.

"Let's drop this. I am surprised at you, Selden." Dodds spoke angrily, but a lurking suspicion lingered in his eyes.

"I am quite convinced," Selden said calmly, "that we shall not get to the bottom of this murder from this end, and that is only between us two. The solution lies at Lydford, or, rather, Cold Stairs."

"You may be right, young man, but meanwhile we'll get hold of our man at Paddington, and find out whether he saw Mrs. Seaton. I shall also get a report from Perkins as to her movements at Lydford, and with whom she talked and so on."

"That would be useful," Selden said, and then added: "It's only right to tell you, sir, that Professor Johnson says he went to meet Mrs. Seaton at Paddington, but missed her."

There was no mistaking the implication.

"Here, go easy, Selden; what are you suggesting?"

"Nothing at present, but I am going to find out."

A knock came at the door, and an officer announced that a gentleman wished to see Chief Inspector Dodds on an important matter.

Selden rose to go, but in answer to Dodds' inquiry the officer handed a card.

"Dr. Hughes from Lydford—you'd better stay, Selden," Dodds said quietly.

Hughes entered and took his seat, nodding to Selden. He appeared to be holding himself in with some difficulty.

"I came to see you about the murder of Mrs. Seaton," he said; "we travelled up together by the same train from Lydford."

Neither Dodds nor Selden gave a sign, but the former picked up a gold pencil from his desk. "Yes?" he said calmly.

"I have heard from our young friend here that you are his chief, and I came on here at once."

"You know, of course, that she has been murdered?"

"I heard in a roundabout way; that's why I came, but it would be better if I told you what I know."

"You wish to make a statement, Doctor?"

"It would be better to have it on paper," Hughes replied. "Selden knows my position, and my connection with the Cold Stairs affair."

"Let's have the story," the latter said eagerly.

"I will be as brief as possible. Mrs. Seaton came to Cold Stairs last week, staying at Lydford. She introduced herself, and told me of her presence on the night of the murder of Sir John Harman. I knew that already. I found her a cultured, interesting woman, and she made no bones about her visit. She believed in some supernatural explanation of the murders, and was trying to find out in her own way."

"Yes, I know that," Selden remarked.

"The house," the doctor proceeded, more at his ease now, "is in the hands of the decorators, and she found no difficulty in getting permission to go over it thoroughly. She also interviewed the Jenkinses."

His eye glanced a meaning look at Selden, who nodded. "I don't know what happened, but she came to me, very determinedly, with permission from the parents to visit the County Institution where their daughter is living. She wanted me to get the official permit, and I saw no reason why she should not go, but insisted on accompanying her myself. Two days ago, we went there. I hadn't seen Anne Jenkins since she had been admitted, and found her much changed. The medical superintendent informed me that she had improved a great deal, and apart from some fits of hysteria was, for the most part, merely childish, and her mind seemed a blank. He allowed Mrs. Seaton to see her, after she had promised not to excite the girl, and they had an interview." The doctor paused and seemed to be making up his mind about something. Then he continued, picking his words.

"You know, Selden, that we have both tried to keep the supernatural element out of this case. I don't know what took place between Mrs. Seaton and the girl, possibly she had some hypnotic power, but when she came out she told the doctor quite emphatically that Anne was perfectly sane, and could be released, but on no account ought she to return to her parents' cottage. Dr. Hopkins, as you can imagine, was very annoyed, and told her it was not a matter for her to decide. Then she made a strange statement. She said quite firmly: 'When I have cleared up these murders, you will alter your opinion, and thank me'."

"What did she mean by that?" Dodds said.

"I don't know. On the way back she was very silent, but came to my house for a cup of tea. She was quiet and thoughtful, and I did not disturb her. Then I thought I must try to get something definite from her, and asked her whether she had solved the problem.

" 'What problem do you mean?' she asked.

" 'Why, the murders, of course,' I said, rather crossly I am afraid.

" 'Oh! Yes, there is no doubt whatever in my mind,' she said confidently.

" 'Then you will, of course, inform the police,' I said.

" 'It is not a matter for the police at present,' she replied.

"The same old thing," Selden exclaimed.

"I don't know, I am sure," the doctor said. "She talked to me in a very similar manner to our conversation, Selden. I suppose I was weak, but I wanted to help, if she had got hold of something, and I showed her the photographs."

"You did?" Selden gasped.

"She showed no excitement, but merely said, 'That is the final proof. I must write to Professor Johnson, and then see him in town.' "

Chief Inspector Dodds looked up in surprise. "What photographs?" he asked.

Selden answered: "Just some woodland scenes taken round Cold Stairs, which Dr. Hughes developed."

His foot touched that of the doctor, who took the hint.

"They were taken at the spot where Anne Jenkins fancied she saw something," he lied.

"So you came up together," Selden said hastily.

"I had to come to town in any case, but this had rather disturbed me, and as I had given no pledge of secrecy, I had decided to tell our young friend here about the whole thing. We travelled together, having lunch on the train, and at Paddington she said good-bye rather hurriedly, and left me abruptly."

"She didn't say where she was going?" Selden asked anxiously.

"Not in so many words, but she had told me she was going to see Professor Johnson, as I have told you. I was not surprised, after that, to see the Professor on the platform, but of course it was none of my business. I had an appointment, and it was only after that was over I remembered they had not met. That is to say, I never saw them do so. I suppose it was fussiness on my part, but I couldn't get the thing out of my head, and called up the Professor's house, where I was informed that he was with Mr. Stevens. So I got on there, and Stevens answered himself. I merely asked for Mrs. Seaton, and he told me the news that she had been murdered, and that you, Selden, had gone to the Yard, so I came on here."

"And that is all you know?"

"Everything—it's all very vague, but I thought any information would be of value."

"We are very much obliged to you, Doctor," Dodds said. "Your statement will be most useful. You are sure Mrs. Seaton did not meet the Professor?"

"Of course I can't be certain, but as she had gone off at once, in an obvious hurry, and I saw him afterwards peering about among the arrivals, it looked as though they had missed."

"It looks to me," Selden said grimly, "as though she had changed her mind. She had asked Professor Johnson to meet her, and then avoided him deliberately."

"If you don't mind, I will get off. I have an important engagement," Dr. Hughes said. "Selden knows my address at Lydford, and if you want me for anything I will come along. I am a coroner myself, you know," he added with a smile.

When he had gone Selden lay back in his chair, puffing smoke idly in rings.

"That's a strange story," Dodds remarked.

"We're dealing with strange people," Selden commented. "Cardigan Street is nowhere on the route from Paddington to Langham Place. Mrs. Seaton was not a young girl, and knew London well. She was also in a desperate hurry to impart her news to the other two. Something made her change her mind. I wonder if the doctor unconsciously did so."

"It's no good asking me conundrums, Selden. What is your next step?"

"I'm going to see the Professor."

"Be careful what you do. Remember he's an influential man. We don't want any scandal."

"You may rely on me, sir."

"Very well. I must wait for reports."

Selden taxied to Stevens's house, and found the two men there in earnest conversation. He was not going to give any information, but rather to ask it, and merely imparted the bare facts, as known to the police, and which had already appeared in the evening papers. Even Selden was shocked at the calm way in which they discussed the murder of their colleague. It was, he thought, either from their fervid belief in spiritualism or sheer callousness. He forced the issue.

"You think you can get in touch with the dead?"

"Dead? We do not recognize that word," Stevens said unctuously, as though quoting from one of his own articles. "She has merely passed on, and is as much alive as you or I."

"As I explained," the Professor said, "it may take some weeks, or even months, before we can establish communication, especially in a case of a violent passing like this."

"You have no idea of your own about this murder?" Selden asked, his eyes on the Professor.

"Of course we should not expect you detectives to accept our reasoning, but in our minds there is little doubt that the Being that was active at Cold Stairs came to London with our colleague, and took her life as she had discovered its secret."

"It's a pity you didn't see 'it' on the platform," Selden said.

The Professor ignored the irony. "It may not even have materialized," he replied calmly.

It was impossible to argue with these people, and Selden took his hat to depart.

"By the way," he said, as though on an afterthought, "you remember telling me about Dr. Gilkie the other day?"

The Professor frowned. "I saw an advertisement in *The Times* by some firm of lawyers asking his son to call on them. Was that your doing, Mr. Selden?"

"I had nothing to do with it, Professor, but it may interest you to know that Sir John Harman *had* left all his property to this son, but had since revoked his will in favour of his widow."

He watched the Professor's face and saw wonder grow, and then a fanatical look of intense excitement. Slowly he looked away from Selden and his eyes sought those of Stevens, who had gone suddenly white in the face.

"There is no suggestion that Gilkie *knew* of the change in the will?" Stevens said in a strained voice, as though more hung on the words than he would admit to himself.

"We don't even know if he exists," Selden answered gruffly. "But if you are suggesting that he murdered Sir John out of revenge, it rather knocks the bottom out of your supernatural theories. It becomes a very material crime."

Something on the faces of the two men caused Selden to stop. It was as though a sudden light came to them at the bare mention of the name.

"On the contrary," the Professor blazed out in a vibrant voice, "it almost proves us to be in the right, eh, Stevens?"

"That is out of my depth," Selden said, noting that Stevens had sunk into an arm-chair and was furtively wiping his damp forehead.

"Mr. Selden," the Professor said solemnly, as though choosing his words, "the subject of Dr. Gilkie is one I do not care to discuss. It is very distasteful to me, but I do not think you will find any trace of his son, nor do I think he exists, as you would denominate existence."

"That remains to be proved, but you may perhaps be able to tell me this. Did Harman—as he was then—know Dr. Gilkie in New Guinea or Assam?"

"He was on the scientific expedition that Dr. Gilkie undertook. Harman knew the country well and offered to act as a guide. That is all I can tell you."

"Very well, Professor, we shall, I hope, meet again and we shall each conduct our researches along our own lines."

The Professor crossed the room in two huge strides, and seized Selden's arm roughly.

"Leave it alone, young man. It will do your reputation no good and may be dangerous. It is only we who understand the hidden Powers who can face intangible risks. Your courage and detective's skill will be of little use."

"We shall see," Selden gently released himself.

The door closed and the Professor turned to Stevens. "Gilkie's son," he muttered thickly. "Then his theories were right after all."

CHAPTER XI

PROFESSOR JOHNSON INTERVENES

T HE INQUEST ON MRS. SEATON was a purely formal affair. Evidence was given that the unfortunate lady had been staying at Lydford, and had arrived at Paddington. After that all trace of her had been lost. Chief Inspector Dodds had decided from the first that the sensational tale that Dr. Hughes had told could throw no light upon the matter, and might hamper the police investigations.

The papers assumed that she had either been attacked in the fog by some gangster, or that she had met someone unknown who had murdered her and stolen her handbag.

The matter had been placed in the hands of Scotland Yard, but Selden had not been asked to carry out investigations. He accepted an invitation from Hughes to stay a few days with him at Lydford, and went off as soon as the inquest was over.

Lady Harman, having triumphantly finished her shopping, returned to Cold Stairs, where the work of renovation had been sufficiently completed for her to take possession.

Jack was left with Sybil at the Mews, under the doubtful care of Mrs. Perks.

One evening Selden walked in unexpectedly.

"Well, what's the latest news?" Jack asked after greeting him warmly.

"Just got back from Lydford." Selden was looking bronzed and fit, after an outdoor existence in the rain and wind. "Our old friend, Sergeant Perkins, has almost given up the case in despair. You see the 'improvements' to the house included scraping off the creepers from the walls, and of course the workmen found those iron rings. It got about, and Perkins has become rather a laughing-stock. The local paper is getting at us for a lot of fools. They say that obviously the murderer came in that way, and had been playing the ghost. They conclude that he was interrupted by Sir John, and there was a struggle in which the baronet was strangled. It sounds most plausible, and Perkins is inclined to believe it. You and I know better."

"Do we? I'm not so certain I do."

"My dear Jack, I thought better of you. On the night of the murder the house was watched and patrolled. It was pouring in torrents, and yet there were no marks of wet feet. Of course you will say the murderer might have changed his footwear, but remember he must have run along that corridor pretty quickly to get to Sybil's room and not be heard, and then slip down the rings into the arms of the police. It's out of all reason."

"So you are no farther with the matter."

"They have taken the Seaton case out of my hands," Selden said somewhat bitterly. "Old Dodds said I should confine myself to the Cold Stairs affairs, as an excuse, but I know he's beginning to lose faith in me. For see, Jack, I'm in the experimental stage. All the old hands are dead against the college, you know the sort of thing—the old school tie cheap sneer, and so on. By luck I happened to come to the front, but they would love to see me downed."

"Cheer up; perhaps another case will come along!"

"There will be no other case for me if I fail now. No, I am going to get to the bottom of it somehow. But let's have your news. You wrote that Mrs. James and Eric had gone to Germany."

Hartley showed slight signs of confusion. "Yes, she is staying with him while he is receiving treatment."

"I see; and what about Sybil?"

"I saw Ned and put that all right."

"You mean that you have constituted yourself her guardian?"

"Hardly that, Dick. Our landlady, Mrs. Perks, is putting her up, and brings her round each morning. Sybil is more cheerful, and is losing a lot of that queer look she had. She's getting more human. I took her over Broadcasting House the other day. You know, Dick, she'll be a very pretty girl when she grows up."

"M'yes! The role of grandfather will suit you very well. I suppose you are teaching her the alphabet."

"Alpha—oh, I see, you're trying to be funny." The door opened and the girl herself tripped in flushed with walking in the cold air. Selden's keen glance showed him that even these few days had wrought a change in the girl. She was more normal, smiling and laughing as he had never seen her before. The heavy mystery that had wrapped her round at Cold Stairs had lifted like an evil fog. He noticed that she and Jack were on the friendliest of terms.

"I have been out shopping," she declared. "Jack thinks it's good for me to go into these big stores and look at dresses and all the things I would buy if I could." She put some parcels on the table. "Here's your tobacco—I bought a pound to save trouble. Here's the papers you wanted, and the socks you asked me to buy." She unfolded a parcel displaying two atrocious pairs of light socks covered with spots of green and blue.

Hartley, who would have thrown them into the dust bin in ordinary circumstances, thanked the girl and praised them—a very bad sign, Selden thought.

Sybil flung her hat and coat on a chair and came to the fire, where she sat on the pedestal of the curb-fender, and warmed her hands.

"Just the way to get chilblains," Selden growled.

"What's the news?" Sybil asked casually, though Selden detected a note of anxiety.

"I've been telling Jack. You wouldn't know Cold Stairs. All the walls stripped of creepers and cleaned up. Fancy *cleaning up* fifteenth century stonework!"

"How horrible," Sybil remarked, and to Selden's surprise, calmly lit a cigarette.

"You are not improving," he said dryly. "It's a good thing I've come back."

"Blame Jack." She smiled at Hartley.

"There is a small army of labourers at work, cutting down trees and laying out the gardens in front. I believe they are putting down new gravel and making a proper drive."

"I hope they are not getting rid of the old tenants and servants," Sybil said, puckering up her forehead.

"No—on the contrary, Lady Harman has taken them all on and added a new butler as she wants to pose as a feudal lady. Your friends, the Jenkinses, have been pensioned off." He looked keenly at Sybil to ascertain the effect of his words.

"I am glad of that," Sybil said quietly. "It would have been a shame to turn them out of their cottage, just because ..." she showed signs of hesitation, "just because they are old."

"Their son is back on leave, a very fine fellow. He's a full sergeant now in the Sappers, and they are very proud of him."

"I can only just remember him," Sybil said thoughtfully. "He must be getting on. He's about twenty-six now."

"He was very upset when he learnt what had happened. His company has returned to England from India, and as the old people can't write, he had heard nothing."

"Well, what about a spot of food?" Jack said with a yawn. "I don't suppose you've had anything since you left Lydford."

"Isn't Mrs. Perks cooking us anything?"

"I gave her the evening off," Hartley said confusedly. "I didn't know you'd be hopping back."

"I see, you and Sybil were going out on a glory bust."

"Just a bit of grub and pictures."

"I think it's just about time I did come back."

"You'll join us, of course?" Sybil asked.

"Not for worlds. You two go and enjoy yourselves."

A ring from the outside door was answered by Selden, who found O'Connor waiting in the rain.

"Glad to find you are back."

"You know Sybil's here," Selden said.

"Sure—didn't I give my leave?" Ned said abstractedly.

"I suppose you came to see them in your capacity of legal adviser."

O'Connor stopped before entering the sitting-room. "Dick, it's a serious matter. I have news for you all."

"In that case it would be advisable to say nothing to these two until you've told me. They are going to the pictures like two dear lambs, and we won't spoil sport. Say you've come to take me out. Not a word to them, you understand."

O'Connor nodded.

They noted with amusement that neither Hartley nor the girl showed any great distress at their announcement. Selden bustled them off, and then poured out drinks for himself and his friend.

"Now, Ned, my lad, let's have it. I am afraid I can guess your news."

"I have two matters, both of urgent importance, for you to know, but I'll take the latest first. The Court has awarded the guardianship of Sybil to Lady Harman. I did what I could, but hadn't a leg to stand on, in fact his nibs got quite cross and wondered what I was after. He asked me straight out whether I had anything against her ladyship. You see, after all, she is her aunt-in-law—sounds funny, but there it is, and therefore the correct person to be appointed guardian. Mrs. James is only a governess, and the judge remarked sarcastically that it would be open to Lady Harman to employ Mrs. James if she wished to do so."

Selden's manner was very grave.

"You know what this means: Sybil will have to return to Cold Stairs and live there, and that's exactly what I wanted to avoid."

"I know, but couldn't she go to a boarding-school?"

"Impossible. She would run away, for one thing, and Lady Harman wouldn't hear of it. I know her type. She will keep the girl there like one of the heirlooms to add what she can't give— tradition and birth to the place. And you mark my words, she'll do her best to get that imp of a son of hers to marry the girl later on, and so add dignity to her own position."

"But surely you are going too fast."

"That's only a remote contingency. What worries me is the thought of Sybil going back to that place."

"You don't think there is any danger?"

"There is very real danger, but in her case to her mental balance rather than her life. These few weeks in London have got her mind off all that imaginative stuff—London and Jack between them."

They both laughed in spite of the seriousness of the situation.

"Once she gets back there with the woods and her mysterious adventures, whether imagined or real, and her wonderful box containing rubbish, all that will be altered and I am sure that Jack won't be allowed there. . . . Is this absolutely certain?"

"I'm afraid so, old man. By this time Lady Harman will have received the news, and you bet she'll be round here to claim her, or send for her."

Selden kicked the coals impatiently. "What a mess. Let me think a moment."

They sat in silence, smoking, the lawyer watching his friend, for whose quick intellect he had considerable admiration. He knew also that the setback Selden had received had hurt his pride and injured his reputation at the Yard. Presently Selden stirred and his face cleared.

"Well, we've got to face it. You had better tell Sybil yourself. Send for her tomorrow. It would be better for Jack Hartley not to be there. He'd only 'create'. Then you can inform Lady Harman that you are bringing her down. It will be quite correct and not bring Jack into it. You, as the lawyer, would naturally do so. Hand her over and obtain a receipt and your job is over."

"You take it very philosophically, my friend," O'Connor said, wondering at Selden's complacency.

"This new move has only made the scheme I had formed in my mind more firmly fixed. I shall go there myself."

"Yes, I suppose you ought to be investigating on the spot."

Selden laughed. "That's a nasty one. But you don't take my meaning. Richard Selden is due for a holiday. He is not at all well, and suffering from strain. He will ask for a month's leave, which his chief will grant all the more readily as he is now out of favour."

"What on earth is all this rubbish?"

"No rubbish, you bright lad. Don't you remember that Lady Harman had eyes on me for 'tooter' to that imp?"

"You are not going to offer your services?"

"That is exactly what I have done. You see, she has no idea that I am a detective, and I have impressed on Perkins that on no account must he reveal my identity to anyone. He and the doctor are the only people who know. What you tell me about Sybil only makes me more firmly resolved. I shall be able to watch things from inside the house, and that is the only possible way."

"You might include Sybil in your instructional work."

"I'll confine myself to the imp," Selden said with a smile; "besides, I don't want to cut Jack out."

"Has it come to that?"

"One never knows with these wireless men. But let's have your second piece of news."

"It's not so pressing, but it's puzzling all the same. We have been searching for that Gilkie to whom the money was first left—making some private inquiries, as it seemed strange that he never turned up."

Selden became acutely interested. "Any results?"

"Rather curious. I can't make head or tale of it. Old Coffin's pretty shrewd. He found out somehow that there was a Dr. Gilkie, an eminent chemist who didn't practise. He did go out East on an expedition and met Sir John there, but this is the strange part. He died from a snake venom when fiddling about in his laboratory, but he died childless. There never was a son. He'd been away nearly two years."

"And Mrs. Gilkie?"

"It appears that she did not see her husband when he came back. No trace of her has been found."

"Oh, well, it doesn't matter much," Selden said lightly. "Perhaps he told Harman he had a son. Anyway, it accounts for no one having turned up to answer your advertisement."

"Perhaps you are right. After all, he would only have met with disappointment."

And so the matter was dropped, but Selden wondered how much the sphinxlike clerk really knew, and how much he had imparted to his amiable chief.

The following day, in the laconic words of the announcer of the weather forecast, "A deep depression covered the British Isles". It was for all of them a day of squalls. O'Connor broke the news to Sybil, and though he was not a man of much imagination or insight, he could not help noticing the subtle changes in the girl's face as he made the announcement.

Something like fear crossed her face—unmistakable terror—and her hands clenched tightly. Then very subtly a change came. He described it as though a man had been asked to undertake some great and dangerous adventure, and the dread of it had first struck him. Then some mysterious fascination engendered by the dread itself had overwhelmed him. Selden knew only too well the underlying meaning of the words.

Then, of course, there had been a scene with Hartley, who declared that they should immediately take Sybil to Germany to Mrs. James, to save her from her fate, and roundly accused O'Connor of being an interfering devil. Selden, having patched up some sort of peace, betook himself to the Yard, where Dodds received him coldly.

"Leave? Certainly," he said. "It would be a good thing for you to have a rest. The Cold Stairs affair appears to have reached a deadlock."

"And the murder of Mrs. Seaton in London," Selden said ingenuously.

"That is still unsolved," Dodds snapped, sensing the reproof in Selden's tone. "Not a shadow of a clue. We can't find a taxi or car that went anywhere near Cardigan Street. The affair is at present on the unsolved list, but something may come along."

"Then I may have a month?" Selden asked.

"Take six . . ." Dodds began, and checked himself. "Go, my boy," he said in kinder tones. "Perhaps you will be in better form after a rest. We can't all rise quickly in this profession."

The inference was so obvious that Selden thanked him and retired at once.

The young people had dinner together at the Mews. Sybil was quiet and subdued, but not unduly depressed, an attitude that made Hartley angry.

"Of course," he said rather unsteadily, "you'll find a large house like Cold Stairs a change from this small place."

"I have been very happy here," the girl said. "If I can't get on with Lady Harman I shall run away."

"You will write to me," Jack implored with a comically tragic face.

"Of course." The girl laughed at him.

"I suppose you will be going down to carry on?" Jack asked Selden.

"I am off on a month's holiday."

"Sure you haven't got the sack?"

"Not yet, but no doubt it will come in time," Selden said calmly.

"Sorry, Dick, I'm behaving badly." He seized his knife and fork and worked off his feelings on the chicken they were devouring. "Ever since we tried that dismal experiment things seem to have gone wrong with all of us."

"You ungrateful beggar. If it hadn't been for that you would never have been to Cold Stairs and met our charming young friend here," Selden declared.

Sybil turned a pair of deep unfathomable eyes on him. "If it had not been for that experiment, perhaps my uncle would have been alive today," she said.

A rather uncomfortable meal was interrupted by the unexpected arrival of Professor Johnson, who had never been to the Mews before. He seemed preoccupied as usual, and wandered on inconsequently before coming to the object of his visit.

"I've been to Scotland Yard, Mr. Selden," he said at last.

"Indeed, Professor? About Mrs. Seaton, I suppose."

The iron-grey hair bristled, and the Professor's beard stuck out aggressively. *"You* ought to know. I've had an inspector round twice asking me impertinent questions, and I am sure someone has been following me about. I have very acute hearing, Mr. Selden. I stood just about enough of it, so I went to Scotland Yard. I knew Dodd's father, and had no difficulty in seeing him. I put it to him straight. Why was I being subjected to this treatment? I was willing to answer any questions they wanted. Then I heard for the first time that you had not been given this case—and had—not to put too fine a point on it—been sent on leave."

"That's quite correct," Selden said, smiling at him.

"It appears that from some remark you made, Dodds had come to the conclusion that I had murdered my old friend, Mrs. Seaton."

Hartley was up in arms at once. "Rot. I'm sure Dick never said such a thing. You must have misunderstood the Chief Inspector.

I'll bet if Dick had thought that he'd have had you in chokee long ago." He scowled fiercely at the infuriated savant.

The interruption saved Selden from answering, for the Professor turned his wrath on Jack.

"Young man, because you happened to be mixed up with that affair at Cold Stairs—as a mechanic, I believe—that is no excuse for addressing me like that."

"Then don't address my friend Dick like that," Jack replied hotly. "I don't wonder Scotland Yard suspected you. I'm not a sleuth, but you went to meet Mrs. Seaton, according to your statement, and said you couldn't find her in a crowd. That was rather childish for a great man of science, and then you turned up afterwards at Stevens's house."

The Professor interrupted in a perfect fury; he was not used to being talked to like this by mere boys, as he considered them.

"So that is the cock-and-bull story that Dodds got from Mr. Selden, the rising young detective. Of all the impertinence!"

His passion was suddenly cooled in an unexpected manner. Sybil had been gravely regarding him with her large searching eyes. She spoke quietly, but brought a sudden hush in the room.

"Professor! You know perfectly well who killed Mrs. Seaton."

The firm, clearly spoken words completely changed the atmosphere. Hartley stared at the girl with a look almost of horror. Instead of the indignant reproof they expected from him, the Professor's hands suddenly clenched tightly, and his leonine face was turned on the girl.

"The third passage, below the threshold, and the sublimation of the unborn," Sybil said strangely.

The meaningless phrases were more horrible than any coherent sentence.

"You!" Professor Johnson gasped. "What do you know of that? Child, take care, you have been in communication with things not good to know. The secret of the woods."

Selden was breathing hard, but outwardly his face showed only puzzle and astonishment, for the curious words she had used were from the book *The Ritual of the Woods* which he had taken from the safe at Cold Stairs. If Sybil had by chance seen them, why should she suddenly quote them to the Professor, whose whole attitude had changed! He looked from one to the other of the three young people.

"How much do you know?" he asked in a stern voice. The faces of Selden and Hartley seemed to reassure him, and he shrugged his shoulders.

"The form remains and does not change," he said idly as though addressing the ceiling.

"But the spirit comes and goes," Sybil said promptly, and the Professor leapt to his feet so violently that Hartley followed suit and stood by the girl.

With an effort the Professor recovered himself and gave a forced laugh. "This takes us nowhere," he managed to say coolly, his eyes on the girl as he spoke. "I hope I managed to convince the Chief Inspector that such suspicions are not only groundless but insulting to a man of my position. I thought I would come and have it out with you, but as you are going on leave and are not on the case it really doesn't matter. As for your foolish statement, young lady, it is not worth answering. I may have my own ideas, but the matter-of-fact policemen would not take the slightest notice if I told them, and it is not in their line. How you have got hold of that stupid gibberish I can't imagine, but I should advise you to forget it. No good will come of it. Get down to your lessons, my child, rule of three and French grammar and so on." He seized his hat and, without saying good-bye, flounced out of the room, his cloak waving behind him like the wings of some evil bird.

"Well, I'm damned!" Hartley exclaimed vigorously when he had gone. "Sybil, you ruffled him up somehow, but how on earth did you get hold of that rubbish?"

Sybil's face was flushed and her eyes were unnaturally bright. "It's not rubbish. It is part of *The Ritual of the Woods*. It came to me quite suddenly."

Selden intervened. "Well, don't let that old ruffian spoil our last evening. I don't think Dodds was playing the game by telling the Professor what he did, but he's annoyed with me."

Later in the evening, when Sybil had gone off with Mrs. Perks for the night, Hartley returned to the subject.

"I don't think we ought to let Sybil go back to Cold Stairs, Dick," he said earnestly. "You remember what she told me. Whatever the truth about that story may be, it can't be good for her to be in those woods again."

"I certainly think, after what we heard tonight, it is highly dangerous, but I see no way out of it. If it were possible to keep the girl here, she would be gradually drawn to Cold Stairs, like a nail to a magnet. She would become fretful and discontented, and it would end in a row. Just at first the novelty of this life, and—I am not trying to flatter you, Jack—your company, have taken her mind off other things. It's better for her to go as a regular member of the household than to run off into unknown dangers in the forest."

Jack was sobered, though not convinced, but Dick went on.

"That old humbug didn't take me in. I said that Dodds was not playing the game, but that was merely for Sybil's benefit. I never even suggested that the Professor was concerned with this affair to Dodds, only that I was going to follow up the question of his failing to meet Mrs. Seaton, which I still think wants clearing up. What the Professor wanted to know was whether he was being shadowed by detectives or—by someone else."

"Great Scot! Do you really think he is being followed?"

"He said so," Selden said dryly. "Sybil's strange interruption prevented me from getting further with him, but it gave me a strong hint."

Jack stared at the detective, open-mouthed.

"I thought—forgive me, Dick—you were absolutely in the cart over this business."

"I'm glad you think that. I want everyone to be of the same opinion. Don't you see the apparent rubbish that Sybil and the Professor were exchanging gives a link between the Professor and the Something we are after? You remember I told you I found the book in the safe. No doubt Sybil had got hold of it. I've read it through. It's just one of those many old secret rites of the middle ages."

"But I don't see. How did that old goat get to know of it?"

"That's the point." Selden gripped his friend's arm tightly. "Don't you remember that there was a fly-leaf and the inscription was to the effect that the book had been given by the Professor to Dr. Gilkie."

"It's too deep for me, old thing. I suppose I'm just a mechanic without imagination." Selden laughed.

"Cheer up! You can at least take it that old Johnson is in a blue funk about something. It would have been a positive relief to him if Dodds had told him that he was being shadowed."

"Dick, I'm not going to let Sybil go. Do you understand? There seems too much funny business going on."

Selden thought for a minute without speaking; then he turned a smiling face to Jack.

"There's one thing I didn't mean to tell you. Not that I don't trust you, you know that, but I wanted you to be in the position of saying truthfully that you didn't know where I was. You are a very poor liar. I am going to take a job as tutor to that dreadful imp, so that I can be on the spot, and actually in the house. That will relieve your mind."

"What a lark!" Jack grinned with a look of immense relief. "Does Sybil know?"

"I shall have to tell her of course, but as all the servants had been given leave, you remember, no one knows me there in my true vocation, except the doctor and Perkins."

"I wish I could come with you."

"I may want your services, Jack. If I wire, come by the first 'plane you can get hold of, for it will mean life and death then."

"That's a bargain. Just a nightcap, and we'll turn in."

CHAPTER XII

ℭᏥᎬ ᏚᏟᏒᏬᏩᏩᏞᎬ ᏆᏁ ℭᏥᎬ ᏔᎾᎾᎠᏚ

OLD STAIRS HAD THE APPEARANCE of a shorn lamb. O'Connor stopped his car in the drive, and drew in a deep breath. All the ivy, clematis, and Virginia creeper that had clung to the ancient walls in a friendly embrace had gone, and the old stones had been cleaned and scraped, so that the house resembled a washed dog fresh from his bath. Green paint had been freely applied to any woodwork that could be treated, but the leaded windows fortunately could not be touched. The massive oak front door glistened in the sunlight with fresh varnish. At the back of the place a number of trees had been cut down, leaving an open space, where men were at work making flower-beds, and laying turf. Bright yellow gravel was being spread along the drive, where a steam-roller was at work.

Anger and surprise showed on Sybil's face at the desecration, as she deemed it, but O'Connor thought it less gloomy and forbidding, and more like a boarding-house or hotel.

Lady Harman's new and beautifully upholstered butler met them at the door, holding a silver tray, into which O'Connor solemnly dropped his business card. He had already seen Lady Harman watching their arrival from the drawing-room window, but this archaic practice was in accord with what she considered proper for a "lady of title".

They waited, O'Connor amused and Sybil fuming, in the oak-panelled hall, which was now covered with white enamel, until the pompous butler returned to say that her ladyship would receive them.

Lady Harman waddled across the drawing-room floor, with her head held high, and greeted them in an affected voice.

"So pleased to see you, Mr. O'Connor. So you have brought the dear child with you. I am sure you will find a great improvement in this place, Sybil."

She kissed the girl coldly on the forehead, and then swept them in to luncheon where the butler, a footman, and two maids were waiting in a row.

"Where is Sir William?" Lady Harman asked imperiously.

"I am afraid I am unable to say, my lady," the butler replied with a profound bow.

The imp strolled in when the meal was half over, and took his seat with a nod to O'Connor and Sybil.

"I've been for a stroll in the woods, Ma," he said, watching the butler pour out whisky. "These peasants are damned impertinent. Don't drown it, James."

Sybil's face flushed with anger, and she bit her lip.

"I shall have those Jenkinses out if they are not careful," he went on with his mouth full. "They had the cheek to say we had spoilt the house by cutting down the creepers, and that hulking soldier son of theirs agreed with them."

After a most uncomfortable meal, Lady Harman handed Sybil over to the housekeeper, and took the lawyer into her own room for a business talk. He was saved from further bother with regard to Selden, for Lady Harman opened the subject at once.

"I am really indebted to you for introducing me to Mr. Selden. I have engaged him as 'tooter' for Sir William, and I think he will be quite satisfactory. He is arriving this afternoon."

O'Connor hid a smile with his hand. "He is a very clever man, and took a good degree at Cambridge."

"So I saw from his testimonials." The butler entered with coffee and she paused while he was in the room.

Like most women of her type, she admired large jolly men like O'Connor and was genuinely grateful for the way he had handled her affairs.

"I like that man, and of course, being a friend of yours is in itself a recommendation. When I told him he would have meals in the servants' hall, he expressed his agreement most charmingly. He said he knew his own place. Of course it would be awkward when I am entertaining to have a 'tooter' dining with us."

"May I smoke?" O'Connor asked to hide his feelings. He could picture Selden, with his keen sense of humour, playing up to this atrocious woman. He dared not trust himself to meet Dick, and made his escape as soon as he decently could, receiving a warm invitation to come again.

As soon as Lady Harman had seen his car vanish down the drive she sent for Sybil. The girl entered quietly, but those who knew her would have seen that she was holding herself in with difficulty.

"Sit down, Sybil. I want to talk seriously to you," Lady Harman began. "Now that I have been made your guardian by the Courts, I am responsible for your conduct, you understand that."

"Yes, Lady Harman," the girl said listlessly.

"You may call me Aunt Hilda. It is less formal. I want you to understand that there will be a rather stricter discipline than under my husband, who was very easy-going."

"Why may I not have my old bedroom?" Sybil flashed out.

"Ah," Lady Harman said. "I am glad you mentioned that, because it brings me to the very question I was about to discuss with you." She breathed hard, and eyed the girl sternly.

"I don't want to inquire into your past conduct, Sybil, but I have my suspicions. I suppose you know the workmen found those rings leading down from your bedroom window, and the faked window. I suppose you used to slip out of the house that way, or perhaps someone used to slip in."

She saw the indignant look on the girl's face at the gross insinuation.

"You need not look like that. I understand you have been staying in London with that engineer, Hartley. It's about time you considered your age. You are not a child now."

"Is that all?" Sybil said, rising.

"Don't be pert with me, child, or I'll box your ears. Until I get a suitable governess for you, I am placing you under the care of my housekeeper, and you will not be allowed to go out alone. You understand that you may accompany William, if he wishes it, or Mrs. Simmons. I shall have to make inquiries about past events. I know what you girls are nowadays. I shall also see any letters you write before they are posted."

When Sybil finally left her guardian, even her young brave spirits were broken. She went to her new room and flung herself on the bed in a passion of weeping.

Not a friend in the house! Even the servants were cold and unsympathetic, taking their cue from the mistress, whom they heartily despised.

Selden arrived in the afternoon, and Lady Harman was more than pleased with her choice. His deferential manner and complete agreement with her wishes touched her vanity.

"You will find my son in the study," she said at the conclusion of the interview. The imp was reclining on a large couch, smoking a cigar.

"Good afternoon, Sir William," Selden said pleasantly.

"So you are the new tutor. You'll understand that I work when I choose, and when I don't want to, then I shan't."

"Of course; that is entirely as you wish. I am here to place my services at your disposal, when you require them." Selden was thoroughly enjoying the situation.

The imp grinned his appreciation of these laudable sentiments.

"Can you play golf?"

"Yes, Sir William."

"Billiards?"

"Yes, Sir William."

"Here, chuck it. You're a gentleman if you are only a tutor. Drop this Sir William business. Call me Harman."

Selden smiled. "As you wish, but I think I'll keep to the title in the presence of Lady Harman."

The imp was no fool; he laughed loudly. "You are right. There's no holding the old girl in nowadays. Have a drink; you're not one of those damned teetotallers, I hope?"

The new tutor soon demonstrated the contrary, and a queer friendship was cemented. Selden felt genuinely sorry for the lad, who had never had any education to speak of, and yet was an admixture of his father's breeding, with its instincts and traditions, and the sheer vulgarity of his mother. A combination that has many times led to disastrous consequences.

One matter worried William. He did not like the idea of Selden taking meals with the servants, and would have spoken to his mother about it had not Selden persuaded him not to do so. Secretly William wanted Selden's company at meals, finding these ornate ceremonies rather boring, but Lady Harman found an ally in Selden himself, who solemnly declared that he had never heard of a mere tutor dining with "the family".

The butler, who had overheard the remark, repeated it in the servants' hall, and in consequence Selden received a warm welcome below stairs. He was sufficiently plain in appearance to cause no qualms in the amorous heart of the footman, and old Mrs. Simmons, the housekeeper, was a motherly body who took to him at once: his method of handling his knife and fork proving him a gentleman born. After supper he played and sang to the other servants, in spite of an intimation from James that her ladyship had invited him to take coffee with her.

With such a promising beginning it was not hard for Selden to arrange with Mrs. Simmons for him to occupy Sybil's old room by special favour.

Had her ladyship seen him unpacking his suit-case when he retired she would have received a shock. Among other strange gear for a tutor, he took out a coil of fine-spun silk rope, with a knot each yard, a dagger in a case, and an automatic.

Things were turning out well for Selden. He had learnt from the gossip of the servants' hall that Sybil was practically a prisoner, and was not allowed to roam about alone. Then, on the following day, the imp had diffidently asked his tutor to teach him how to shoot, as he did not like to display his ignorance before the gamekeeper, and wanted to be able to take his rightful place with the gun.

This enabled Selden to explore the forest depths, as William desired solitude for his practice. He was solemnly introduced to Sybil, who showed no sign of recognition. She had been warned by O'Connor on the way down, and the thought of Selden in the house had been her one comfort.

Day followed day in seeming tedium. The imp was delighted with a tutor who took him out into the deep recesses of the forest, where he "potted" various objects, and learnt how to load and hold a gun. Lessons were perfunctory and usually confined to wet days, and after luncheon when the lad felt like it. Lady Harman was delighted. Even to her obtuse mind, the change for the good was evident. The lad was smarter in his dress, more alert and active, and less boorish.

And every night when the household was asleep, Selden slipped down his silken rope and disappeared into the forest on his relentless quest after that strange Something that lurked there.

Every day Lady Harman motored out to pay calls, with complete disregard of etiquette, and was careful to take Sybil with her. Several of the families round about had known the child, and out of pity for her received the terrible woman, but Lady Harman returned each time raging at the "snobs" as she styled them.

Already she was discussing the question of going to London for Christmas, when an event occurred that brought matters to a head.

Snow had fallen, but the clouds had passed away, and a full moon was shining in a clear sky on the white woods and fields. Selden opened the window of his room, and drank in the pure cold air. The dead silence of midwinter brooded on the forest. Beasts in byre and stable waited patiently for the coming of spring, and humans tucked themselves snugly in warm beds. The hibernating instinct still held sway in the countryside. Selden fastened his rope, and slid down cautiously to the ground. He had put on a thick woolly and a sports coat, but the keen air was exhilarating. He shook his head over the footmarks he was compelled to make. A thaw or a further fall of snow were unlikely before daylight, and if some prying gardener came round in the morning he would see the tell-tale marks.

There was nothing for it but to get up early and do some brushing before the others were awake. He ought to have provided himself with a broom.

He set off briskly across the space made by uprooting of old trees and plunged into the dark forest. He knew his way perfectly by this time, having made a mental map of the forest and its devious paths, and went straight to the cottage of the Jenkinses with steps which were soundless in the snow that had fallen through the leafless trees.

The clearing in which the cottage stood was flooded in moonlight, and the snow-covered roof gave the cottage the appearance of a Christmas card. Not a light showed in the tiny diamond windows, but Selden skirted the clearing and came to the tunnel in the woods, no longer green and dry but with a brook in full spate, flowing too rapidly for freezing. Along the bank he went towards the old mound where a farm had once stood. Here again the clearing was bathed in silver and looked the picture of peace. Suddenly Selden's hands tightened and he gave a shuddering gasp of apprehension. His heart missed a beat as his eyes were fixed on the ground before him. The marks of naked human feet in the snow issued from the wood, and he saw the track in the clear moonlight leading to the humped mound. Night after night he had watched this place unsuccessfully. A sense of terrible danger, imminent and real, filled his mind with unnamable fear. He dashed across the open space, whipping out his revolver as he ran. At the mass of bushes that closed the entrance to this strange place he paused. Someone was there, for the snow had fallen from the tangled mass of dry twigs and lay in a heap on the ground. With a sickening feeling of dread he saw the footmarks passing through the screen of bushes.

He pushed the branches back, as noiselessly as he could, but a dry branch snapped loudly in that stillness. A dim greenish light showed inside, but was immediately extinguished, and utter darkness came down. Selden put caution to the winds, and threw himself forward through the branches that lashed his face, flashing his torch round the interior. The next moment something rushed with a snarling noise, and an arm closed round Selden's throat like a bar of iron.

Selden was a highly trained athlete, and strong beyond his appearance, but was powerless in this relentless grip. He felt his eyes starting from his head, and there was a singing in his ears. Fingers were feeling for his throat while the other arm held his head back. It was fortunate indeed at that vital moment that the training he had received had included meeting any kind of attack. Without attempting to force away the arm, which would have been useless, he bent suddenly forward, almost double, with a mighty heave which nearly split the muscles of his neck. The suddenness of the movement forced the thing that was strangling the life out of him completely over his head, and the arm relaxed. There was something awful in this struggle in the dark entrance among the bushes. The torch lay on the ground sending a beam along the floor.

The thing had struck the ground, and it was no time for polite fighting. Selden lashed out with his boot with all his strength and heard a stifled cry like that of a wild beast, as his foot met soft flesh. He grabbed for his automatic and torch and flashed the light down, but there was nothing there. For a moment even Selden's heart quailed at the awful possibility that he was fighting something not human; then he flung aside the bushes and emerged into the bright moonlight. For one moment he saw something crouching low, and running with incredible pace. He steadied himself and fired, but the Thing had sprung into the overhanging branches of the trees, and was lost to sight. He emptied his automatic at the spot, more to relieve his feelings than in any hope of hitting his adversary, and then tottered, sick with loathing, back to the entrance to the chamber.

The chamber was dark inside. For a moment he fancied it was empty. The same heavy, overpowering smell pervaded the place as he had noticed in the room where Sir John had been killed. Then he saw Sybil lying crumpled in a heap on the floor, clothed only in her nightdress, with a dark coat thrown over it. The black tumbled hair concealed her face, and for a moment he feared the worst. He picked her up and carried her into the open, when to his intense relief the girl opened her eyes and looked at him with a vacant stare. Then recognition came and she struggled violently.

"Steady, Sybil," Selden said firmly. "You are quite safe now."

"Oh! It's you, Dick." She looked round in a puzzled manner.

"I came just in time."

"But where is . . ." she paused abruptly and her glance was directed to the dim entrance.

"Whatever it is it has gone," he snapped. "I would have gone after it but for you. Are you feeling better?"

Selden saw the same secretive look come over the girl's face like a mask. "You followed me, then?" she asked.

"This is no time for explanations. Can you walk, do you think, or shall I carry you?"

"I'm all right now, Dick," she said with a nervous laugh.

Selden hastily removed his boots and socks and handed the latter to the girl. "Put those on, Sybil, anyway. You'll catch your death of cold."

She obeyed mechanically, as though her brain was not fully functioning and she was afraid of saying something before she had collected her wits.

"Oh, my box!" she cried, as they stood up. "I must get it!" She rushed back into the cavernous aperture, and Dick followed with his torch. The place was empty. Sybil put her hand to her head. "I remember now—he took it."

"Come on," he said almost impatiently, and they started to walk back.

"You must tell me everything," Selden said sternly. "Things have gone too far for any more secrets." Her sudden recovery from the faint appeared suspicious to him.

"You haven't taken any harm, Sybil?"

She looked at him with clear, honest eyes. "I? None whatever. I suppose I must have fainted when I heard a struggle at the entrance."

"Who was that with you? Tell me the truth."

"Why, the king of the woods, of course," she said innocently.

"King of rubbish," Selden muttered to himself.

"He told me to come and bring my box," Sybil added.

It was the old story again, and Selden bit his lip with vexation.

"Called you—how?"

"I heard him from my window last night. I was leaning out, and he said, 'Come tomorrow night, and bring the secret box.' "

"And this is the first time that you have been out at night since you came back to Cold Stairs?"

"Of course. I couldn't get out, and it was so cold."

"But how did you get out of the house?"

"I crept downstairs and out of the side door that leads into the garden, and then out into the woods. They had not locked the garden door."

So that was why he had not seen her. The old walled garden at the side of the house had supplied vegetables and fruit, but now, covered in snow, it had been left deserted. She would have been completely hidden from his sight by taking that way.

The girl was showing signs of exhaustion. This strange, almost hypnotic influence that drew her to the woods had exhausted itself, and the bitter cold had taken hold of her.

Selden thought of the Jenkins' cottage, but felt that he must get her back before their absence was discovered. He sat down on a fallen tree-trunk, and took the trembling girl on his knee. He took off the wet socks and rubbed her feet till some slight warmth returned. She was deadly white now, and put her head back on his shoulder.

"I'll carry you now, Sybil. Before we go on, I must ask you one question, and then I won't worry you. What have you got in that box of yours?"

Her answer startled him. She sat up on his knees, and looked him fairly in the face. "I don't know. I have never opened it. He told me not to."

"All right, Sybil, now we'll get along."

A slight touch on his hand made him look up, and silently through the trees he saw the flakes of snow descending. Since they had left the clearing the sky had become overcast, but in the excitement of the events of the last half-hour he had not noticed it. Now the snow was falling fast.

He picked the girl up in his strong arms, and went forward through the forest by a track she pointed out that skirted the Jenkins' cottage, and twisted away to the left. It was a "ride" similar to the one in which the constable had been murdered, and emerged at the gate in the wall of the old garden, which was open as Sybil had left it.

"I can walk now," she said. "It's only a step to the side door."

Selden placed her gently on the ground, and she ran lightly across the garden path. The snow was coming down heavily, and Selden was pleased to think the tracks would be covered by the morning. He saw the girl fumbling at the door, and a sudden misgiving seized him. She hurried up and he saw her face white in the semi-darkness. "It's locked," she whispered.

CHAPTER XIII

ȚȟҼ ȞȚȚȞCK ON ȚȟҼ
DOCȚOR'ș ȟOUșҼ

S OMEONE HAD LOCKED THE DOOR while they had been out, but the house was grimly silent, and Selden hoped that perhaps the butler had been round and fastened it up.

"There's only one thing to do, Sybil," he answered her mute inquiry. "We must climb up to my room—your old room."

"The rings have been taken away," she panted.

He took her icy hand and they ran through the garden and skirted the wall to the back of the house. Selden breathed a sigh of relief when his hand touched the silk cord.

"Cling round my neck," he whispered, "only don't strangle me."

He felt the girl's numbed fingers close round him, and, setting his teeth, ascended the slender cord with hands and feet, slowly pulling at the knots. His hands grasped the sill, and he made one frantic effort and pulled himself up. Sybil's hands relaxed their grip as she seized the window-sill, and he was able to scramble into the room and drag her after him. He stood panting, exhausted by the strain, which would have been too much for the average man.

"Better not switch on the light," he whispered. "I'll let you out, and you can slip along to your room. Change your things, and pile everything you can on the bed, or you'll get a fearful cold."

He advanced cautiously to the door and turned the key noiselessly. The girl was just behind him, as he slowly opened the door. The corridor was in complete darkness, and he widened the entrance for Sybil to slip through.

Without warning the corridor light was switched on, and the glare blinded them. Selden sprang back, placing Sybil behind him, but it was too late. The burly butler stood in the entrance in trousers and shirtsleeves and the footman stood by him, ready to assist if required. Selden caught a fleeting vision of the imp in the corridor grinning sheepishly.

"Here he is, my lady, and the young lady with him," the butler said in the unctuous tone that servants adopt when they discover scandals in their employer's affairs.

Lady Harman advanced along the corridor like an angry virago. "So this is what has been going on in my house!" she screamed. "You little—"

She lifted her hand, but Selden stood firmly before her. Selden's mind, even at that moment, was moving like lightning. If he told the truth, not only would he have been called a liar, but all his plans would be ruined. If he accepted the situation obviously implied, Sybil's reputation was gone.

"You are entitled to an explanation, Lady Harman," he said calmly.

"Explanation—what more do I need than the testimony of my own eyes? Explanations, indeed! You wormed your way into my house for this purpose, I suppose! You immoral scoundrel."

She was hysterical with fury, and it was impossible to argue with her in that state.

"Go to your room at once, girl. I'll speak to you in the morning. You will find Mrs. Simmons there, who will see that you don't come out." The girl turned and went without a word, her head drooping with fatigue and shame at the titters of the servants.

"As for you," Lady Harman said, addressing Selden, "you'll pack your bag at once, this instant, and leave the house, unless you want me to order the *other servants* to throw you out."

"I will certainly go," Selden said coldly. "But I warn you not to lift a finger against Sybil. I shall inform Mr. O'Connor of what has taken place and if you strike her you will lose your guardianship."

The firm words, coming from a mild tutor, staggered her for a moment.

"James, stay here with Williams, and see that this person is out of the place in ten minutes." She turned on her heel and stamped down the corridor to her room.

"I'm sorry this has happened, Selden," the imp said awkwardly, when his mother had gone. "I had no idea you were such a goer— and Sybil, my word! It's always the quiet ones."

Selden laughed rather bitterly. "My boy, you must not jump to conclusions, like your mother. When you come to know the truth you will realize that Sybil has come to no harm, but I have rescued her from a grave danger, and perhaps you and your mother as well.

Leave me now. Your mother is within her rights, but look after Sybil."

He held his hand out and the young man seized it warmly. He had a high regard for his tutor, whose mind had completely dominated his own weak nature.

Selden turned back into the room, and started to pack quickly. He went to the window, as though to shut it, and swiftly wound up the silk cord. James was watching from the door but did not come into the room, with a courtesy that Selden was not slow to notice.

"I'm ready now," he said cheerfully, picking up his suit-case.

"I'm sure all of us will be sorry to lose you, Selden," James remarked as they went down the stairs. "You have behaved like a gentleman should while you have been with us." He hesitated. "I heard what you said to Sir William. I believe you, and I hope her ladyship will when she's calmed down a bit."

"That's good of you, James. Tell me, how did you come to be waiting outside my door?"

"That's very simply explained," the butler answered. "Her ladyship had told Mrs. Simmons to keep an eye on Miss Sybil, and she heard a door banging in the night. It kept her awake and she went to close it. She found it was Miss Sybil's room and that she was not in her bed. She went to her ladyship, and she told Mrs. Simmons to wake me and the footman. We searched everywhere for Miss Sybil. Of course we thought she couldn't have gone out on a night like this, and all the doors were locked."

They were standing in the hall and Selden had his hand on the door. He stopped, rigid.

"You are quite sure all the doors were locked?"

"I locked them myself last thing before I went to bed."

"Yes, but when you searched for Miss Sybil did you examine them again?"

"Of course." The butler seemed surprised at the question.

"How long ago was this?"

"About half an hour, I should say. Her ladyship told us to wake you, but we couldn't get an answer, and then she told us to wait till you came out."

"You are quite certain—it is most important. The side door, for instance—you found that locked?"

"Why, what are you getting at, Selden? I've told you already."

"James," Selden placed his hand firmly on the butler's fat arm, "there is something here I don't like at all. If you will take my advice you will see that everyone in the house locks their doors, and don't go to bed. Keep the lights on and get the footman to stay up with you."

The butler's eyes grew large and round with fear.

"What is it, then?" he asked.

"I can't be certain, James, and I can't explain more, but someone locked the side door from the inside, and is in the house now. I have a suspicion that it is the murderer of Sir John Harman."

"Oh lord!"

"You need not be frightened. If I am right, he will not want to be seen. Carry out what I have said and patrol the house, and no harm will come to you."

"But why not ring up the police and have him arrested?"

"It's not so easy as all that," Selden replied with a smile. "By the time the police got here he would be gone; in fact he may have gone already, hearing all this disturbance. I rather fancy when I leave this house I shall draw him off in any case," he added grimly.

"I'll do what you wish," James said in a humble tone.

"All right; I'll go, there is not much of the night left now. Here, take this."

He produced his automatic from his pocket and gave it to the butler.

"I'm afraid I'm not much used to these things," the latter said doubtfully.

"Never mind; it will make a noise, and give you confidence."

"Thank you, sir—I'm sure I wish you weren't going."

"I shall see you again before long," Selden said confidently, and went out into the blinding snow before the other could urge him to stay.

It was a long and weary trudge to Lydford, but Selden never faltered, swinging along through the snow that was now covering the ground in deeper folds and obliterating tracks. He reached the house of Dr. Hughes and rang the night bell. A speaking-tube by the front door answered him.

"Who's that?"

"Selden. Come down like a good fellow and let me in, I'm frozen."

"It's not another murder?"

"Not this time, but hurry up," Selden called.

"Well, young man, perhaps you will give me an explanation for routing me out at this time of night," Hughes said, as he opened the door, clad in a dressing-gown and slippers.

He took the detective into his study and roused up the smouldering embers in the grate.

"You're frozen, man. Not a word till you've had a good stiff brandy. I can see something important has happened."

He bustled about, and soon had steaming hot brandy and water with some lemon in it by Selden's side. The look of utter fatigue on the face of the young man had aroused all his professional instincts.

"I'm very tired, Doc, and I can't argue tonight. I came to you for a bed, which I knew you would not refuse, and for your help which I know I can rely upon. I'll tell you what happened. You know I asked you not to reveal my true profession to the people at Cold Stairs?"

"Yes, and I wondered what you were up to—something to do with the murders, I suppose."

Selden, warmed by the fire and his hot drink, narrated the story of his visit to Cold Stairs. The doctor, a good listener, remained absolutely silent, puffing at his pipe.

"That's about the queerest yarn I've ever heard," the doctor said when Selden had finished. "But the attack on you was real enough, and disposes of the supernatural theory."

Selden felt his throat. "But for ju-jitsu, and the fact that I was able to throw my opponent, I shouldn't have been here now," Selden remarked without replying directly to the doctor's implication.

"The method of attack was so exactly similar to the other two cases, that I am convinced it was by the same assassin, but there are difficulties about the case. For example, supposing there is some monster living in the woods, how is it possible for it to have been there for years without being discovered, and how does it subsist? Again, there is method and reason in everything that has been done. How does that agree with some semi-human creature?"

"It's a tough nut to crack," the doctor commented slowly. "It's a pity you didn't wing him when you fired."

"If he could be injured by a bullet. I'm a first-class shot, Doctor, and I could have sworn I shot him clean through, but he got away. But the girl Sybil frankly puzzles me. If we accept as a basis that there exists some Thing, let us call it, we must picture It as of some frightful appearance. It caused the tragedy of Anne Jenkins, and so scared the policeman that he ran for his life. It frightened young Eric so badly that he crashed down the stairs, and lastly there is that grisly photograph of yours. All these agree, but, on the other hand, Sybil has this strange delusion of a being mysterious, and almost holy, for whom she has a sort of worship, and I am convinced there is not a trace of sex in the case. She talks of It in an awed way. It's morbid and unhealthy, but there's not an atom of passion. But how can she be totally immune from harm, and in fact, fascinated by such a monster?"

"Unless she is under some spell; there have been cases of that."

"Granted, but this savage killer has spared the girl, not only from death but from other things. I am like a man who has had a half-truth revealed, but there are baffling gaps. It's altogether outside the line of ordinary police investigation. Perkins and his men have searched the forest from end to end, and I have been out every night on the watch. Now I've been turned out of the house I fear the worst, for the creature is at large, and has been beaten for the first time."

"What about dogs?"

"Perkins has tried, without any success; in fact the hounds refused the scent, with every sign of terror."

"Well, I think bed's the best place for you. Good counsel comes with sleep," the doctor said with a yawn.

"I ought not to have come here," Selden said gravely. "It is just possible that I am bringing trouble on you."

The doctor grinned. "I'm not afraid. I only have my old cook sleeping here with her husband who does odd jobs and cleans my car. The maid comes from the village. But I'll load my gun."

Selden did not respond to the other's amused tone.

"We'll go round the house, Doctor, and see that everything is fastened."

The doctor glanced uneasily at Selden. He rather fancied the adventure of the night had upset him more than he cared to own. To humour him, he made a tour of inspection. Front and back doors were securely locked and bolted, and the ground-floor windows, though devoid of shutters, were hasped.

"Well," the doctor said as they stood in the hall, "I hope you are satisfied."

The words died on his lips as a crash came from the study, and the sound of falling glass.

"Switch off the hall light," Selden called urgently, and dashed into the study. A huge hole had been made in the window-pane, and a large stone lay on the floor. Selden saw that much with his torch, and then went to the broken aperture and gazed out into the darkness. The snow fell silently but heavily, and the night was intensely black. Selden noiselessly pushed up the sash and scrambled out.

"Come back!" the doctor cried, terror of the unknown seizing him. Then he followed Selden.

"Where are you?" he called softly. The next moment a beam of light shot from Selden's powerful torch and turned the snowflakes into iridescent particles of rainbow. For one fleeting moment both men saw a form of horror half hidden in the bushes. The grinning skull and hideous shapeless arm uplifted, as though in menace, gleamed a moment in the ray, and then disappeared with the suddenness of an apparition.

The doctor gripped Selden fiercely by the arm. "Come back, you young fool," he cried frantically, and almost dragged Selden to the house.

"What a pity I gave my automatic to the butler," Selden remarked calmly when they stood inside the study.

The doctor was panting, and his eyes were fixed uneasily on the broken pane.

"Thank goodness we saw it, though I'm sorry about your broken window," Selden remarked.

"Whatever do you mean?"

"I mean just this, Doctor. I was afraid that Thing was in Cold Stairs, and warned the butler, but I have drawn it here."

"We can't stay here, anyway." The doctor furtively helped himself to a large brandy and drank it down.

"We'll sit up in another room. This is too draughty. It won't be long before dawn, though this snow will delay daylight."

"You're a cool customer, Selden," Hughes said.

"Not cool except physically, but perhaps I can see further than you, Doctor. I have studied this case more closely, that's all."

They moved into the doctor's dining-room and lit a fire. The doctor went to explain to the startled servants that nothing was wrong, and that they could get dressed.

"You ought to get some sleep, you know," he said, as he entered the dining-room carrying his sporting-gun, at which Selden smiled.

"I am quite awake now and we can talk. I mentioned I have thought this problem out pretty deeply. You will observe that in all the three murders in which this being has been concerned, he has only used his bare fingers. This use of a stone, I believe, was in fury at being baffled in the wood. He disappeared quickly enough when I fired, and when, just now, I flashed the torch on him."

"That, at any rate, is reassuring," the doctor said, fingering his gun.

"Men like darkness rather than light, because their deeds are evil," Selden quoted.

There was a ring in Selden's voice that made the doctor look at him curiously. The tone of fatigue had gone and he seemed almost triumphant.

"You seem quite satisfied," Hughes said, almost annoyed at the other's manner.

"I believe I am seeing light at last. If you are not too tired, I'll tell you."

"There will be no sleep for me. My cook is getting us some early breakfast. Go ahead."

"It will be interesting to hear your reactions. Take the events from the beginning. Sir John may have brought his death on himself by going up to investigate alone. The constable saw what we have seen, and had to be killed." The doctor was about to interrupt, but Selden went on, "Mrs. Seaton had discovered the truth—I have no doubt of that—and had to be silenced. But there was that mysterious box of Sybil's, which she had taken to London. She tells me she does not know what was inside. It had to be got back by the Creature for some reason. He called Sybil, as she says, and she took it back to the ruin."

"What are you hinting at?" the doctor said hoarsely.

"Now follow this. Mrs. James opened that box on the night of the first murder, and declares that there was nothing inside but rubbish. But would the assassin take the risk of coming back for rubbish?"

"Are you suggesting a sort of 'gin' or ogre in the box, like the bottle-imp in the story?"

"However incredible and monstrous it may appear, I believe I have hit upon the solution. Nothing more now, Doctor, or you'll certify me insane. Let's talk of other things, or play cards."

Not another word would Selden say on the subject, and the arrival of coffee and eggs and bacon gave them other things to think of.

CHAPTER XIV

SELDEN'S REVELATION

L ADY HARMAN WAS GRAVELY DISTURBED. Thinking over the events of the night, she wondered whether she had acted wisely. In the morning the sleepy-eyed butler had informed her of Selden's warning, and produced the automatic as proof of his valiant vigil. Perhaps it would have been wiser to have kept the erring tutor until she could fetch O'Connor from London.

And William, her son, was cross and irritable because he was badly scared. A talk with the butler had brought to his rather dull mind the recollection that the last baronet had been murdered in this house, and the murderer was still at large. He had grown attached to his easy-going tutor, and, having no moral sense, did not regard the episode, even considered in the worst light, as a very heinous crime.

Snow was falling inexorably, and had completely obliterated all footmarks round the house. Lady Harman dispatched a telegram over the 'phone to O'Connor asking him to come immediately, and the lawyer received this and one from Selden at the same time.

After breakfast Lady Harman fortified herself for the interview with Sybil with a stiff glass of gin, her favourite beverage, and sent for the girl.

A thrashing, of course, would be the best punishment, but Selden's warning about the guardianship had produced its effect, and the girl was already suffering from the beginnings of a snuffy cold in the head. She came in, defiant and completely under control, and the interrogation began.

"Have you any explanation to offer for your disgraceful conduct?"

"None whatever," Sybil answered quite calmly.

"Don't be impertinent, child. You are under my charge and I am responsible for you. What were you doing in Mr. Selden's room?"

"I think, Lady Harman, it would be better if you asked him." Sybil had made up her mind that nothing should be said by her about the midnight expedition.

"Answer my question, Sybil." Lady Harman's hand itched to box the girl's ears. "I suppose you were carrying on a clandestine love-affair. How long has this been going on?"

A bright red colour dyed Sybil's face, and tears started to her eyes, but tears of anger. She knew Selden would never allow such an insinuation to be made.

"You are making a great mistake," she said firmly. "Mr. Selden is not a tutor, as you imagine. He is a Scotland Yard detective, and is investigating the murder of my uncle."

The good lady was staggered. "Detective! What rubbish are you talking?"

"It is easy for you to find out," Sybil retorted. "Mr. O'Connor knows quite well, and so does Jack—I mean, Mr. Hartley."

"Do you mean that he was masquerading in my house under false pretences?"

"He was acting as tutor, but in your own interests. He feared that the same fate would overtake your son and you, as my uncle. He did not wish to appear in his own capacity."

"And you knew this and never told me—but that does not explain your conduct."

"Mr. Selden is the soul of honour. I was merely having a conversation with him."

Lady Harman was shaken and frightened, for this agreed with the warning given to the butler.

"Go to your room and remain there. I shall send for this Mr. Selden. Meanwhile my housekeeper shall have charge of you."

Lady Harman was vulgar and ill-bred, and what she actually said would hardly bear the cold light of print. When the girl had been escorted to her room by Mrs. Simmons, James the butler asked permission to speak with Lady Harman.

The interview was short and stormy. The butler and footman wished to give immediate notice. Lady Harman threatened, abused, and finally tried to bribe the butler to stay, but James was adamant. He had already heard strange stories from the gardeners about this place, and the happenings of the night before had, as he expressed it, "put the lid on it". He was too old to tackle murderers that sprang out at one in the dark, and choked one's life out. He knew the law concerning such subjects, he declared, and had "buttled" for thirty years in the best houses.

Lady Harman, who had always employed a "general", was overawed by his pomposity, and gave way. And then came Sir William, very angry and rather the worse for liquor.

"We have got to clear out of this damned place, Ma. I always said it was a mistake. It's only because you want to get into society and cut a dash."

"I did it for your sake, William."

"Well, now we'll pack up and go to London for my sake," he sneered. "The sooner the better."

O'Connor arrived by the express, and motored with difficulty through the thick snow to Lydford, where Selden and the doctor were waiting for him. He listened eagerly to the story they had to tell, and gazed at the new pane of glass that a local glazier had fitted.

"We must get the household to London," O'Connor declared emphatically. "I saw Jack last night. He's like a rampant lion, because Sybil hasn't written to him and he's heard nothing from you. I believe he'd have come down here."

"I expect Sybil's letters have been opened and destroyed," Selden said briefly. "I had no time to write."

"But surely," the doctor suggested, "now that we know there is a being of touchable qualities, who can throw stones and attack you, aren't you going to hunt him out?"

Selden pointed to the snow. "His tracks will show wherever he goes. It would be so easy to follow them, wouldn't it?"

"I don't follow you," Hughes said in a puzzled tone.

Selden was strangely irritable; he had not slept a wink the whole night, and there seemed something on his mind that was weighing heavily.

"I mean just this. Do you suppose for one moment that the assailant of last night would be quite such a fool as to roam the forest leaving tracks and freezing to death? Don't forget he has been to London once, if we accept that the murder of Mrs. Seaton was his work."

O'Connor looked serious. "I see what you mean, Dick. We are planning to take the whole family to town for safety, and you think that the murderer may have gone there already."

"I'll tell you what I think," Selden said in a sudden burst of confidence. "I believe he came down here to get that box—why, I can't tell you. It couldn't have been pleasant in the forest at this time of the year. He got Sybil to bring it to him by some strange power he has over the girl, and, having got it, he made a break for

Lydford. A fit of passion, which may be a useful hint to me, induced him to storm this house, and then he went. But not back to the woods. It makes our task a thousand times harder in London."

"Then really," O'Connor said, "if that is so, the family would be safer down here at present."

"Look here, you two"—Selden placed both his arms on the table and spoke in an earnest manner—"I have taken both of you into my confidence because I can trust you both. I shall tell Perkins as much as is necessary for him to know, and he will get his man out to watch for tracks, as long as the snow lasts. But remember I am on a month's leave and can do what I like. There is one other point I wish you both to notice. The side door of Cold Stairs was undoubtedly locked last night, and no one in the house did that. The murderer had a free run of the house, and a flabby butler and a weak-kneed footman would not have deterred him if he had wanted to do further mischief."

"But isn't that assuming too much? Someone in the house *may* have locked the door."

Selden's face was troubled, and he looked older in the watery sunshine. "Unfortunately," he said with decision, "I *saw his marks in the snow,* outside the side door."

The doctor swore softly. "The same marks as when the constable was killed?" he whispered, gazing fearfully round the room.

"The same marks, and they were on the carpet in the passage, though fainter as they dried."

"I can't understand it," O'Connor said. "What on earth should he go to the house for? You said there are no secret chambers or anything of that sort."

"He evidently got to the house before us, which wasn't difficult, as I was carrying Sybil. I would hazard a guess that he had been watching the house to see whether Sybil was coming, and had seen her leave by the side door. He entered and locked us out, but I expect he meant to do some mischief, when the great search for Sybil all over the house prevented him."

Selden's eyes were unnaturally bright with coming fever, and the doctor looked anxiously at his flushed face.

"But still I don't understand," he said soothingly. "One moment you say that a weak-kneed footman would not have deterred him, if he had meant mischief, and now you say the search disturbed him." Selden laughed bitterly.

"It was me he was after. I have no doubt he knew all about my rope, and hoped I should return that way, and that Sybil would have gone to her room. I should have stayed there all night in spite of Lady Harman, but I thought it wiser to draw him off, as I did."

"But why did he not attack you on the way here?" O'Connor asked.

"He already knew I had a revolver, and didn't know I had given it to James."

"That was rather a foolish thing to do."

"I wanted him to attack me," Selden said deliberately. "I have a very useful dagger here."

"But supposing someone had seen him?" O'Connor asked, wondering whether the strain of the past few days had proved too much for Selden.

"The doctor and I saw him last night," Selden replied. "I saw him in the forest when I had a shot.

This creature is—" he stopped suddenly, and his mouth set firmly. "I'll say no more."

"Dick," O'Connor said with a nervous laugh, "I believe you know who the murderer is."

Selden had sunk his head between his hands in utter weariness. He looked up at O'Connor's words, and laughed harshly. "Of course I know. But if I were to go to Dodds and tell him, he would have me examined by a medical alienist, and put away. Don't ask any more questions."

"You must lie down, Selden, and get some sleep," the doctor said soothingly.

"I think I will, while O'Connor goes to Cold Stairs, and with his pleasant Irish way placates the angry Lady Harman. You can say what you like, Ned, but this conversation is confidential."

"You think you will be able to bring the criminal to justice?" O'Connor said in a practical manner.

"If I can find him." Selden's manner suddenly changed. "I have a bigger task on hand, Ned. Don't think me theatrical. I am fighting for that girl's very soul. If this goes on, her reason will be unseated, like Anne Jenkins'. Worse, for when the devil goes out of a man, there may enter in something too awful to contemplate. Hartley is our one hope. Love can be stronger than death."

The doctor glanced significantly at the lawyer, and gently touched his forehead.

"Come along, Selden," he said in a hearty voice. "I'll give you a sleeping-draught." But Selden's head had fallen forward, and they carried him, fast asleep, to the doctor's bedroom.

"Humph! As I expected," Hughes said, examining his clinical thermometer. "101.8. A bad chill, if not pneumonia."

It needed all O'Connor's tact to smooth matters over at Cold Stairs. The fact that Selden was an old friend, and now in danger from exposure through being turned out, alarmed the woman. He scorned with some heat any suggestion that his friend was carrying on a secret liaison with Sybil, and hinted broadly that Lady Harman's guardianship must include charity in its composition.

"The fact is," Lady Harman declared at last, "I'm town-bred, and I can't stand this place in winter. These snobs won't call on us, and I want the lights and the noise of London. Give me the neon signs of Piccadilly Circus—that's where I am at home."

"Then I'll arrange for you all to come to London," O'Connor agreed. "You can stay over Christmas there in any case, and we'll see then about other arrangements."

Having disposed of this question to his satisfaction, O'Connor had a talk with Sybil. His interest had been aroused by Selden's words, though, like the doctor, he thought they were due in part to the high temperature and partial delirium that had overtaken the detective.

The girl was listless and almost sullen at first, but soon thawed when O'Connor informed her that he and Selden and Jack Hartley had been old friends together at Cambridge.

"I wrote to Jack three times," she said, with a slight flush on her pale face. "He never answered."

"He never got your letters," O'Connor replied. "And he never heard from you. He was nearly coming down here to look you up."

To his surprise, instead of pleasure, a look of terror came to her.

"He mustn't do that. When I go to London, I can't see him. Don't let him try." She spoke in a hot whisper, as though the walls had ears.

"All right," he said cautiously, remembering Selden's words. "You shall please yourself, but I hope to see you, and can take any message you care to give me."

"I am glad we are going to London," the girl said, to his immense surprise. "Now that I no longer have my box, there is nothing to keep me here."

Truly the atmosphere of Cold Stairs was not conducive to sanity, O'Connor thought, but he made no comment.

CHAPTER XV

ᴛʜᴇ ᴀʀʀɪᴠᴀʟ ᴏf ᴡɪʟfʀᴇᴅ ɢɪʟᴋɪᴇ

N ATHANIEL COFFIN WAS IN SOLE CHARGE of the office. The responsibility caused him no uneasiness; he had been in virtual charge for many years. But clients had a habit of getting annoyed when they called and found only a clerk.

Many times in his dark cynical mind Coffin had wondered at their stupidity. He knew the limitations of his "chief" whom he had watched from boyhood. Because he had been to Cambridge and stumbled through a law "special" and was his father's son, he was the man whose advice was sought on difficult matters of transfers, conversions, titles, and the like, on all of which matters he, Coffin, was an expert, though only a clerk.

His appearance, grim disposition, and perhaps his name, had proved an effectual ban on matrimony. Who would care to be known as Mrs. Coffin, or stand at the altar beside a man with a face like death itself?

No one could be more utterly isolated than he. A small flat in an old neighbourhood—a bachelor flat of three rooms—was his home. No servant ever crossed that threshold. He did his own meagre cooking, washing-up, and cleaning. His dark sitting-room was completely surrounded by books on every conceivable subject, but folklore and mediaeval legends formed his favourite subjects.

Had he died in his sleep no one but O'Connor would have missed him. He had no kith or kin. There are many such men, and women too, in this fast spreading octopus of London.

When O'Connor had made his sudden dash for Lydford, the clerk merely moved into his chief's room and carried on with the correspondence; the sole difference being the letters "p.p." to the signature of letters he would in any case have dictated. The junior clerk, typist, and boy all feared him, a sentiment that gave him secret joy, for like so many of his type he desired fear when love was denied him.

No visitors were expected, and no appointments had been made for that day, so he was rather surprised when the lad announced that a gentleman wished to see Mr. O'Connor. He fully expected that the visitor would go when he was informed that the head of the firm was away, and was mildly interested when the boy opened the door after a decorous knock and ushered in a stranger without giving any name.

Coffin saw before him a lithe, well-built man under thirty with a dark face, either through long sojourn in the tropics or an origin not altogether European. The face was dark mahogany colour, and the eyes of blue formed a striking and unpleasant contrast. The hair was black as jet, carefully brushed, and the whole bearing of the man was that of a well-educated gentleman dressed in good taste.

Coffin rose to his feet and scrutinized his visitor while he waited for the other to speak.

"You are the chief clerk, I understand," the stranger said in a well-modulated voice.

"My name is Coffin. I regret that Mr. O'Connor, the head of the firm, is absent."

The stranger smiled, showing fine white teeth which contrasted strongly with his dark skin.

"I have often found," he said suavely, "that chief clerks are more versed in the business of their firms than the chiefs. But pray sit down, Mr. Coffin."

He placed his hat and stick, which Coffin's experienced eyes identified as a Penang cane, carefully on a chair, and then seated himself.

"My name may be not unfamiliar to you, though we have never met. I am Wilfred Gilkie."

In spite of his strong self-control, Coffin started.

"Of course, Mr. Gilkie, your name, as you say, is familiar."

"I have just returned from Assam, where I have lived most of my life. You probably know the reason for my call."

Coffin rose and lifted down a box from the shelf to gain time. Gilkie went on.

"I saw an advertisement in *The Times* newspaper, and as I had not been home for many years I thought I would take this opportunity of doing so. You have some information to give me, I understand."

"Yes, Mr. Gilkie, quite so. We inserted that notice in perfectly good faith. You are not acquainted with the reason?"

"I know nothing. It rather surprised me that anyone knew of my existence."

"You have heard of the late Sir John Harman of Cold Stairs?" Coffin asked, fingering the papers he had taken from the box.

"I believe he was a friend of my father's, but I have never met him. But pardon me, do you object to smoke?"

"Not at all, sir." Coffin was glad of the diversion.

Gilkie handed a handsome leather case filled with Indian cheroots to the clerk. "Will you try one of my native products?" he said with a smile.

Coffin took one and lit it with murmured thanks. "You have not heard that Sir John was murdered?"

"I saw it in the papers, but as I say, I never met him, and was only interested in the name."

"You were then unacquainted that he had married secretly. It was quite an unexpected romance. His wife, or, rather, widow, turned up after Sir John's death, and established her claim."

Gilkie flicked the ash from his cigar into a tray and laughed softly.

"This is interesting, Mr. Coffin, but I hardly see how it bears on your wish to see me."

"I am afraid I have some rather bad—or, shall we say, disappointing news for you. The fact is that Sir John had made a will leaving almost his entire fortune to you, but of course," he went on hurriedly, "that will is now superseded by a later one in favour of his wife."

"Why on earth should he leave anything to me?"

Coffin was relieved at the cool way he took the loss of a small fortune.

"It was rather queerly worded: he left the money to the son of his old friend, Dr. Gilkie."

"Of course that is so much waste paper now?"

"I am afraid so. Lady Harman's rights have been proved, and probate granted. She has taken possession of the old place."

"And has she any progeny? I mean did they have any children legally born?" There was a slight irony in the words.

"There is a son, Sir William, about eighteen years old, who is now the new baronet."

"Well! Well! The age of romance is not dead. She was his cook I suppose?"

"No, she married him when he was plain Mr. Harman; but you will pardon me, Mr. Gilkie, you take this uncommonly well."

"As I never expected a penny, there is not much cause for disappointment. If I had known out there, it might have been different. I might have gone on the bust a bit and possibly sold up my small property. I was coming to England in any case." He gave an amused laugh. "It might have been a little awkward if the good woman had turned up after I had taken possession."

"I am very glad, sir, that contingency did not arise."

"I suppose," Gilkie said whimsically, "I should then have been compelled to marry the widow. By the way, it may sound stupid to you, but did they find out who had done the murder?"

"Not yet," Coffin said guardedly. He did not want to tell the whole story. He would leave that to O'Connor.

"I am much obliged," Gilkie remarked. "Of course I should have liked this unexpected nest-egg. It would have come in very handy. But it's no good worrying about it now. I would like to see the first will out of curiosity."

"I am afraid that is deposited with the Court," Coffin lied.

"Oh well, it's no matter. I am a complete stranger in London. I don't know a soul. It will be interesting to see the place. I just remember it as a child."

"I am sure Mr. O'Connor would like to see you, if you would care to leave your address."

"I am staying at the Victoria Hotel at present. I would like to meet him, but of course the legal aspect is all done with. I really must not take up more of your time."

He picked up his hat and stick and held out his hand in a friendly manner.

"Fancy. I might have been walking out of your office with a large bank balance, and an old estate belonging to me. How queer a thing is life. The East teaches philosophy, Mr. Coffin."

The clerk went with him to the door, glad that the interview was over. He returned to his desk and made a *précis* of the conversation, placing it in the tin box.

Gilkie stood on the pavement a little bewildered. He walked up Bedford Row, that quiet backwater in the middle of crowds, and hailed a taxi.

"One moment," he said to the driver, as the latter carefully put down his flag. "I've got the address here." He searched in a bulky pocket-book. "Here we are." He handed a card to the driver.

"Right-o, sir."

He drove to Professor Johnson's house in Cromwell Road, glad of a respectably long drive. With the acuteness of the London taxi-driver he summed up his fare as a stranger to London, and made a detour therefore to increase the amount on the clock.

Gilkie pulled some silver coins from his pocket and puzzled over them; then he put them back and handed a ten-shilling note to the driver. The Professor was in, the maid told him.

He was conducted into Professor Johnson's large study with double doors opening on to the garden. The old man was standing before the fire holding Gilkie's card with a look of positive amazement on his face. He looked up quickly as the stranger entered.

"You are Professor Johnson?"

The Professor's hand trembled as he took the other's.

"That is my name, and you, I see, are Mr. Gilkie."

There was something rigid and stern about the old man.

"I believe you knew my father, Dr. Gilkie," the younger man said urbanely. "You will pardon my calling, but I haven't a friend in London. I have just arrived from Assam."

"May I ask how you knew my name and address?"

Gilkie seemed surprised at the cold tone.

"I found it among some papers, some old letters you had written to him, when he was in New Guinea on an expedition. Perhaps I should not have presumed upon that."

"You were quite right to come," the Professor said with obvious effort. "I am glad to see you," he swallowed hard. "You knew your father, I suppose?"

"I never knew him," Gilkie said sadly. "He died before I was born. I believe he was a fine man and a very clever one from what I have heard."

"Your mother, of course, you knew?"

"She is dead," Gilkie said softly. "She died of malaria some years ago."

"I am sorry for that. And you have come to England?"

Gilkie laughed. "On a fool's errand it appears."

He recounted his interview with Coffin while the Professor watched guardedly. His whole mind was in a whirl though he showed no outward sign. All the theories and ideas he had built up in his mind were crashing about him.

Gilkie watched him and evidently thought the Professor imagined he had come to borrow.

"Fortunately," he concluded, "although, of course, this legacy would have been a help, I am unmarried and have money of my own. I won't say enough—no one has that—but sufficient for my wants. I mention this in case you might think I had come to borrow money."

"Such a thought never entered my head," the Professor said angrily. He took a few brisk paces up and down the room in evident excitement, and then faced the young man. "I suppose you are able to prove your identity?"

Gilkie lifted his eyebrows superciliously.

"I don't know that I am called upon to do so to you, Professor Johnson, but as I had come in answer to the advertisement, not knowing its bearing, I certainly brought all the necessary papers for the lawyer. I don't know that there is any particular reason why I should produce them to you. I will wish you good day."

"No, no." The Professor clutched him with a damp hand. "You must not go. I mean, I must apologize for my cavalier manner. Really, Mr. Gilkie, I am pleased to see you, but I was so taken by surprise. Your father and I knew each other very well, though we did not see eye to eye on some matters; scientific theories. You must tell me about yourself. I am most interested."

He ran on, fearing the other would make good his threat of going. "I would be pleased if you care to come and make this your headquarters. I am all alone and it is more homelike than a hotel."

Gilkie sat down and lighted one of his Indian cheroots. "I would like to know," he said with quiet determination, "why you are so interested in me."

"Well—I knew your father."

"With whom, from your statement, you quarrelled."

"Purely on scientific grounds; I admired his genius."

Gilkie gave a cynical laugh. "Sir John Harman was also a great friend of my father's, wasn't he?"

The Professor started. "You heard about that?"

"My father kept a diary." Gilkie spoke slowly with his eyes on the Professor. "A most interesting document. It taught me quite a lot."

"So you thought that possibly Sir John might have left you something in his will," the Professor said with an attempt at heartiness.

"I had read of his death in the papers; but I had no suspicion that he had left me a penny; why should he?"

The Professor spread out his hands. "Of course not. You just came back when you saw that advertisement."

"By air, yes. I was coming in any case for a holiday. Can you throw any light on the matter?"

The Professor moved uneasily. "Naturally you will want all the facts. I'll introduce you to the detective in charge of the case if I can get hold of him."

"I would like to see him," Gilkie said suavely.

"I'll try him on the 'phone," the Professor said hurriedly. "If you would not mind waiting a minute."

He went out to the 'phone and called up Stevens, who answered at once.

"Young Gilkie has turned up from Assam."

The Professor heard a gasp from the other end and an expletive. "He is in my house now, but is very suspicious of me. I don't want to lose sight of him. It all seems wrong somehow."

"You doubted his very existence."

"I can't say more now; he is waiting, and I promised to 'phone Selden. I'll keep in touch with you."

He hurriedly rang off and got Scotland Yard, where he was informed that Selden was on leave and not expected back for some days.

He returned with this information to Gilkie.

"I should have liked to have seen this detective," Gilkie said. "On leave, is he? Then it looks as though he has either given up the case, or it has been taken out of his hands."

"I am sorry as well, Mr. Gilkie." The Professor had recovered his poise now, and was quiet and dignified. "I would tell you the whole story myself, but my account would be necessarily biased by what my friends and I consider to be the explanation. Selden would give you the official version."

A slight sneer came to the other's dark face. "I have heard of your work, and even read a brochure by you. You are one of the shining lights of Spiritualism. My father was not!"

"I would prefer not to discuss that," the Professor said firmly. "Selden lives in a mews with his friend Hartley, who is a wireless man employed by the B.B.C. He might give you as good an account as anyone. I will write the address for you as London must be strange, and you can take a taxi."

"Thank you. I will call on him, and may perhaps catch him at home."

"I shall hope to see you again." The Professor held out his hand to Gilkie.

"I shall make a special point of coming to see you after I have the full account of . . . Sir John Harman's death."

The cold emphatic tone in which these words were spoken sent a chill to the Professor's heart.

"Very well then," he said, as though accepting a challenge.

CHAPTER XVI

A DANGEROUS INTERVIEW

A LONG SLEEP, with the help of aspirin and a strong constitution, enabled Dick Selden to rise from his bed in the evening with a temperature slightly above normal, but without any more serious effects. The doctor advised a couple of days in bed as quite essential, and Dick might have acquiesced when the arrival of O'Connor changed all his plans.

He had received a telegram from Coffin, telling him of the call at the office, and a subsequent telephone conversation had given more details.

"This means my instant return to London," Selden said when he had been told the news.

"Impossible," the doctor declared. "You would only be laid up for six weeks."

"My dear Doc," Dick said sententiously, "there is such a thing as the influence of mind over matter. Keep me here, and the mental strain would break up my constitution, whereas in town the activity of my mind will—"

"Shut up that nonsense for the love of Mike," O'Connor broke in. "It's no good, Doc, I know the headstrong nature of the beast. He'll go."

Dick was already searching in the time-table for a train.

"I can catch one at midnight at Gloucester. Sleeping-car and all. If you'd like to be a Christian, Doc, you'll run me there in your car."

"The roads are blocked with snow," Hughes said sullenly.

"Not the main roads, my friend. They will have cleared them, and if you don't I must expose myself to a local train, and probable pneumonia."

It was no good arguing with Selden when he was in a persuasive mood. He had everything arranged before the other two could intervene. O'Connor was to bring the Harman party to town as soon as possible, and see to their comfort. Coffin could wait.

After a meal, the grumbling doctor got out his car, and they took the road, warmly wrapped up.

"You seem to attach great importance to the fact that this man Gilkie has turned up."

"The very greatest," Selden replied in a tone of satisfaction.

"Well, I wish you luck. I should like to hear how you get on."

"I shall let you know," Selden said when he had taken his seat in the well-warmed express. "Meanwhile sleep safely in your bed. There will be no more stones thrown through your window."

The doctor could wait for no more as the guard had already sounded his whistle. He hastily got down from the train, and saw it glide from the station like a bright caterpillar, glittering in the dark.

It was still dark when Selden arrived at Paddington, but the city was astir. A bitter wind blew sleet into the faces of early pedestrians, and men hurried along with hats pulled tightly down and coats firmly buttoned. Slush from melted snow lay yellow and mushy by the roadsides, and taxis went warily along the slippery roads.

Jack was still in bed when Selden arrived at the Mews, but Mrs. Perks had lit a fire in the sitting-room, and was busy cleaning up.

"Wake up, lazy-bones." Dick shook the recumbent figure vigorously.

"What a time to come back," Jack grumbled sleepily.

"Put on your dressing-gown, and come into the sitting-room. I want a bath and a shave, but we must confer first."

Jack knew his friend by this time, and hopped out of his warm bed at once.

"Mrs. Perks," Dick said, "could you get us some tea? You can leave the cleaning up. I shall make a mess in any case."

"So you've come back, and never had the decency to write." Jack kicked the log in the grate savagely and Dick laughed.

"Splendid weather for a fine holiday. I was too busy to write." He cast an amused smile at Jack. "You seem like a bear: what's the trouble?"

"It's not very lively being alone in this place, and the weather is not pleasant enough for going out much."

"Had any letters lately?"

"I heard from Mrs. James. She's furious about Lady Harman collaring Sybil, and blames me. She's at some German spa, and says that Eric is getting on well, but can't leave off the treatment yet, and she can't leave him."

"She hadn't a leg to stand on with regard to Sybil. By the way, have you heard from her at all?"

A dusky red betrayed him. "There was no reason why she should write. I dropped her a line, but she didn't answer. You saw her, of course."

"And so poor Jack got no answer! Cheer up. Your letters—not 'a line you dropped'—were intercepted by Lady Harman, and Sybil's were opened and read. So take that to your comfort."

"What damned cheek!"

"I have returned defeated and disgraced," Dick grinned. "As a tutor I proved a distinct failure, and was accused of making love to Sybil and dismissed."

Jack turned round and shot a glance at his friend.

"Make your mind easy, Jack, my boy. I was not trying to cut you out. Now you know that she did write to you your mind is in a fit state to receive my rather sensational story."

As Dick detailed the happenings at Cold Stairs in quiet unemotional sentences, Jack's eyes grew wider, and his fists clenched with anger as he heard of the girl's danger.

"Then that tale of hers was true after all," he said, half in relief at finding that she had spoken the truth, and half scared at the mystery of it all.

"I never doubted it for a moment, Jack. I now have very tangible proof."

"And yet you have come back," Jack said uneasily.

"For two very good reasons: the family are returning to London, and the missing man Gilkie has turned up."

"Good lord—he'll be furious about that will."

"Possibly. Old Coffin saw him and told Ned that, as he knew nothing about any legacy, he did not expect anything. Now for a bath and a clean up. One feels all sticky after sleeping in a train."

When Dick returned from the bathroom, breakfast had been laid, and the post had arrived.

Dick saw the neat scholarly handwriting of Professor Johnson and, ignoring the others, opened it with a feeling of misgiving.

Dear Selden (it read),

You will be surprised to hear that young Gilkie, for whom your friend O'Connor advertised, has turned up from Assam. He called upon me today, and I have referred him to you. I told him you were on leave, but gave him your address, so he may call. Be on your guard. There is something about that man which I cannot tell you, but you will judge for yourself.

Do not be misled into wrong inferences. After he had gone I took steps to verify his story. He undoubtedly landed at Marseilles last Friday, and came straight through by air. He is staying at the Victoria Hotel. He has his identification papers on him. If he calls on you, be careful. I fear the worst.

> *Sincerely yours,*
> *Andrew Johnson.*

Selden read the letter aloud, and whistled softly. "What do you make of that, Jack my lad?"

"I give it up. That Professor's an old fool—why can't he say straight out what he means?"

"If I'm any judge, he's in a blue funk."

Breakfast had been cleared away, and the two friends were smoking before a roaring fire. Outside, hail was beating against the windows like small shot, and the day was so dark that electric lights had been switched on.

A ring sounded from without, and Jack started.

"That's our man," Dick affirmed. "Jack, give him your seat, then we'll have the light right on his face."

Mrs. Perks entered, announcing that Mr. Gilkie had arrived, and was followed by the man himself.

"Mr. Selden?" Gilkie said, looking from one to the other.

"That is my name. Come in, Mr. Gilkie, and take that wet coat off—Mrs. Perks, will you get it dried?"

Gilkie slowly divested himself of his coat and hat and handed them to the housekeeper.

"Cigar?" Jack said, passing the box.

"If you won't think me rude, I'll have one of my cheroots. I've got used to them."

He took Jack's seat by the fire, and cast a puzzled glance at Selden.

"Professor Johnson, who was a friend of my father's, told me that you were the Scotland Yard detective in charge of the murder of Sir John Harman."

"That is so. Does that surprise you?"

"A little; you will pardon me, but you are rather young for a job like that."

"My friend Selden is one of the bonniest detectives at the Yard," Jack said indignantly, and Gilkie bowed, slightly, ironically.

"Naturally I am interested," Gilkie went on. "That Professor has some bee in his bonnet. I'm not going to waste your time. After seeing him I went and hunted up the old copies of the most sensational of the daily papers, the *Daily Wire,* and read all about the murder of the constable and of a certain Mrs. Seaton. That old fool told me nothing of these two events. I want to know the connection."

"I would like to know that myself," Dick said suavely. "It has completely baffled me, and in fact my chief has taken the Seaton case out of my hands. I shouldn't be surprised if he did the same with the others."

Jack gazed keenly at his friend. This self-depreciation, he knew, was for some purpose.

"It's as bad as that, is it?" Gilkie spoke superciliously.

"It was bad luck for you Sir John's wife turning up like that."

"It all comes in a day's work. I never expected anything, so it doesn't matter. But surely in England . . . I always thought our police were the smartest in the world. And three murders!"

"You have lived in the East, Mr. Gilkie, and have doubtless come across matters that hardly come within the scope of material things," Selden said solemnly.

"All fraud! Like the Indian Rope Trick. Clever fakes. You don't tell me you think there was anything of that sort about this business!"

"There are some strange features about it—but you would not be interested. London must be quite changed since you were last here."

"I don't even remember it at all. I went out East with my mother when a tiny child."

"I suppose," Selden said idly, "you have no idea as to the reason why Sir John Harman's first will left practically everything to you?"

"I can only conjecture that as an old friend of my father's, and a bachelor at the time, he had no one to leave his money to. I expect he did it as a sort of joke."

"You never met him—when a child I mean?"

"That is a question I can't answer. My mother never told me. He may have seen me as a baby and been struck by my beauty. I wanted to ask you about these people who have inherited the property."

"They consist of Lady Harman, Sir John's widow, the young baronet, Sir William, and Sir John's young niece Sybil, a child of fifteen."

"Sixteen now," Jack said unguardedly.

"Quite so," Selden smiled. "That's the family."

"It's a curious story altogether," Gilkie remarked. "You really have no idea at all about the murders then?"

"They're a complete mystery. I was really rather hoping you could give us some help."

"Me? Whatever should I know about them?" Gilkie laughed.

"Nothing about the murders, but you might have known someone in the past who had a grudge against Sir John. Of course," he added quickly, "now that I know you never saw Sir John, it isn't likely. But you knew the Professor?"

"Only by name. I met him for the first time yesterday. I must say I was not favourably impressed, but, then, I had heard that he quarrelled with my father."

"Really! I rather agree with you, he's a bit of a crank."

"Are you staying long in England, Mr. Gilkie?" Jack asked.

"I don't know, I'm sure. Not if the weather keeps like this. I shall run over to Paris and Rome, and probably Algiers."

"You wouldn't care to see Cold Stairs, I suppose? It could easily be managed while the family are in town."

"I don't think I should particularly care to see an old property that nearly came into my hands," Gilkie said. "It was always what I longed for—a snug place in the country, and to live in England. However, that's that. I have no particular wish to see it now."

"This might interest you though," Selden said, and went to his desk. "Here is a plan of the place I made on the spot, showing the ground floor and the first floor." He demonstrated with a pencil. "Here is the room in which we all sat with the loudspeaker that my friend Hartley rigged up. Here is the room in which Mrs. James waited, and from which Sir John went out to his death."

Jack's eyes were fixed on Dick. He knew that innocent bland manner of his, and he also knew the keen look that came into his eyes when his mind was focused on one subject. There grew in his mind a sense of intense horror, unmeaning and yet real.

Gilkie scrutinized the rough sketches with interest. "It's quite a large place," he commented.

"I've got a photograph here." Dick went to his desk, while Gilkie examined the plans. "This photograph was taken before Lady Harman made alterations in the appearance of the place."

"A fine old house, but very gloomy I should imagine," Gilkie said without taking the photograph from Selden.

"Jack, you are forgetting your duties as a host. You will take a drink, Mr. Gilkie?"

"It's rather early—we never drink in the East in the morning. Still, with your English weather driving the vitality out of a man, I won't refuse. A little whisky. Three fingers, please."

Jack poured out the fluid mechanically. A queer feeling came over him that he was watching some gruesome play that had a tragic ending, but in which he could not play a part. He was certain a grim silent struggle was going on between these two men, and yet the conversation was conventional and even banal.

"Thank you," Gilkie said, as Jack poured in soda-water. He was idly toying with the sketches that Selden had laid before him, and lifted the glass, wishing them luck vaguely.

"Professor Johnson holds strongly that there is a supernatural explanation to these murders. He is a great spiritualist, you know." Gilkie laughed scornfully. "You, as a detective, would hardly accept such a theory I should imagine."

"We cannot neglect any solution, however fantastic it may appear," Selden answered.

Gilkie shrugged his shoulders. "Well, I hope you are successful in your researches."

"Thank you. I have your address, and if you should change your mind, and care to meet the Harmans, my friend Hartley would be pleased to take you to call on them, when they come to town."

"I don't think I should care to intrude on them. After all, I have no standing, and they might think it impertinent after that first will. The dispossessed heir of romance, you know."

In answer to Selden's ring, Mrs. Perks brought in Gilkie's coat and hat, now warm and dry, and Jack held them for him. For a moment Gilkie's back was turned, and Jack nearly dropped the coat. Like a flash Selden had seized Gilkie's half-finished drink, and had placed his own in the same spot on the table.

Gilkie slowly drew on a pair of fur gloves.

"I rather fancy," Selden said in a deliberate voice, "that a romance is brewing up there. I think Lady Harman is set upon making a match of it between her son, the new baronet, and Sybil."

Two pairs of angry eyes met his, Jack's and Gilkie's, and then the latter quietly picked up his glass. "I may as well finish it," he said, rolling the tumbler round in his gloved hand.

"Have another?" Selden asked.

"No, thank you—excuse my glove." Gilkie held out his hand, which Selden took, and then Mrs. Perks held open the door, and Gilkie went out.

Jack turned angrily on his friend, about to demand an explanation of his remark about Sybil, when he saw the transformation that had come over Dick. The easy, rather diffident manner had gone, and his eyes flashed in sudden energy. Jack was startled to see him produce a handkerchief and wipe the perspiration from his forehead. "Phew! Jack, I owe my life to your presence, perhaps. Of all the infernal cheek—coming here!"

"I don't understand—" Jack began.

"There is no need to, Jack," there was a tone of exultation in the voice. "We've got him or I'm a Dutchman. But I couldn't have kept it up much longer. He's a clever devil."

"For goodness' sake tell me what it's all about, or I shall go crackers."

"One moment, and I'll tell you all I know."

He seized the telephone and called the Yard. When he had been put through to Dodds, he spoke calmly.

"Will you put your best plain-clothes officer to shadow a man called Gilkie, dark, swarthy, blue eyes, just arrived from Assam? Staying at the Victoria. On no account lose sight of him. He has just left here."

"Hello, Selden, so you're back from leave," Dodds said. "You seem to have got busy on something."

"I can't say more at present, sir. I'll make you out a report, but I have several things to do at once."

"All right then," Dodds said, "I'll do what you wish."

Selden rang off, and turned to Jack.

"Now, my friend. You are entitled to an explanation, but I warn you much is obscure still. You saw me change those glasses."

"I suppose you wanted his for fingerprints."

"Bright lad—I did, and got them; but what was of greater importance was that Gilkie saw the danger, and put on his fur gloves, and deliberately rubbed them round the glass he thought was his."

"But I thought you had no fingerprints of the unknown assassin."

"Steady—you are going too fast, Jack. I said your practical mind would be of use to me. Just sit there and listen, for I tell you this has been a strain. It was a sparring match, and I can't say at present who got the better of it. I caught him in one or two obvious slips. The moment he came in, I knew that colour was not sunburn from the East, though it might deceive the ordinary person who did not already suspect. It was either walnut juice or some other dye. Then he had walked—he came in dripping wet. He said he knew nothing of London, and we live in an obscure Mews. Surely a man straight from the East would have taken a taxi. On a day like this, he preferred to walk."

"I suppose he wanted to," Jack said doggedly.

"Yes, my boy, he wanted to—because the evidence of a taxi-driver who had driven him here might have been useful if he had been driven to extremes. He did not expect to find you here, and Mrs. Perks could easily have been disposed of."

"Lord! You are suggesting murder!"

"He hedged about Assam and India, and was smoking cheroots to keep up the illusion. I don't believe he's ever been there."

"But you had evidence that he had just come from there!"

"No, Jack; we had evidence that he had come from Marseilles, having landed there. Have you never heard of the Air Service? A clever man would fly to one of the ports of call, and join the boat there. That I shall find out. But these were small points. I watched him very carefully, and he could not altogether control his face. Is it reasonable to suppose that a man who had lost a fortune would take it so calmly, and not want to see the Harmans and find out exactly what had happened? Again, why should he connect Mrs. Seaton's death with the other murders when you remember Dodds very carefully kept any connection from getting known publicly?"

"That's certainly suspicious," Jack said judicially. "When I shot the bolt that made you so annoyed—about Sybil and young Harman—you were not the only person who was angry. He positively glared at me for a moment, and then picked up his glass to cover up."

"I didn't notice that," Jack said with a sudden bashfulness.

"All these points weighed with me, but this is of far greater importance." Selden picked up his sketches from the table. "I made these sketches of Cold Stairs for a purpose, and made deliberate mistakes. I put the front door in the wrong place, and the room where Sybil slept on the night of the murder on the other side of Mrs. James's room, and wrote the names in, as you see. I deliberately engaged him in conversation while he was looking at the sketches. He had my pencil in his hand, and subconsciously rectified the mistakes."

Dick triumphantly showed the slight thin lines that Gilkie had traced.

"It all sounds very ingenious," Jack said doubtfully.

Selden sprang to his feet. "Exactly, Jack! That's what I wanted from you. You have intelligence above the average and say that. If I went to Scotland Yard with what I have told you, they would take precisely the same line. That is why I asked Dodds to have him watched. We have no evidence whatever to warrant an arrest, and the authorities have a horror of arresting on suspicion. So many criminals have slipped away from insufficient evidence."

"Then what are you going to do?"

"He will be watched, but if he smells a rat he'll be off like a shot. That's why I can't watch him myself."

"But who is he? You say he's never been to India or Assam."

"I can tell you *who he is not*! He is not Dr. Gilkie's son."

"That's too deep for me. You think he's the murderer?"

"Perhaps, but he may have employed Something to help him."

"Here, you give me the creeps," Jack said, looking round the room fearfully. "You keep on dropping hints, but won't say what is in your mind," he added fretfully.

"I can't say more than this. I may be all wrong, but the picture is shaping itself in my mind. There is this strange immunity from danger to Sybil, for which we are thankful. Now follow carefully. Sir John Harman leaves his property vaguely to 'the son of my old friend' Dr. Gilkie. Now that's curious; he gives no Christian name, and there might conceivably have been more than one. He knows there is not. He gives no address for the son in question, or even 'late of so and so', as is usual. He cuts out the said Gilkie from his will, though he would have inherited if Sir John had died before he made the second, which was only executed recently. Is it too much to suppose that the son knew of the first will, and was content to wait. But that second will, we know now, was made under threats from Lady Harman that she would come to live at Cold Stairs."

"He didn't want to own her," Jack put in.

"I don't accept that. He was hardly that type. It seems more probable to me that he wished his marriage kept a secret from the one person who would be affected by such a marriage."

"You think, then, that Sir John met his death because this person you say is not Gilkie's son at all found out about the marriage."

"It is possible," Dick said coolly, "or he may have got tired of waiting, or, what is more probable, it may have been because Sir John interfered, and found out something that had to be kept secret."

"All this is mere speculation," Jack said restlessly.

"Quite so, but what about the situation now!" Dick said grimly. "Will such a man be prepared to sit down quietly and watch the Harmans enjoying what he thinks is his?"

"But what good would the death of Lady Harman and her son do for him? Really, Dick, your imagination runs away with you."

Selden lit a pipe before he replied. "You are such a confoundedly hot-headed fellow I'm almost afraid to go on."

"For goodness' sake don't put on those airs. You can trust me."

"If the Harmans were out of the way?"

"I suppose the old will would come into force." Selden laughed for the first time. "You are a wireless expert, but haven't much knowledge of law. The old will was revoked and is so much waste paper. It's a deeper and more diabolical plot than you think. Lady Harman cannot make a will. The property is only hers for life and then the imp gets it. But if both perished, who gets it?"

Jack sat up very straight, and gave a gasp. "Sybil," he murmured, as though light had dawned on him.

"Exactly. Sybil. She has been free from physical danger, but mentally has been under the dominance of some strange being, as she thinks. So that the one way of getting the property would be by marrying the heiress."

"That's preposterous, Dick." Jack's eyes blazed.

"Jack, old friend, I'm going to ask you a question; don't go off the deep end. Do you care enough for the girl to marry her?"

"What rot you are talking," Jack said nervously. "She's only sixteen."

"I don't mean now, Jack, but later on."

"I don't suppose she cares two hoots for me."

"You are wrong; she does very much. Her attachment for the other, whatever it is, is mental only. I am fighting for her reason. Go to her and tell her what you like, and if she falls for you, you may save her soul. I'm not raving, I mean it."

"Dick, I do care. I'd do anything for her."

"You may go through hell, but it's not a contest between rivals, Jack. It's nothing so easy as that. On your side will be human love, and on the other—" he paused—"the Powers of Evil."

CHAPTER XVII

PROFESSOR JOHNSON'S SUICIDE

ICK SELDEN WAS SHAVING the following morning when the telephone-bell rang. At this time any call was alarming, and he hastily picked up the receiver, not knowing what news might be awaiting him.

Dodds was speaking from the Yard.

"I've got some rather bad news, Selden, which may have a bearing on your case. Professor Johnson poisoned himself last night."

"Suicide?" Dick asked laconically. He had paid a visit to Scotland Yard the day before and imparted as much as he thought fit to his chief.

"I don't think there is any doubt about it. I have just received a full report of the case, and I'll give you the bare facts. It appears the Professor's servant, Bartlett, went to his room as usual with a cup of tea at seven o'clock. He could not wake his master, and ran round to a doctor who lives near. The medico declared him dead—poisoned. There was a bottle of Prussic acid by his bedside, and the doctor states he had taken enough to kill twenty people. That's all. The place was in perfect order, and there is no reason to suspect foul play. The servant says that a man called last night, and was with the Professor about two hours, but Johnson let the man in, and afterwards saw him out, so Bartlett doesn't know who he was. The only other point of interest is that, as the servant was locking up, the Professor came from his study with a letter in his hand. Bartlett offered to take it, but he says the Professor turned on him with a sort of snarl and rushed across the road to the pillar-box as he was, in spite of the storm that was raging. That was the last time he saw his master alive. This report has just come through on the 'phone from Sergeant Cummings of that division, and I thought I'd let you know."

Dick thanked his chief, and replaced the receiver. Jack was standing behind him looking as though he had not slept a wink. "What's up?" he asked anxiously.

"Professor Johnson has poisoned himself."

"Not murdered?"

"You've got murder on the brain," Selden said, clapping him on the back. "Pull yourself together, man. We've lots to do today."

They had scarcely taken their seats for breakfast when the bell rang, and Jack started uneasily. "I'm all jumps today," he remarked.

"Mr. Stevens to see you," Mrs. Perks announced.

"I expected him," Selden said. "Now we shall hear something."

The man himself appeared. His dark complexion was almost green with fear. His sleek hair had lost its glossiness, from his habit of brushing it with his hands when nervous.

"I came to you at once," he panted. "I suppose you have heard the dreadful news?"

"Have some breakfast?" Selden said composedly.

"I couldn't touch anything, but please go on with yours."

"The Professor has poisoned himself I hear," Selden remarked as Stevens sank into a chair.

"There is no doubt whatever, unfortunately, that he committed suicide. I received a letter from him by the first post, and immediately rang up the house, and was informed."

"That would be the letter he posted late last night I expect," Selden remarked. "Have you got it with you?"

Stevens fumbled in his pocket, and produced an envelope, which he opened with shaking hands. "Shall I read it to you as you are eating?"

Selden nodded.

"There is no doubt that my poor old friend was mad when he wrote this. It starts without any formal beginning. I'll read it right through, and we can discuss it afterwards:

"The step upon which I have determined is the only logical conclusion after what I have heard tonight. I have listened to such a tale of horror that the very foundations of my life are shattered, and the ideas I have maintained in my writings and in controversy are falling in ruins about me.

"I have been brought face to face with the brutal and vile example of misapplied science crashing into the beliefs that we have held. I know now what Clare discovered at Cold Stairs,

and sent her hurrying back to her death. Pray to heaven that you do not learn the truth. Standing as I do on the threshold of that mysterious change that men call death, my earnest advice to you is to have nothing more to do with the Cold Stairs affair. Drop it altogether, and, if you can, eliminate it from your mind.

"As for myself, my life's work is over and I fear wasted, for if such things can happen in this world I would rather pass over to where the truth will be revealed. I can say no more, for I have pledged my word. Tell young Selden, who is but on the threshold of life, that if he wishes to retain his sanity he must give up any attempt to solve the problem of these murders, for he will never bring to justice That which caused the deaths. His own life is at stake, as the least penalty he will suffer.

"My affairs are in perfect order, and there is nothing for the police to investigate. Doubtless the coroner will advise a verdict of temporary insanity, though my brain is alert and only too clear.

"My works and money I have left to you, but I ask you to destroy the treatise on Psychology on which I have spent years of work, for it is based on fundamental untruth.

"I am posting this letter myself before I pass painlessly.

"One item I will add, though here I am in danger of breaking my pledged word. If you have any power to do so, get Sybil, Sir John's niece, right away. Let her be placed in a convent school abroad or in some other secluded and guarded retreat, but on peril of her very soul let her not return to Cold Stairs. If she found out the truth I doubt if her reason would stand it. Burn the house down if possible, but if not let it stand empty and desolate for ever.

"There the letter ends abruptly," Stevens said, "but he has signed his name in a firm hand, as though to show that his mind was clear and he was in full possession of his senses."

At the mention of Sybil, Jack had dropped his knife and fork and stared with startled eyes at Stevens.

Selden went on quietly with toast and marmalade, as though the reading was merely an extract from the daily paper. "I think," he said cheerfully, "if any doubt existed in the minds of a coroner's jury as to the sanity of the writer, that letter would remove it."

"You think he was mad?" Stevens said sharply.

"On the contrary I think he was perfectly sane, but I don't expect a dull coroner or twelve good citizens from the suburbs to accept my views."

Jack gasped. "But if so, what about Sybil?"

"It merely bears out what I told you yesterday. The situation has become acute and we must act at once."

"What am I to do about this letter?" Stevens asked.

"You had better leave it with me."

Stevens handed over the letter with a look of relief. "I shall be glad to do so. I don't mind telling you this has upset me badly. Johnson was my oldest friend, and after the murder of Mrs. Seaton—"

"I should do as the Professor asks; drop the whole thing. I will take care that you are not referred to in connection with this letter. There will be no difficulty in that as he does not even mention your name."

"Thank you so much, Selden. I was hoping you would, but I felt I must come to tell you."

"You have done quite right. We have been associated right through in this business. And now it remains for you to tell us what you know."

The quietly spoken words had a remarkable effect on Stevens. The sickly pallor grew more marked. "What do you mean?" he spluttered.

Dick rose from his place at the table, and stood with his back to the fire-place, facing the cringing man.

"I mean just this, Stevens," he said sternly. "It is not sorrow for your friend that brought you round here, or anxiety to impart the information to me. To put it in plain blunt language you are in a blue funk for your own skin. One of you three has committed suicide and Mrs. Seaton has been murdered. You are wondering whether you will not share their fate."

The face of Stevens passed through the phases of anger and terror as he listened to one whom he had regarded as rather an aimless young man.

"I suppose you realize that the visitor who came to see Professor Johnson, and whose revelations appear to have caused his suicide, was the man about whom I questioned you both?"

"You mean Dr. Gilkie's son," Stevens said haltingly. "I was afraid so."

"That won't do, Stevens. I saw your face when I was questioning the Professor. You know quite well. Now I want the truth if I am to help you."

The stuffing seemed to have gone out of Stevens, and he gripped his chair in silence. In his mind the danger of saying anything that might draw vengeance on himself was in conflict with the desire to help.

"I only know what Johnson told me," he said doggedly. "When Dr. Gilkie came back from his expedition in the East, he wrote to the Professor, a terrible letter it appears, saying that he was going to put into execution an experiment he had planned after years of research. It was connected with the possibilities of extracts from the ductless glands, as they are commonly called. He and Johnson had quarrelled bitterly over this very question. Gilkie claimed that he could manufacture, by chemical means, something beyond the wildest dreams of human reason."

"He hinted at something of that kind to me," Selden said sternly.

"I don't want to be drawn into this case," Stevens said wildly.

"You have gone too far now; you must tell us the rest. I am absolutely certain that a man of the character of Professor Johnson would not commit suicide for the reason he gives in his letter to you. There is something behind it."

"There was! I suppose I must go on. The Professor was so upset that he went round to see Gilkie, much as he hated the man, to implore him to desist from such a course. Gilkie told him that his wife had gone away before he returned; he didn't know where, and that the servants had also left. He had only a Malay servant he had brought with him. I have no very clear impression of what happened, because the Professor, when he told me, was very reticent, and also took more of the blame on himself than I believe was justified. They met in Gilkie's laboratory, and argued the case out. The Professor has always been convinced that Gilkie had killed his wife, but of that there is not the slightest proof. At any rate a quarrel grew, and words were said between them. Johnson told me how wild he got because all the time they were talking Gilkie was calmly going on with his experiments with snake venom, and seemed quite unmoved. You have seen the Professor when worked up—he was a passionate man. He seized Gilkie's arm, whether merely to make him listen, or whether for a diabolical purpose, we shall never know, but the test tube broke in his hand and cut his thumb.

"Johnson said the man had amazing courage and nerve. He seized an axe used for opening crates, and deliberately cut off the thumb.

"The Professor rang for help, and then he saw Gilkie's face turn rigid, and he fell on the floor. Johnson fled from the room, and only when he read the evening paper he knew that Gilkie had died. That's the whole story, and now you can understand why Professor Johnson said that Gilkie had no son, and why he was so upset when a man calling himself Gilkie turned up."

"You think, then," Selden said guardedly, "that this Gilkie became possessed somehow with this knowledge and threatened the Professor with exposure."

"I suppose so," Stevens said sullenly. "But there must be more than that."

"Shall I tell you what is in your mind, Stevens?" Selden said with conviction. "Both you and the Professor think that Dr. Gilkie had become possessed of some deadly knowledge, perhaps buried for centuries. Science, as Johnson said at your house, may have discovered what the old wizards knew. In other words, Gilkie's death came too late. *The experiment had already been made.*"

"Stop, for God's sake!" Stevens cried. "I know what you are going to say. That is what the Professor and I feared. I shall resign my position and go abroad." He rose, shaking like a leaf. "I must go—can I get a taxi? I shall have no peace now. I shall dream of it at nights."

"Have a drink?" Jack said.

Stevens assented with a nod, and seized the stiff whisky from Jack, and they heard the glass clinking against his teeth as he swallowed it down. "Thank you," he said in a calmer voice.

"Face it like a man," Selden said scornfully. "Which of us is in greater peril: you, who were merely a friend of the Professor's, or I who am hard on the track of a murderer, or even Jack here, for another reason?"

"But young Gilkie had nothing whatever to do with the murders at Cold Stairs," Stevens asserted, "he was away in Assam."

"Quite so; you still hold to the supernatural theory." A look grew in Stevens's eyes, as though they saw something beyond the bright untidy room; the dim shadow of a horror.

"It can't be!" he shouted, putting out his hands as though to ward off an unseen enemy. "I never thought of that," he muttered brokenly. "Then Mrs. Seaton knew . . . and the Professor knew . . . last night." Not another word would he say, and Selden refrained from asking anything more. A taxi was fetched, and the wretched man was sent off, mumbling his thanks, and gazing with bloodshot eyes to left and right as he drove out of their tiny yard.

"Thank goodness he's gone," Selden said; "we shan't see anything more of him. He's a miserable specimen, and only joined the others to run his paper, and claim friendship with Professor Johnson. But he hasn't told us the whole truth. He wouldn't be in such a funk merely because he was one of the Committee. The murderer is after bigger game than him."

"I thought he was talking a lot of nonsense," Jack remarked with a puzzled frown on his open face. "Surely if Gilkie had been away for two years, and never saw his wife again, there may be a simple, though rather beastly explanation of the birth of this son?"

Selden looked quizzically at his friend. "Harman made a will in favour of this man, with some degree of uncertainty about his name and address. You are suggesting that this son may have become aware of his origin, and took his revenge for the wrong done him?"

"That's what I mean, Dick, and if so, what becomes of all these wild theories and awful secrets? I believe that's all humbug."

"We'll leave it at that, Jack," Selden said with a smile. "I wish it was so simple. Now we've had enough of talking. Can you get the day off?"

"Easily. I am on experimental work just now, and my time is more or less my own. We must do something about Sybil at once."

"Not at once, Jack," Selden said with an amused smile. "We have a less pleasant job first. We are going to the Victoria Hotel."

Jack caught his breath. "You are going to beard the lion in his den!"

"With the knowledge I now possess I am going to have matters out with this person. You 'phone for leave, while I get the car out."

The manager of the hotel, on seeing Selden's card, took him to his private office, and sent for Pierce, the plain-clothes officer who had been shadowing Gilkie.

"Everything O.K.?" Selden asked.

"He's in his room, sir. He led me a pretty dance last night. I followed him to Professor Johnson's house and waited over two hours. Then he came back here, and I saw him safely to bed. The night porter kept an eye on him while I got some sleep, but he was all right this morning, and asked the maid who took him up tea for all the morning papers. When I saw the account of the suicide this morning, I thought you'd be around."

"He is still in his room?"

"Still there, sir. I got a waiter to take his breakfast up to him, and then later I sent a whisky up that he had ordered."

"Very good, Pierce, we'll go up and have a word with him, but I warn you he's a desperate character, and further: *don't be scared by anything you may see.*"

Pierce led the way to the lift and they ascended to the third floor.

A small page-boy was pottering about aimlessly and grinned at Pierce. " 'E's in there; no one ain't come out."

"All right, my lad."

Selden approached the door and knocked softly; there was no reply. A louder knock produced no result, and with one hand significantly in his coat pocket he turned the handle. To the surprise of all three men, the door opened, and they entered an obviously empty room. It was just an ordinary well-furnished hotel bedroom, with no possible place of concealment. The window was shut and hasped, and outside there was a thirty-foot drop to a closed space in the centre of the building. The door to the bathroom was slightly open, and Selden dashed into it, but like the bedroom it gave no result.

After the talk he had had with Dick, Jack felt a sense of horror creeping over him. The man had clean gone. He saw Selden's face was hard and stern as he turned to Pierce.

"There is a door here into the passage," he rapped out.

"Why, yes, sir—there nearly always is with attached bathrooms, so that a servant can enter that way, or the bathroom can be let separately."

Selden walked to the door and opened it; the empty corridor lay before them. "It's all too simple," he groaned.

"He couldn't have got out that way," Pierce declared stoutly. "I was watching except when I went to breakfast, and that boy is pretty sharp. He had an exact description of the gentleman, and had corroborated that by knocking and asking if he had rung his bell."

"Jack," Selden said sourly, "what would you do if you went to an hotel and wanted to disappear at a moment's notice?"

"I don't know I'm sure."

"Pierce, if you knew you were being watched what would you do?"

"I shouldn't have come back to the hotel at all—that's what puzzles me, but I'm sure he never suspected me."

"You are wrong. He had to come back for his bag, but he has done exactly what I would have in the same circumstances, unless I am much mistaken. He came here and booked a room, paying in advance, and giving his own name. He then walked casually out of the hotel, before he had made any calls, remember, and came back in another capacity, an entirely different person, and took another room. It's quite easy in a large hotel, and would not require an elaborate disguise. Then he has two rooms, and if he is a clever man he will arrange for the two to be as near as possible."

Pierce uttered an exclamation of anger.

"Ask the manager to come here at once with his register."

Pierce got on the 'phone.

"Jack," Selden said, "he's tricked us. Why the devil didn't I take this on myself, in spite of the risk of his recognizing me?"

The manager came bustling in, anxious that there should be no scandal in his hotel. In answer to Selden's inquiry, he opened the register and showed the clear firm signature—Wilfred Gilkie, and the number of the room, 254. Others followed, some Americans and two women, but Selden placed his finger on a small crabbed signature—Hiram Smith of Chicago with the number 255 against it.

"I remember him, Mr. Selden," the manager said. "I was in the hall when he arrived. A typical American gentleman. He was about sixty I should say, with a grey pointed beard and a moustache, and he had very large round glasses. He left this morning."

"Any other feature you can remember about him?"

The manager thought for a moment. "He walked with a limp, using a stick, and his hair was rather long."

"Anything else?" Selden said with great patience.

"Now I come to think of it, he had very curious blue eyes, china blue I should call them."

"Ah! The only feature he could not change even with glasses."

"May I ask what these inquiries are for? Is the gentleman who occupied this room wanted for anything?"

"He has paid his bill, and I suppose the other—the American settled up?"

"Oh yes, we had no trouble. Mr. Gilkie was out nearly all day."

"Thank you," Selden said with an easy change of manner. "I won't detain you."

When the manager had gone, Selden turned to Pierce. "That was your man. As I thought, he took the next room. He went into the bathroom, made the necessary changes in his appearance, and slipped out into the other room. It is quite unlikely that the page, however sharp a boy he may be, would watch the bathroom door. Hiram Smith then came from his own room, summoned a porter and calmly walked out of the place."

"I'm afraid you are right," Pierce said ruefully.

"You can return to duty," Selden said. "Don't look so down-hearted, you were dealing with an exceedingly clever man, and you are lucky to have escaped with your life. You need only say that I don't want your services any more. I shall report what is necessary to Chief Inspector Dodds, and shall throw no blame on you."

"Thank you, sir," Pierce said warmly, and hurried out full of gratitude to the young detective.

"Now, Jack. This has taken a very serious turn and we haven't a moment to lose. Either Gilkie read the account of the suicide, and feared that the Professor might have broken his word, and written a statement of what took place at that interview last night, or Pierce bungled badly and Gilkie knew he was being watched."

"That seems most likely."

"There is a third possibility," Selden said gravely. "He may have learnt more from me at our meeting than I did from him. I am certain he came for that purpose. But he's got away, and is at large and dangerous. Of course I shall circulate a description and so on, but we shall never see the man we saw at the Mews again I am sure of that."

"What are we to do?" Jack looked appealingly at Selden.

Selden led the way to the lift and they descended to the hall, where the manager was fussing about, evidently eager to see the back of unwelcome visitors.

Selden had a word with the hall-porter, who had got a taxi for Mr. Hiram Smith and had received a large tip from that gentleman. He remembered the American telling the driver to go to Liverpool Street as fast as he could.

Selden started his car, and when they were on the way to the Mews Jack was astonished to see Dick give a grin.

"Another slip, and a bad one," he said.

"Whatever do you mean?" Jack asked.

"A long shot, Jack, my boy, but if a man wants to lay a false trail natural instinct makes him give a direct opposite. I have found that useful before now. If he wishes to disguise his appearance he will make a complete change altogether instead of some slight change which is more effective. Now here he gave Liverpool Street Station. What is the exact opposite to Liverpool Street?"

Light dawned on Jack. "Paddington," he said with a shudder.

"Exactly," Dick said sharply. "He's gone to Cold Stairs, and we'll have him now. Thank goodness the family will have moved to London; they were only just in time."

Jack grew pale at the words. "We ought to find out where they are staying and warn them."

"The Mews first—there may be news from Ned."

CHAPTER XVIII

JACK AND SYBIL

SELDEN DROVE INTO THE COBBLED YARD, and jumped out. Mrs. Perks had opened the double door for them.

"There's a visitor to see you," she announced.

Without waiting to inquire who it was, Selden brushed past her, and opened the sitting-room door. Perhaps here was the final meeting.

Someone rose from a deep arm-chair, and Selden gave a laugh of utter relief. Sybil came forward, tired-looking, but smiling.

Dick took both the girl's hands in his. "Thank God it's you, Sybil—but what are you doing here?"

Jack hung back bashfully, but his face showed his feelings.

"I hope you won't be angry, Dick," the girl said wearily, "I had nowhere else to come."

"Sit down, and tell me quietly." Dick seemed to have forgotten the very existence of Jack, his mind only concentrated on the problem before him.

"Lady Harman was absolutely beastly to me, and accused me of all kinds of things. I was practically a prisoner there, and she said I was never to see you or Jack again. Last night I ran away."

"How did you manage that?"

"I had to sleep with Mrs. Simmons, the housekeeper, but there was an awful row going on. The butler insisted on going and then the footman, and Mrs. Simmons said she would not stay in such a house. Lady Harman was very rude to her, and that made her take my part. I persuaded her to help me, and she fetched my clothes, which had been taken away. She let me down from the window. She said she wasn't going to help a woman like Lady Harman in her plans, and . . ." The girl stopped and gave a quick nervous laugh. "She said she liked you; she thought we were lovers." She looked frankly at Dick as though she thought the joke was a good one.

"I heard you were staying with the doctor, and went there. He was awfully decent, and lent me money, and took me to the station. He seemed only too anxious for me to get away, I don't know why; and promised not to tell anyone."

"And so you travelled up all night?" Jack asked, but Dick's eyes were fixed on the girl with an expression she could not understand.

"What's the matter, Dick? You didn't mind my coming?"

"Why should I mind? I am delighted to see you," he said with an effort.

"I mean after sending that telegram telling us to stay on at Cold Stairs."

Dick's mouth closed firmly, but he showed no other sign. Only he gave a warning glance to Jack.

"Mr. O'Connor showed it to me," the girl went on easily. "He said he couldn't quite understand it."

"I don't wonder," Dick said grimly. "Can you remember what it said, Sybil?"

Fear sprang to the girl's eyes, and she clenched her small hands convulsively.

"It was something like this, as far as I can remember: 'Will you all stay at Cold Stairs for a few days, I am coming down there'. It was roughly in those words, but, Dick," she seized Selden's arm, "didn't you send it?"

"So Lady Harman and William are remaining," Selden said sternly.

"Yes, of course! But what's the matter?"

"I never sent any telegram," Dick replied. "I'm doubly thankful that you came." He laughed rather harshly. "The sender never realized that he was telling the truth. I am going there."

Dick cut short any remark Sybil might have made. He turned sharply to Jack. "Do you mind going into the next room for a minute, old lad? I want to speak privately to Sybil."

A sudden suspicion came to Jack's mind. "I don't see why I should go; you can speak in front of me surely?"

"You can trust me—I'm not making love to Sybil, if that's in your mind. But run along like a good boy, and I'll fetch you myself."

When the door had closed behind the reluctant Jack, Dick placed Sybil back into the big arm-chair, and stood by the fireplace.

"I can't tell you what is happening," he said gravely, "but things are nearing an end, and I must go. You must trust us to do the best for you."

"I'll do whatever you want as long as you don't send me back to that hateful woman."

"That is precisely what I have no intention of doing. If I can manage it, you shall not see her again. I'm going to put a straight question to you, Sybil. Do you love Jack?"

The girl looked furiously at Dick, and then her eyes dropped and her face became tinged with red.

"Don't get offended," Dick said almost roughly. "Things are too serious for that; only if you do care for him it will simplify matters."

"Did he ask you to say that?" Sybil said scornfully.

"He'd be the last to do that. I know he's desperately keen on you, but he's too shy to say a word, and thinks you are much too young for that sort of thing. I've studied you and know better."

The earnestness of this plain red-haired young man, with his grandfatherly manner, touched Sybil's latent sense of humour. She laughed a little hysterically.

"You've got some cheek, Dick. What on earth have my affairs to do with you!"

"I'm not asking you to become engaged formally, or anything like that, but a girl of sixteen can choose her own place of abode. It makes all the difference." He stumbled badly over the words.

"I'm very fond of Jack," Sybil said coolly. "But I've never thought of him as anything but a good pal. Why are you so keen to know?"

"Because I know I can trust you both, and, if you are willing, I want to pack you off together. It will make things easier if you are really keen on each other."

Dick's argument would have shocked Mrs. Grundy, but he was in deadly anxiety to have a protector for the time being for this girl, and one who would get her thoughts away from Cold Stairs and its horrors.

"Jack's a white man, and will guard you with his life, though I hope it won't come to that, but you must be out of everything."

"Jack brought us up here from Cold Stairs, and gave me a rattling good time. I think . . ." she hesitated, "I'd be all right with him; but can't we stay here?"

"That's impossible; I'll arrange. I just wanted to know that you were agreeable."

Sybil's face showed a smile of intense amusement.

"I'm sorry for the girl you make love to, Dick. You are too much the detective. It's not done that way, you know."

"I'll tell Jack then," Dick said, ignoring her banter.

He found his friend angrily pacing the floor outside the sitting-room.

"It's all fixed up, Jack, my boy," Dick said, slapping the other on the back, "it's a load off my mind. Now I can get away to Cold Stairs."

"Are you mad? What's fixed up?"

"Sybil's all right, only she doesn't like to say too much. You are going to take her away and hide her till this business is over."

"What do you mean?—for heaven's sake talk sense."

"Get this into your head. I'm going to have the final round—you know what I mean. By an extraordinary stroke of luck Sybil has come here. Now it's her reason I'm concerned with. She must never know what has taken place at Cold Stairs in the past, or what may happen in the next day or so."

"But, Dick, what about her reputation? After all—"

"Damn her reputation and yours as well. Now listen. You know my bungalow at Selsey?"

"Contraption made of railway carriages. Oil lamps and no water laid on. I know it."

Selden grinned. "That's the place. Take Mrs. Perks with you, and motor there as soon as you can. Better get some food first, but I believe there's a lot of tinned stuff in the cupboard. Don't let Sybil hear the wireless, put it out of order—that's your pigeon. You'll be all right there."

"Here, steady on. In the middle of winter, and the place as damp as hades!"

"I've no patience with you. All this protesting is because you are afraid of being alone. You're in love with the wench, and I am a pretty shrewd judge of character."

"Go on! Don't mind me. You have come to the conclusion that she loves me!"

The door opened and Sybil came out. "Whatever are you men arguing about?"

"It's all fixed up, Sybil. You are going with the good Mrs. Perks to my famous bungalow."

"Is Mrs. Perks absolutely necessary? Jack and I will be all right by ourselves."

"Babes," Selden said, and summoned the housekeeper to give her rapid but concise instructions, together with money for running expenses.

He looked at the radiant face of the girl, and the look of smug contentment on Jack's, and he knew he had won the stern battle. The mysterious glamour of the creature of the woods would gradually fade from her mind.

"Are you sure you can spare the bus?" Jack asked, feeling some diffidence in taking Dick's car.

"I shan't want it; I'm going by train," Dick answered. "Besides, you'll want it down there; it's hardly weather for sun-bathing. If I can drop you a line, I'll do so. Now I really must go. Good luck to you both."

He went out rather hurriedly, hating good-byes, and yet fearing that perhaps it might be the last time he would see them.

Sybil remained staring at the door, a little flushed and excited at the expedition, but also rather annoyed at the way in which she and Jack had been ordered about by Selden. She belonged to the type that can live on nerves for days, seemingly tireless, but in danger of a subsequent reaction.

"Well, Sybil," Jack said, feeling somewhat foolish, "I suppose we had better go. I must 'phone for leave, and then we'll buy some stores as I don't expect there's much there, and the bungalow is right away from the village. By the way, I must get some money."

"Mr. Selden gave me money," Mrs. Perks said, "and, if you like, I'll go and get what is necessary just for tonight."

"I like his cheek," Sybil said when the good woman had gone. "He bundles us off in a hurry, and then pays for our expenses as though we were a couple of children."

"He knows a good deal more than we think," Jack remarked. "I am certain he must have had some good reason for it. He thinks you are in danger."

Sybil's eyes flashed indignantly. "I'm not a baby. If he had thought that, he should have told us. Besides, if there is any danger we stand a better chance in London than in a desolate bungalow."

Jack saw clearly that Sybil was on the verge of refusing to go.

"Wait while I 'phone my chief," he said gently, "and then I'll tell you what has happened."

The girl lit a cigarette, and turned to the fire without a word, kicking viciously at a log.

When Jack came back to say that everything had been fixed up, he found her staring moodily into the fire. He took a seat opposite, and related the story of Gilkie, and the interview in that room. At first she seemed hardly to listen, but as he proceeded he noticed her eyes were fixed gravely on him, hanging on every word.

"I don't understand it," she said when he had done. "What possible connection can this man have with the murders at Lydford?"

Jack had confined himself to facts, and had refrained from telling of Dick's conversation with him.

"Dick seemed to think there was," he said. "Anyway, there's something peculiar in the way he disappeared, and there is no doubt the Professor committed suicide after having talked with this man."

"It's a pity," she said bitterly, "that Dick didn't take us both more into his confidence. I could have told him something. It's too late now. No, Jack, I am not going to say another word. Here's Mrs. Perks."

She sprang up briskly, but Jack saw that she was holding herself in tightly. He supposed the experiences she had been through had partially upset her mental balance.

It was a depressing day, a typical London December day of fine drizzling rain and a gloomy sky. Even in the country the rain was falling and the air cold and damp. Sybil said little as they made their way along wet roads through Surrey and Sussex.

They stopped at Horsham for food. Both were ravenously hungry, but until now the stirring events of the day had prevented them from feeling the need for a meal. Sybil roused herself under the influence of food and warmth, and Jack was glad to see that she was more normal, though there was an obvious restraint between them.

It was dark when they squelched along a half-made track to the bungalow. It was one of a group, but the owners of the others, having a little common sense, had shut theirs up for the winter. It was constructed of two railway coaches, with a space between which was covered with a pent roof, and formed the lounge; pleasant enough in the warm summer months, with the sea just outside, but drear and desolate now.

But both of them were young, and something of the picnic spirit came over them, as they set about making the place habitable. Blankets were hung before the Canadian stove, soon in full blast, and oil lamps were trimmed and lighted. Mrs. Perks was busy in the tiny kitchen unpacking stores and overhauling the cupboard where "emergency rations" were kept.

She glanced through the door and saw that the young people were busy. With a smile of anticipation on her face, she brought out a bottle of whisky and drew the cork, helping herself to a liberal dose.

When Sybil and Jack had completed their work, Mrs. Perks announced thickly that the meal was ready.

Jack looked quickly at the woman. She had, he knew, a weakness for liquor, but under the strong influence of Dick she had kept her habits well under control while at their Mews.

"Mrs. Perks, have you got anything to drink in the house?" he asked.

"I'll have a look, sir," she muttered, and went out unsteadily.

Sybil leant forward and whispered, "She drunk," quite calmly.

"I hope not."

"You forget, Jack, I stayed with her every night while I was with you. She drinks like a fish."

Mrs. Perks returned, carrying a bottle of burgundy in one hand and one of port in the other, which she placed with some slight difficulty on the table.

"Found them in the cupboard," she said thickly, and lurched back into the little kitchen, once a compartment in a railway coach.

"That's a nuisance," Jack said, when the door was shut. "I suppose that was why she offered to get supplies."

"It doesn't matter much—she'll sleep it off," Sybil said lightly.

Jack was not thinking of the wretched woman, but of Sybil.

"We'd better leave these things here," the girl said when they had finished. "We can't get her to wash up, and we can't very well go in there."

Jack assented and they sat by the fire. The wind had got up, and it was eerie alone in the wild, with the dark shapes of the deserted bungalows, like rotting hulls of ships, and the sad wash of the waves outside. A feeling of depression came over Jack, and he cursed Dick for having sent them here.

The girl seemed desperately tired, and Jack saw the long lashes close over her eyes several times, and then she woke with a start. "It seems so long ago," she murmured half asleep. "It's all happened so quickly. I can't believe it yet."

Jack stirred the fire; he did not want to hear any confidences from her when in this state.

"Why, Jack! I believe I was nearly asleep. Oughtn't you to go and see what's happened to Mrs. Perks?"

"I suppose I had better." He rose to his feet stiffly, and opened the kitchen door. A lamp was smoking badly on the shelf that did service for a table, and an empty whisky bottle lay on its side. Mrs. Perks had gone.

"Damn the woman!" he exclaimed heartily.

"What's the matter?" Sybil called.

"She's done a bolt, or else fallen down outside." He seized the lamp and went through the door.

A search in the pouring rain was not pleasant, but Jack conscientiously cast his light round the ground outside, and went into the muddy track. There was no trace of the missing woman, and he returned, angry and wet.

"What are we to do?" Sybil said. "She may have started walking, and then fallen down somewhere."

"It's three miles along the coast to the village," Jack grumbled. An uneasy feeling gripped him. Was it natural that a half-drunk woman should go off like this?

Sybil put his thoughts into words. "Jack, do you think she went of her own accord?"

"I'm not going to worry about her. When she wakes up she'll come back, I suppose. If she gets pneumonia it's her own fault."

Jack was not going to leave Sybil alone while he searched for the woman, and was certainly not going to expose her to the bitter rain.

"You had better get to bed," he said, "you're half asleep as it is."

The bedrooms were queer little "cubby holes" made from the compartments of the carriages, but the spirit of picnic had gone out of these two wayfarers.

Jack saw Sybil safely into hers, and carefully locked up the doors. Then he went to his own, and lay down as he was, with the lamp burning,

He was fast asleep when a hand touched his face, and he woke with a start, to see Sybil standing beside his bed. She had thrown a coat over her nightgown.

"What is it?" he asked, sitting up at once.

"Jack, I can't sleep—there are such queer noises all round the place, and I am sure someone is outside."

"It's that damned woman—I'll go and see."

He searched again round the place, but could find no one, and returned to the girl, who was still seated on his bed, listening intently.

Here was a pretty situation for a modest, almost prudish man.

"You had better go to bed, Sybil," he said. "There's no one there, but I'll sit up."

"I'm not going," she said firmly. "I can't sleep."

"Then hop into my bed, and I'll stay in the sitting-room."

For the first time Sybil smiled. "Afraid, are you, Jack?" She pulled back the bedclothes and got into the bed. "Sit there and let's talk. Jack, I'm going to tell you something. I nearly did when we were in the car. I ought to have told Dick, but somehow I didn't like to."

Jack lit a cigarette and offered one to Sybil.

"It's about Cold Stairs," she said when the cigarette was well alight. "You probably know that Dick came after me that night when there was all that row, and he had to leave."

"Dick told me," he said simply.

"He found me in the place you know of in the woods, where we went that morning—it seems so long ago now."

"I know," he said grimly. "Where you used to meet someone."

"He called me the night before, to bring my box. I went there, and found . . ."

"What?" Jack said, seeing the girl's white face.

"It was my fault," she said haltingly. "I should have gone blind-folded, but it was so cold, and I was in a hurry. I went in, and the place was lit with a greenish light, and then I looked up and saw the man you described to me as Gilkie."

Jack took a deep breath, and his hand closed convulsively on Sybil's.

"I can't make it out." A puzzled frown came to her face. "He seized the box from me, and hid it in a corner, and then he turned to me. I don't know what would have happened, but the shock was so great that I staggered back when he came towards me. Then we both heard a sound outside, and I thought it must be the king of the woods coming. I must have fainted, and when I came to I was being held by Dick."

Jack smiled at the girl. "Don't you realize what this means?"

Her eyes fell. "I have been trying to puzzle it out ever since."

"Of course, you see that your so-called king of the woods was this fellow," he said brightly. "He worked on your imagination."

"I don't know—it has upset everything, Jack. I begin to feel that I have made a fool of myself. I ought to have told Dick."

"I think Dick has a good idea about things," Jack said confidently.

"It's an awful shock," she repeated. "I did most firmly believe it all."

"My dear Sybil, we all did when we were young; Santa Claus, and fairies, and all that. Living down there, I don't wonder you got those ideas. I should try to forget them now."

"It's not so easy, but perhaps when Dick has got to the bottom of it all, we shall know better."

A great joy stole over Jack. The glamour was being rudely shattered, though there was much to explain.

"Jack, do you think he's followed us down here?"

He knew what she meant, and his own mind had been on that since Mrs. Perks had left them.

"Dick was going to follow him to Cold Stairs," he reassured her.

They sat in silence, immersed in their own thoughts, while the rain beat against the windows in fitful gusts and the moaning of the sea came to their ears like a soul in pain. But in Jack's heart was a great feeling of contentment, for the desire for the woods had gone from her.

Presently she spoke, half dreamily. "Jack, I wonder what's going to happen to me? I shall never go back to Lady Harman again."

"There will be no need for you to do so," he said firmly.

"You two boys can't permanently adopt me, you know, and Mrs. James is in Germany."

Jack braced himself for the plunge. "Of course we could get married," he said quite loudly, through nervousness.

Sybil laughed outright. "What a way to talk. But, Jack, do you know Dick told me that you were very fond of me?"

"Of course I am, and have been from the moment I saw you," he blurted out.

"But that doesn't prove that I am fond of you," she said softly.

"Dick told me you were."

For a moment a look of anger crossed her face, and then she laughed merrily. "Of all the cheek! Dick posing as a matchmaker. I suppose they taught him at his precious college."

"It's only what Dick said"—Jack was growing bolder. "I'd rather hear it from you, Sybil."

"Well," she said evasively, "I've read many books about love-making, but I've never heard of a proposal under such circumstances."

"I'm awfully sorry, Sybil," Jack said, contrition seizing him. "I ought to have waited—I'm a clumsy lout."

"If you weren't such a great dear," she said very softly, "I might have thought this was a put-up job, Mrs. Perks and all; but I can trust you, Jack, otherwise I shouldn't—be so fond of you."

"Then you do love me?" He made a movement towards her, but Sybil gently removed his hand, which had been holding hers for some time. "I think I'll try to sleep now—you can sit up in the sitting-room, as you proposed to do."

She drew the bedclothes over her head, and Jack rose to his feet, realizing that for all her youth she was wiser than he.

He made up the fire and sat by it, lost in happy thoughts, till sleep overcame him.

When he woke, the sun was shining into the bungalow and he heard the sound of clattering plates from the kitchen.

The table had been cleared, and the place tidied up.

"Is that you, Sybil?" he called.

The girl came in, looking radiant in the morning light, and with the heavy look of worry gone.

"So you have woken at last, Jack! No signs of Mrs. Perks. I'm rather glad."

For one brief moment Jack wondered if the conversation of the night had been a dream, but the quiet, watchful look on the girl's face enlightened him.

He got up, regardless of cramp, and seized her in his arms. Sybil was unversed in the ways of women; she had a simple and sincere nature. She put her arms round his neck and returned his bear's hug.

"You ought to have a shave first," she cried, feeling her chin, between laughing and crying.

"I'm sorry—I couldn't help it. I'll go and have a wash, and then we'll have breakfast."

Inquiries at the village elicited the fact that a woman answering to the description of Mrs. Perks had caught an early train to London, and there the matter rested. Jack and Sybil had too many things to say to worry about her, but on the following day a letter arrived from her, an illiterate scrawl rambling over three pages.

The gist of it was that when Gilkie had called at the Mews he had held a conversation with Mrs. Perks before going off, and had bribed her to keep an eye on the movements of all of them, and report to him. He had been so plausible and she saw no harm at the time. When she went to Selsey she had meant to write to him, but then the drink and a feeling that she was doing a dirty trick had made her go off. She had actually gone to the Victoria Hotel, but found that he was no longer there. She would never come back again, she declared, and felt "rotten" after all Mr. Selden's kindness.

"So you have lost your chaperone," Jack grinned when they had finished the letter.

"And you have lost your cook, and Dick's money."

"I can get plenty," he said with large generosity.

"We can't stay here, Jack. I mean," she added with a blush, "I don't mind staying in the least, but it's rather dismal, and I feel happy now. Let's take the car and go for a tour. I've never seen places. Let's go to Devon and Cornwall—anywhere. Do you think we could?"

"Of course, darling—it would be lovely, and I know Dick won't mind, as he was afraid only . . ." He stopped.

"I know," she said seriously, "he was afraid for my sanity. Well, he needn't be now. Come on, Jack, let's pack and see places."

They wired to Dick at Cold Stairs telling the news and their intentions, little knowing what had taken place at that grim house.

CHAPTER XIX

CHE FINAL ROUND

WHEN SELDEN HAD SEEN THE CAR START, he returned to the Mews and locked the place up, wondering whether he would ever see it again. He took a taxi to Scotland Yard and saw Chief Inspector Dodds. To him he gave a detailed account of the events of the last two days.

"So you really think you have got hold of something at last," the Chief Inspector said when he had finished.

"I think this is the final round," Selden said grimly.

"I hope you are right, but you are not very informative about the affair."

"You must forgive me, sir. I would tell you everything I know, but I am not certain in my own mind with regard to the whole truth. I am going to Cold Stairs to make certain."

"But why not bring the Harmans to London, if, as you say, they have been induced to stay there by a false telegram?"

"Mrs. Seaton was in London," Dick said seriously "The man who calls himself Gilkie outwitted Pierce, and caused Professor Johnson to commit suicide. He would have far greater opportunity in London than at Cold Stairs."

Dodds moved restlessly in his chair. "I don't like it, Selden; you are using the Harmans as a decoy."

"In a sense I am. But I am going there myself, and I fancy that I am the chief object of destruction."

"How can I help you then?" Dodds asked, convinced that he had better let Selden have his head.

"I want three of your best men from the Special Squad and a sub-machine gun."

Dodds laid down the pipe he was smoking on to the desk, and looked straight at the young detective.

"This is a serious matter; it means shooting."

"I know, sir, but we are dealing with a desperate creature."

"Look here, Selden," Dodds said quietly, "I know you are not a timid man, in fact you are foolhardy at times. You tell me there is one man, and yet you ask for three crack shots to help you. Several times you have used a strange expression, 'a creature'. I think I am entitled to some explanation when I give you these men."

Selden looked frankly at his chief. "I can assure you, sir, that if I could tell you I would do so. I am not superstitious, and I know who is at the bottom of this, but there are unique features here that have caused me at times to think that something outside our ordinary conceptions of human beings is at work, with powers with which we can't cope by usual methods. That is why I can't use the local police. Already a constable has fled from some fearful sight and met his death. I want tough men who won't do that. Remember, the lives of the Harmans are at stake, and I don't know what subtle trick I may have to meet. If we can take the creature alive we will do so."

"Very well, Selden, I trust you, and hope you will be able to clear up this mystery, which has been a confounded nuisance. The Press have been making very nasty remarks about undiscovered crimes lately."

"I promise you, sir, that everything shall be cleared up tonight."

"Then I'll detail the three men you ask for to be at Paddington. I'll send Graham for one; he's about the toughest man I've got, and a dead shot."

"At 3.15, then. Good-bye, sir."

Dodds held out his hand. "Good luck, Selden, and be careful, won't you? We don't want any killing if it can be avoided,"

"I will do all I can, sir, but we are dealing with a triple murderer and he will hardly be taken without a fight."

He took his leave rather hurriedly, in fear lest Dodds might revoke the order, and taxied to Bedford Row for news of O'Connor. The clerk informed him that his chief was still at Lydford, and that Mr. Coffin had left that morning without saying where he was going.

Selden proceeded thoughtfully to a post-office where he dispatched a wire to Perkins, asking him to meet the train at Lydford with a car, and a cable to Germany to Mrs. James, requesting her to return to London, and to bring Eric with her if he could be allowed to travel, asking for a reply to be sent to Cold Stairs.

He had some time at his disposal, and after a brief lunch he took the underground to Paddington Station. The express from Lydford was coming in as he arrived there, and he recalled that it was by this train that Mrs. Seaton had come up on her fatal journey.

Idly he watched the passengers emerge from the train, and then took a taxi, directing the driver to proceed to Cardigan Street. During the journey Selden watched keenly the streets through which he passed, holding his watch in his hand.

"What number?" the driver asked.

"You can drive me back again," he said coolly, to the driver's astonishment.

Three quiet, unassuming men were waiting on the platform at Paddington, one of whom was carrying a long leather case.

"Good afternoon, Graham," Dick said. "You are just the man I want for this job."

"Shall we separate, sir?"

"There is no need, the enemy has gone before us."

Graham lifted his eyebrows and laughed. "I thought, by the orders, we were after a gang, and might be watched even here. It's one man then?" There was a note of disappointment in his voice.

"If I could be quite certain that it was a man, Graham, I would tackle the job myself. As it is I prefer to have three of you, and risk being called nervous."

During the journey Selden outlined as much of the case as he thought necessary.

"It's no good looking out for this creature—I've tried that," he said. "We must use Lady Harman and her son as the bait. Don't be alarmed at anything you may see."

"You seem to have got on the track of a rum bird, Mr. Selden," Graham remarked. It had been an even chance whether Graham had become a professional burglar or joined the police force. He had excellent qualities for either, but a good home life and the influence of a Sunday School teacher for whom he had conceived a schoolboy passion, had weighted the balance, and instead of shooting policemen he had become a stout defender of law and order, and could head off and overturn a stolen car as well as any tough guy in America.

Sergeant Perkins was waiting at Lydford for them, a little worried-looking. He had hoped sincerely that nothing more would be heard with regard to the murders, and the sudden recrudescence of the affair had puzzled his head.

He had searched the woods again and again while the snow was on the ground, and tracks must be visible if made by human feet, but without result.

Selden wasted no time on explanations. On hearing that up till then nothing unusual had occurred, he drove straight to Cold Stairs, leaving his henchmen in charge of Perkins.

Lady Harman was in a very chastened mood. The disappearance of Sybil, and O'Connor's stern remarks about her suspicions of Selden, had had their effect.

The servants, following the example of the butler and footman, had packed up and gone, and she had been compelled to enlist the services of the Jenkinses as temporary helps. But for the presence of O'Connor and the telegram from Selden she would have fled to London.

Coffin had come for O'Connor's signature to documents that would brook no delay. He had merely obtained the necessary signatures and discussed business, and had then left the house as silently as he had come.

Selden took O'Connor into the study, and carefully shut the door.

"Look here, old man," the lawyer started at once, "I can't make head or tail of what is happening, but there seems to be some monkey business going on. We ought to have had these people safe in London if there is going to be trouble."

"Safe in London?" Selden echoed. "That would have been fatal. I have every reason to believe that the assassin is down here."

O'Connor stared at his friend. "And yet you keep us all here."

"Certainly; the assassin is anxious to dispose of Lady Harman and her son, but there is one person he must first get out of the way, and that is the troublous and interfering detective who is hard on his track, as he knows. That's why I have come."

"You're a brave lad," Ned said admiringly.

Selden smiled broadly. "So brave that I've brought three of the toughest of the Special Squad armed to the teeth. I'm taking no risks."

"What do you want us to do?"

"I came quite openly in a car, and he probably saw me. That will puzzle him, and he may expect us all to pack up and go. Nothing will happen till tonight, so we have time to decide on our plans."

"You know best, Dick, but I'm hanged if I can see what one man can do against such an army as you have brought."

"If we were dealing with an ordinary gangster, or even more than one, Ned, I should feel safe in my plans, but here we are up against something different, and we don't know what form the attack will take. Remember when Sir John was murdered every window and door was sealed, and yet murder was done."

"Oh, but I thought that was all accounted for by those iron rings and the faked window."

"I allowed that explanation to pass without comment; it was better so, but it's not true. Ned, the assassin was inside the house that evening."

"Then what are you going to do?"

"Leave the windows and doors as they are, and the side door unfastened. The Jenkinses will go to their cottage, and I shall have the Harmans in the dining-room where we stayed that other night. I want you to go to the village quite openly in this car, and fetch my three thugs. You must stow them away somehow out of sight, they are used to that sort of thing, and bring them here."

"That will leave you all alone."

"Exactly, and possibly an attack will be made then; I hope so, as this waiting frets one's nerves. If not, we must have an all-night sitting." Selden gave a dreary laugh.

"But why are you so certain that action will be taken tonight?"

"Because he can't afford to wait. Don't you see, Ned, that he will know that the faked telegram has been discovered by now?"

"Faked telegram?" O'Connor exclaimed.

"I never sent it, but it has helped a lot—that and Sybil's escape. She is quite safe, and out of the reach of the law, my boy."

"I thought that was your doing," O'Connor said with a grin.

Lady Harman entered the room without knocking, and came forward with her lips tightly pressed together, a sure sign that she was on her dignity.

"I would be glad to know the meaning of all this, Mr. Selden. It is quite impossible for me to continue here without servants, and I must make inquiries with regard to my ward. The whole thing seems most irregular to me."

"There are a great number of things that have seemed to you to be quite wrong," Selden replied, "including my posing as a tutor, but I can assure you that you will not have to put up with this after tonight."

"I have no intention of staying here tonight. My son and I are leaving at once for London."

O'Connor shrugged his shoulders in despair, but Selden's face assumed a stern look.

"Don't you realize, Lady Harman, that we are not playing a game? If you do as you suggest, you will meet with death. Do you understand?—Death."

The woman paled, but muttered something about the police.

"If you leave, we can do nothing for you. I won't hide from you that there is danger here, but that we have to face. Once in a London hotel, you and your son would be found strangled next morning, as Sir John was strangled in this house."

"I am entirely in your hands," Lady Harman said in a feeble voice. "Only tell us what we have to do."

"I am glad you take that line," Selden said dryly. "Send the Jenkinses home; we will manage a meal somehow. Then I want you and your son to go to the dining-room."

"You are not leaving us?"

"On the contrary, I am coming with you. Ned, off you go, and do your job."

A heavy thaw had set in, and the snow had melted, leaving thick slush on the ground. The leafless trees dripped in a melancholy fashion on the mush of dead leaves below.

The night was pitch black when O'Connor returned from Lydford and drew up at the front door.

Selden was waiting, and in a low voice instructed him to turn the car so that the back was towards the door, and the brilliant lights were shining into the darkness. Under this light-screen three silent figures slipped into the house,

Selden raised his voice.

"Thanks for the letters," he said. "I shan't want the car again, O'Connor. You had better catch the night train, which leaves at ten o'clock. See you in town."

"What's the meaning of that?" Ned whispered fiercely.

"The fewer he thinks are here, the better," Selden whispered back. "Sorry, old man, but I want him to think I'm alone here with the Harmans. Go to the doctor's house, and wait there. We may want him."

O'Connor gripped Dick's hand and started the car.

"I shan't be sorry to get back to town," he called, and started off down the drive.

The three men were waiting in the hall, and Selden led them into the study, and switched on the light. The shutters were closed and curtains drawn, and no chink of light showed outside.

Graham removed his heavy coat. "Phew! It's a muggy night, Mr. Selden. Pretty hot lying at the bottom of the car almost on top of the engine."

"Anything to report?"

Nichols and Burton, the other two, exchanged glances.

"I was in the back, sir," the former said quietly, "and I had a squint over the edge as we came up the drive. I thought I saw something, but I won't swear. This is the queerest business I've ever been on."

"What was it, Nichols?" Graham asked sharply.

"Well, I don't want to be called a frightened fool, but 'pon my soul I could have sworn I saw something in the bushes by the light of the car as it passed, but we were going a good pace."

"You need not hesitate to say. I told you not to be scared at anything."

"Well, it looked to me like a skull grinning at me, and then it disappeared as quickly as a flash of light."

Selden rubbed his hands together. "That's good," he said, to the astonishment of the others. "He's here then, and watching every movement."

Selden switched off the light and led the way into the big dining-room, where Lady Harman and William were sitting by the fire. A look of relief came to her face when she saw the stout reinforcements enter. William was white with unknown terrors, and had built up his shattered nerves with whisky.

The table was spread with a cold meal, and Selden's thoughts went back to that other night when they had all had supper in this very room. Since that night Sir John, the constable, and Mrs. Seaton had been murdered, and the Professor had died by his own hand. He shook off the gloomy thoughts, and they sat down at the table.

The police officers ate heartily, but Lady Harman and her son could scarcely touch a thing. The silent house and dark forebodings pressed heavily on them. Even a storm would have been preferable to this dead stillness, only broken by the ticking of an old grandfather clock.

Young William broke the silence. "Hang it all, Selden," he said in a rather thick voice. "Surely to goodness you could have chosen some other method than this. Why couldn't you have a man-hunt with dogs and round the beast up."

"That would be worse than waste of time. We should find nothing, and then you would have this terror hanging over you day after day. Believe me, I have thought the whole thing out, and this is the only course."

"And we have to stay here all night?" William said irritably.

"It would be wiser," Selden replied with a grim smile. "I should not advise you to wander about as Sir John did."

The baronet swore forcibly, and seized the decanter. "Now for our plans," Selden said when they had finished. "Graham, you have your automatic gun. I'm going to station you near the side door leading to garden. If anything comes along, no matter what it is, challenge, and then fire if it won't stop. Aim at the legs."

"Right, sir," Graham said with a look that boded no good to a possible assailant.

"You two will work together. You will be in the kitchen, with the window slightly open. That will command the back of the house and the passage as well. Stretch a trip cord across the passage." The two men nodded.

"But you're not going to leave us alone in here?" Lady Harman cried in alarm. "I shall remain here," Selden said calmly. The officers proceeded silently to their stations, having been cautioned not to smoke or show any light.

Selden returned to the dining-room and knocked softly as agreed. Lady Harman opened the door and let him in, and was about to lock it when Selden stopped her. He closed the door softly, and came into the room.

"You had better occupy those two arm-chairs," he said quietly.

"Lord!" William said sleepily, "I feel like bed."

"You can sleep if you like," Selden said cheerfully.

He cleared a space on the table and laid a large tray he had brought from the kitchen on it, pouring a greenish powder from a packet into a heap. The others watched him, while he fastened a wire to a small box, and buried the other end in the heap.

"What's that?" William asked.

"Emergency measures," Selden replied. "It may not be wanted, but we can't neglect any precautions."

He viewed his preparations with satisfaction, and then walked to the telephone and made a call. He waited, depressing the lever, but there was no sound. Then he slowly replaced the receiver.

"I expected that. The telephone had been disconnected."

Lady Harman's face went ashy in the white electric light.

"Then we're cut off; we can't summon help."

"It shows that our enemy is close on the track," Selden said. "I was afraid he had discovered the trap and would not act."

"I wish it were all over," Lady Harman wailed. "I feel like screaming."

"You must control yourself," Selden said soothingly.

Selden had taken a seat by the side of the table, near the door, and had placed his automatic by his side.

The fire had sunk to a dull glow, but the room was warm with a clammy, oppressive heat. The waiting time was telling even on Selden, but William lay sprawled in the arm-chair, fast asleep.

Lady Harman was trying to read, but every now and then she glanced apprehensively round the room. And then the light gave a flicker and for one second the bulbs became red globes and went out, leaving darkness behind; palpitating blackness except for the dull glow from the dying fire. Lady Harman shrieked, and clutched at Selden wildly.

"Sit down," Selden urged roughly, pushing her back. "I was expecting that."

She shuddered in his hands, but instinctively obeyed. William had started up in alarm at his mother's cry.

"We shan't have to wait long now," Selden said in a harsh whisper. "Keep quiet, both of you."

Selden was standing now, his automatic in one hand and a torch in the other, every nerve on the stretch. A slight noise, so slight that only trained ears could have caught the sound, reached him. It was as though the door were being slowly opened. Like a panther Selden crept forward and laid his hand on the door, but it was fast shut. No one could have entered in that brief space of time. He flashed his torch round to make sure, but the room was empty except for themselves. What was the meaning of this? Selden's thoughts were moving wildly. Was it some trick? There came to his nostrils a faint smell, the bitter, acrid smell he had sensed in that haunted room, but here there was something deadly behind it. A feeling of giddiness stole over him.

"What's that horrible smell?" Lady Harman gasped.

Selden clapped his handkerchief to his nose and flashed his torch on the carpet. Just inside the door lay a small wooden parcel, or so it appeared, and sudden realization came to Selden. He sprang to the window, and with desperate haste undid the shutters and flung back the casements. Then he seized the parcel and flung it out into the night and stood back choking.

The whole thing was the work of a minute, but he felt horribly sick with the heavy fumes.

"What is it, Mr. Selden?" Lady Harman whispered. "I feel quite faint."

"Some poison gas," he whispered back. "I was only just in time. Keep quite still."

He tiptoed to the window and drew in great draughts of the cold night air, staring out into the darkness.

This move on the part of the enemy was new and unexpected.

A shriek of utter terror broke the stillness, echoing through the silent house. Inhuman as it sounded, Selden recognized William's voice. He sprang to the table and touched a button and a red flare lit the room. By its lurid light he saw a thing of horror, the skull over William's shoulder, and a bony skeleton arm thrust round his neck. The lad's head was bent back and his face was purple. The grinning skull turned towards Selden as he fired at the creature's right shoulder. There was a very human yell of pain, and then William collapsed into the arm-chair. Something rushed at Selden before he could fire again, and he was hurled to the floor as the creature swept past him, a form horrible beyond words in the red light of the burning strontium powder.

Selden picked himself up like lightning as the creature disappeared through the open window. He gave one glance round. Lady Harman had fainted, but William was twitching and his hands were clutching at his neck. Selden leaped out into the darkness, and saw dimly a moving object, at which he fired.

He heard the rush of feet behind him, as Burton and Nichols came through the window.

"What is it, sir?"

"Fools, why did you leave your posts? Come along now—spread out and round the house."

A burst of fire came from the garden entrance, and Selden ran round to find Graham standing with his automatic-gun at the "ready".

"Gosh! He gave me a fright, and I'm pretty tough—what in the Lord's name is it?"

"Did you hit it?" Selden cried.

"I let drive, and I believe I did, but it sprang on me so suddenly out of the darkness. I was listening to the firing and didn't know quite what to do."

"I've hit it in the shoulder," Selden panted.

"Do you think it *can* be hit?" Graham said doubtfully.

"Very much so—but come along. I think I know where to find it. Go easy; it isn't armed, but may have poison gas. I ought to have guessed he would do that. He nearly had me."

He led the way rapidly through the woods, the others following in Indian file and past the cottage of the Jenkinses, where lights showed in the window. The cottage door opened cautiously and the old man looked out.

"Is that you, Jenkins?" Selden called softly.

"Ay, sir, what is the matter?" the old man said in a shaky voice.

"Get your wife up, and both of you go to Cold Stairs. You will find Lady Harman and her son in the dining-room. The window is open. Stay with them till I come."

He saw the door close quietly and joined the officers. "Follow me." They crept through the darkness, among the rotting vegetation by the stream, and emerged in the clearing that Selden knew so well. "Spread out—you see that mound—he's in there."

"But surely he would want to get right away."

"He had to go there; I can't explain now," Selden cried. "Spread out."

The men obeyed at once, Graham running round to the right, and the others to the left, stumbling in the pitchy darkness. Selden waited till they had taken up their positions and then advanced straight towards the entrance. Not a sound came from behind the screen of branches, and he pushed them aside. The next moment something leapt at him. He fired desperately, but two bony hands laid hold on his left arm which instinctively he had held out for protection, and with almost supernatural strength broke the bones of his forearm like a stick. The sudden, intense pain made him cry out, and a flash of light came from the automatic-gun behind him.

"Got him," Graham shouted, "a full half-dozen shots."

He came forward and flashed his torch on Selden's white face. "Are you hurt, sir?"

"You only fired just in time, Graham. He's broken my arm."

Selden reeled sick and giddy against the doorway. Then with an effort he went on with Graham, the others following. The bright gleam from the three electric torches illuminated the inside of the strange place. Lying on the floor with the arms wide spread was the figure of dread, motionless now and looking like a grotesque dummy.

Selden came forward gritting his teeth with pain.

Seen closely, the disguise was evident. The head was a huge skull, and the body was clothed in close-fitting black, on which had been sewn the bones of a skeleton, while a black, flowing cloak of flimsy material hung from the shoulders, obviously with the intention of covering the whole form if necessary.

Graham knelt by the body, from which blood was oozing, and his fingers found a hasp and hinge on each side of the skull, similar to a casque in the Middle Ages armour. The whole skull opened, and could be removed like a helmet. Before them, when this had been taken off, the watching men saw the dead face of Eric James, beautiful as in life, the blue eyes widely staring, and the lips slightly parted. He had staggered in, to die in his retreat like a stricken animal.

"Take that disguise off," Selden said. "No one must see it."

None of the other men had seen Eric in life, and Selden alone knew of his existence.

They stripped the corpse of its gruesome covering and the pitiful form of a man of remarkable physique, about twenty-five years of age, small but very powerful.

Selden groaned and caught the side of the door for support.

"This won't do, Mr. Selden," Graham said, and with practised skill bound up the broken arm with an improvised splint and made a rough sling. He offered a flask of brandy that he always carried, and Selden took a deep pull.

"Who is it?" Graham asked when Selden had thanked him.

"The son of Sir John Harman and Mrs. James, presumed to be a cripple. That's all I can tell you now. We must bring the body along, and have a search of this place tomorrow by daylight. You see, I suspected that he would have to come to this place to divest himself of his disguise and get his own clothes. If I hadn't winged him, he would probably have had time, and would have disappeared completely. Then no connection between the cripple and the murderer would have been discovered."

"It's all Greek to me, Mr. Selden, but as far as you are concerned it's bed for you for some time."

They carried the poor relic of humanity back to Cold Stairs, and Nichols was dispatched for the doctor and O'Connor. Graham took charge, as even Selden's astonishing vitality had given way, and he was put to bed.

A grey dawn was breaking when the doctor and O'Connor drove up to the house.

CHAPTER XX

SELDEN'S CASE

WHEN DR. HUGHES EXAMINED SELDEN, he found him in a bad way. In addition to the fractured arm, the fumes of the deadly gas, with which the murderer had hoped to overpower his victim, had affected him far more than either Lady Harman or her son.

Selden had picked up the deadly packet before it had time fully to discharge its contents, and had flung it out of the window, thereby saving their lives.

He lay in a high delirium for days. To O'Connor and Hughes the final revelation had come with stunning effect. All these terrible events, and the gruesome horror that had rested on Cold Stairs and the grim forest, had apparently been the work of that soft-spoken crippled boy. They could hardly credit the statement, even though they had the evidence before their own eyes. From hints that Selden had dropped from time to time, they had pictured some mysterious thing of evil, possessing magical powers, and able to change its shape and come and go unseen.

They waited impatiently until such time as Selden could impart to them the meaning of it all. In the meantime, at Selden's earnest request before he lapsed into a semi-conscious state, the identity of the dead man had been kept a secret. If Selden's remark to Graham were correct, this strange being was certainly not entitled to the name of Eric James, but was legally Wilfred Gilkie, whatever the mystery of his origin.

Lady Harman and her son had packed up and gone on the day after the attack. The good woman was highly indignant that she should have been exposed to danger, and blamed Selden, not appreciating the fact that she owed her life to him. She declared that never again would she set foot in Cold Stairs. She departed in a whirlwind of abuse and lamentation, leaving everything in the hands of O'Connor, who, she stated, was the only man she could trust.

Graham and his assistants had carefully searched the strange place that Eric had used as a "dressing-room", and found the box wherein he had kept his awful disguise, and other things no less important.

Dr. Hughes had been adamant in his orders that on no account should the detective be allowed to talk till his temperature had gone down to normal.

And then Chief Inspector Dodds, having been informed of the bare facts, came to Cold Stairs to hear the story first hand, and the doctor granted permission for Selden to tell his tale. He was propped up in bed with pillows, with his left arm heavily bandaged in a sling.

"Well," Dodds said heartily, "I congratulate you, Selden, in having run the criminal to earth, at the expense of a broken arm, but I'm hanged if I understand the meaning of the whole business, nor how you have managed to solve the mysterious affair. Now you mustn't talk more than the doctor allows, but of course we are all most anxious to hear all about it."

The doctor was sitting by the side of the bed, while O'Connor and the Chief Inspector took their places by the fire, prepared to listen.

"I will tell you all I can, and try to make it as short as possible," Selden said, "but there are some points that may be unexplained, and upon which I can only offer suggestions."

"The difficulty, of course, is Eric James."

"Poor fellow, yes," Selden said, to the astonishment of his listeners.

"A triple murderer, and you feel sorry for him!" Dodds exclaimed.

"When you have heard the whole story, you will feel the same about him. Perhaps I had better begin at the beginning, though in that mysterious box of Sybil's I found the diary of Sir John Harman, and that has revealed a lot that was unknown before. I had imagined that Eric had destroyed it when he tore it from the cover, but evidently he kept it for some purpose."

Selden put his hand down beside the bed, where the wonderful box lay open, and produced a tattered manuscript book, closely written in pencil.

"Here it is—we'll come to that in time. Perhaps I'd better tell you what I know in proper order. When I was young I used to love to put together those jig-saw puzzles; you know, the ones with an enormous number of pieces of every shape, and with no picture to guide you—that's the important point."

The doctor looked anxiously at his patient, and Selden laughed.

"No, Doc, you needn't think I'm delirious; I shall have stranger things to tell before I've finished. This problem was my jig-saw puzzle.

"The main difficulty from the very beginning lay in the fact that the actual murders were surrounded and overshadowed by the supernatural element. The whole atmosphere of this place, the wild superstitions of the people, and the fact that we were investigating manifestations of a ghostly character, distracted one from the actual blunt fact that murder had been done by human agency.

"When I came down here with Jack, I expected to see some possible phenomenon or some skylarking; I was prepared for either. The murder of Sir John came unexpectedly, so to speak. It did not seem to be part of the show, if you take my meaning. All through the investigations I tried to keep that firmly in my mind, in spite of the overwhelming evidence that something not human was at the bottom of it all. Now we know that both suppositions were right."

"You are not suggesting that Eric James was not human?" Dodds asked sharply.

"I wanted to keep that till later on, but since you have asked, I will tell you. Eric James was the son of Sir John and Mrs. James; I have ample proof of that from the confession he made. Legally he was Gilkie's son, but Gilkie, as you know, died before he was born. Dr. Gilkie had been conducting some experiments with his wife; diabolical experiments, which would, he thought, produce something outside the laws of nature. But his death put an end to the process when it was half completed, with terrible results.

"Professor Johnson knew about the experiments, but thought that Mrs. Gilkie had run away from her husband before he returned, and believed he contemplated the creation of some monster by chemical means. Everything he and Stevens said seemed to point to that. In my opinion Eric was the opposite to a moron, if you understand what I mean."

"You mean," Hughes said, "that, whereas a moron is one whose mental development has been arrested, while the body grows, here we have a case where the body development had stopped while the mind went on growing."

"Exactly. That is with regard to the outward appearance of the body, for there is no doubt that he possessed more than average strength, as I know to my cost."

"I should hazard a guess," the doctor said gravely, "that development ceased at the age of puberty—that would account for much."

"That is the conclusion I came to," Selden agreed, "but we are drifting off the narrative. To come back to the night of the murder here, I tried desperately hard to eliminate the supernatural from the case if I could. These facts were clear. No living being could have got into the house that night with all our precautions, or got out. That was certain. Very well then, logic told me that someone in the house had done the murder. We five were in the dining-room, and so could be ruled out, and I first discovered the body. There remained then Mrs. James, Eric, and Sybil. It seemed quite incredible that any of these could have strangled two vigorous men like Sir John and the constable. Any of them *could* have done it, given the necessary strength, while we were in the dining-room. Although I dismissed them entirely from my mind at the time, I am certain that subconsciously that first put me on the track of Eric. Here, at any rate, was a little bit of my jig-saw fitting in, but detached from any other piece.

"That mysterious box of Sybil's puzzled me from the first. I was certain that it played some part in the tragedy. Remember, Mrs. Seaton and Mrs. James opened it that night, and found nothing but rubbish, but Sybil said it had been entrusted to her care by this mysterious being, and she did not know what it contained. Of course we know now that Eric kept his disguise in it, and, what was almost more important, this diary.

"Somehow, I think from the beginning, I felt these gruesome trappings were too theatrical, and were a disguise, but I was surrounded on all sides by tales of the supernatural, and I could not make up my mind on that. Up to the very last, as you know, sir"—Selden turned to Dodds—"I thought Eric had some powers not human, and I had every reason to think so. Now we know that his development was abnormal, not supernatural. By the way, Doctor, those grisly marks on the constable's throat, which you said were made after death, were done with a skeleton upper and lower jaw of one of the carnivora, which we found in the box.

"There was a very peculiar smell in the room where the murder of Sir John had taken place, and that was puzzling me until I ascertained from a chemist friend of mine that this was a combination that would prevent hounds from picking up a scent in that room, and then in a flash I understood why there were no skeleton feet. They would have shown outside the room and could have been tracked. The murderer had carefully covered his feet with some material, rendering them shapeless, and leaving only flattened marks in the dust."

Selden leant over the edge of his bed and drew from the magic box two shapeless pieces of thick felt fastened to a pair of slippers.

"It all seems so simple and crude when one knows the explanation," Dodds said, examining the objects, "but go on."

"Let's take things in order. The constable's death introduced a new element. He had seen this thing escaping from the house. He was a local man who had heard stories of horrible things from his boyhood, and no wonder he fled. But he could not be allowed to get away or he would have given an accurate description. We know what happened."

"But if Eric James was at the bottom of all this, why should he want to leave the house?"

"That I only learnt when I talked with Mrs. Seaton. What I think happened was this. He kept his disguise in that box. It was the only safe place in the house. He had taken his disguise out and left rubbish in its place. Then Mrs. Seaton brought the box into her room, and she and Mrs. James were talking. He must have been furious. He could not leave the disguise in the house, which he knew would be thoroughly searched. He had to make a break for it to the woods. You remember the ambulance came, and you, Doctor, and it would not be difficult for him to slip out then. But the unfortunate constable saw him, and fled panic-stricken. He had to be silenced at all costs. After changing in the woods, he returned by the secret window, without disturbing the seals, and went to his bedroom."

"That seems logical," Dodds remarked.

"What happened next? Jack and I went through the forest and had a talk with the Jenkinses, and learnt about their daughter. I had no doubt the same creature had frightened her, but the case was so shrouded in mystery that I could not be clear in my mind that there was some evil being behind it all. Then you, Doc, gave me a very valuable clue, by showing me that spirit photograph. Here again Eric appeared. If I could accept the seemingly impossible explanation that he was not really a boy, he could quite easily have faked that by taking two photographs on the same plate one of the woodland scene, and another of his disguise propped up against the tree. His story then would have been made up for your benefit."

"But what was the object?" the doctor asked.

"Let's take things in order," Selden said. "I went over the events in my mind. It was very peculiar that neither of the children had heard that shriek which echoed through the silent house. Mrs. James said they had not been disturbed. But I felt she was lying for some reason.

"I told you, Doctor, you remember, that you had not told me everything and I might ask for your assistance. You were not called in when Eric was supposed to be injured? Why not? It hurt your pride, I know, and Mrs. James stated that she had taken Eric to a specialist in London on several occasions, but there was nothing but her word. I felt that something was wrong here. Had she a secret about Eric she could not allow a doctor to investigate? Later on I put it to the test. When I saw Eric in London at their lodgings, I offered to help with his cushions, and in doing so took his arm. It was like a bar of iron. Here was another little bit of jig-saw, but if I had told you, sir"—he turned to Chief Inspector Dodds—"that this boy, a cripple, was the murderer, or even that I suspected him, you would have said I was mad. I had then no motive and nothing to go upon. Only wild speculation. All I had at this time was a suspicion that the boy had been playing about with this horrible disguise, had frightened that poor girl Anne out of her senses, probably by accident, for she too was included in the 'secret of the woods' that possessed Sybil."

"But why should he have run about in the woods like that?" the doctor asked.

"That is obvious. If he were seen as himself something would come out, but to get to his secret den he had to dress up. You must remember he kept his disguise in the house in Sybil's box. Then we come to Sybil's wild story, which was most illuminating. She used to slip out by that window, which, by the way, is very old, and was probably constructed by some amorous Harman in the past, with the rings, for his own purposes. Her tale told me quite a lot. It was imagination mixed with truth. She said the strange being called her. At once my mind went to the fact that Eric slept in the next room, and could have opened the faked window and spoken through his own. Then when the girl had gone down the rings, he could follow and get to the place first."

Selden picked up the contents of the box from the floor. There were tinsel adornments and a sort of spangled dress or robe, looking shoddy in the daylight. "He used to dress up and pose as a sort of mystery creature, the god of the woods, as she called him, and taught her that rigmarole which surprised Professor Johnson, and gave me another piece of my puzzle.

"If my theory was true, then Eric, or some 'familiar' at his disposal, for I could not entirely eradicate the supernatural idea from my mind, had got the inhabitants thoroughly scared, and had obtained a hold over the girl, so that her whole soul was absorbed in this queer woodland mystery.

"By this time I had got to the stage when I began to think that Eric was, in some strange way, an older person than anyone had imagined. My talk with the Committee of Three was startling. Professor Johnson slipped out his hatred of Dr. Gilkie and his experiments, and at the same time declared that he had no son. Again the Frankenstein idea came to me, but I firmly dismissed it, and sought a reasonable explanation. Gilkie's son, if he existed, would be about twenty-six. There was a strange mystery about his birth, but he had been left the entire property.

"No one seemed to know where or who he was. But the will had been revoked, and this man had been done out of his inheritance. At once all my theories about Eric seemed to crumple like a pack of cards. It seemed so obvious then that this mysterious Gilkie was at the bottom of the whole business, with powers perhaps beyond nature. Everything seemed to fit in! The manifestations had begun, you will recall, at the very time that Lady Harman came to Cold Stairs and forced Harman to alter his will. If Gilkie had been aware of this, it was only too likely that he would first create an atmosphere of the supernatural, so that when he actually murdered the man who had done him this wrong, the stage was all set for a sensational crime. The visit of the Committee of Three provided him with an opportunity he could never have made for himself."

"All that is quite clear now," Dodds said, as Selden paused to take a drink that the doctor held out for him.

"Fool that I was," Selden went on. "I had two large pieces of my jig-saw, but they did not connect. One was Eric and the other was this mystery man, whom, of course, I had never met at that time. Then came Mrs. Seaton's death, and that seemed to rule Eric out for the moment."

"I thought you were trying to bring the Professor into that," Dodds said with a smile.

"Deliberately—I wanted the murderer to feel secure. On the day of Mrs. Seaton's murder, I had been round to the lodgings where Mrs. James was living with the two children. That was when I discovered that Eric had strength far above his appearance. Directly I left Stevens's house, I went back to the lodgings, and found that Eric was not there. A cripple, mind you, and he had gone out into the London streets, for Mrs. James and Sybil had gone to the pictures.

"I think it was then that I guessed that Gilkie and Eric were one and the same person. Then things shaped themselves in my mind. Undoubtedly he had staged that accident, partly to take any suspicion from himself, and partly to make the tale of the apparition more plausible. It also gave him the opportunity of coming to London ostensibly to see a specialist.

"Eric went to Germany with his mother; I verified that. They did go to a spa and consulted a specialist, but it was not about his back, which was perfectly sound, but with regard to his strange condition. I have heard the story from the German doctor, though only after telling him what I already knew.

"As long as he was there I could get my facts together, but the sudden arrival of Gilkie brought matters to a climax. It was a strong move on his part, for he was free to move about as he liked as Gilkie, but could at any moment return to the cripple boy. But he just overreached himself. He could disguise his face and hair and voice, but there was one feature he could not alter: his strange china-blue eyes. I recognized him by that when he came to my room, but I am afraid he also saw that I had recognized him, and that was fatal. If Jack had not been present, I believe he would have attacked me then and there. War was declared, and I could see what he was after. He knew I was on his track, but, trusting to his disguise, he hoped to get away to Germany.

"I saw imminent danger to Lady Harman and her son. He wired to keep them at Cold Stairs, and hoped to get them before I found out. He might have succeeded but for the lucky chance of Sybil coming to town."

"That's a part I don't understand," O'Connor interrupted. "What did he want with her?"

"He had an immense hold over her, and I think he hoped that he could continue to dominate her will, and prevent any love affair. His motive, I suppose, ultimately, when the time came, was to marry her, as Eric. That is guess work.

"I had his fingerprints, and had already got those of Eric, and they were identical. I had a case almost complete, but there was no time for reports or waiting. I came straight down here, with the result you know."

"It's a most amazing story," the doctor said. "We have no real explanation of Eric's strange condition, and I don't suppose we shall ever know now."

"The only person who could tell us is Mrs. James. I had an answer to my wire from the German doctor to the effect that Mrs. James and her son had left the spa some few days ago, and left no address."

"Well," Dodds said, rising and stretching himself, "that's about as far as we can take the matter, I'm afraid. At any rate you have solved the problem of these murders, Selden, and I congratulate you on that. We shall have no more mysterious business down here. I really think all that need be made public is that Gilkie, having been dispossessed of what he thought was coming to him, took his revenge on Sir John Harman. It is quite true as far as it goes, and avoids anything sensational."

"The difficulty is," Selden said, "the identification of the body. Of course we know it is that of Wilfred Gilkie, but if any of the jury want to see it, as is their right, there may be some bother."

The doctor looked across at Dodds. "You forget you have been laid up here in bed. That difficulty will not occur. He is already buried."

"Without identification?" Selden said incredulously.

"Hardly; we did not tell you until you had told your story, but now we can do so, because it proves, if any lingering doubt remained, that what you have put together with such care is the truth. When I examined the body, as soon as I arrived here, it was that of a boy, undeveloped except for extraordinary musculature. It was without a single hair on face or body, and smooth as a child. The following day, when I went to the mortuary, a startling change had come. I simply can't account for it, except from what you have told us. The mysterious influence that had arrested development seemed to have been lifted with death, and to all appearances there lay the body of a man of twenty odd years, with full development, unrecognizable as Eric, but with a very strong resemblance to Gilkie when he had disguised himself."

"Now there is nothing more for you to do except get well," Dodds said briskly. "I must return to London, and get along with my arrears of work."

"I've had a wire from Jack," Dick said with a laugh. "As I hoped, they have fixed things up, and are off on a joy-ride somewhere. That will end all this mystery of the woods business."

CHAPTER XXI

MRS. JAMES EXPLAINS

Three years had passed since the death of this mysterious creature, victim of a scientist's evil experiment, and the case had merely become a record in Scotland Yard.

Lady Harman had absolutely refused to return to Cold Stairs, and had led a wandering life such as a woman of her tastes would find most interesting. She was well known at most of the higher-class boarding-houses both in English and foreign spas.

Although there was nothing really the matter with her, she had convinced herself that she had never got over the shock of that awful night, and was never tired of telling the story with embellishments.

The death of Sir William had aged her. The youth had run riot with his unexpected money, and had taken to road-hogging. While at Oxford, after a "binge", he had gone for a joy-ride, and nothing but the battered fragments of his car and the body thrown into a field remained to tell how he had met his end.

O'Connor had tactfully dealt with the new situation, and had been able to fix matters so that Sybil should have Cold Stairs, which Lady Harman was only too glad to relinquish, and a sufficient sum from the estate to maintain her position until such time as Lady Harman departed to another world.

Jack and Sybil had read the account of the events at Cold Stairs, as far as the newspaper accounts went, and decided to cut short their joy-ride and return to Lydford.

Jack felt that there was no need to keep the news from the girl, and was anxious about Dick.

One fact Selden insisted on keeping from Sybil: the connection of Eric with the crimes, and she was informed later that he had died in Germany.

Jack and Sybil falteringly announced their engagement, and the only comment Lady Harman had made was that it was the only honourable course for Jack to take.

Sybil had absolutely refused to return to Lady Harman, and as she was too young for any thought of immediate matrimony, things had reached a deadlock when Dodds, who had been immensely interested in the story, offered her a home with him and his wife.

And so, after three years, Jack and Sybil returned to take up their residence at Cold Stairs, after their honeymoon.

Selden had been busy with his work, but he and O'Connor frequently slipped down for week-ends, and Dr. Hughes joined them at bridge.

It was on a calm spring evening, when the country was looking at its best, and the whole party were gathered for a week-end, that a telegram arrived for Selden.

He read it through, while Sybil watched him, fearing bad news.

"I am very sorry," he said, "but I shall have to return at once to town."

"What a nuisance," Sybil said. "Why can't they leave you alone over the week-end?"

"My time doesn't belong to me," Selden said with a light laugh.

"One of your cases, I suppose?" Jack asked, too absorbed in watching Sybil to notice the grey look that had come to Dick's face.

"Yes, one of my cases."

He pushed the telegram carelessly into his pocket, and went indoors to pack, but his mind was full of excitement and dread, for the wire had read: *Mrs. James dying in St. Barnabas Hospital. Asking for you. Come at once or you will be too late.*

He travelled up by the night train, and in the grey morning stood by the bedside of the dying woman.

He would hardly have recognized her. The hair was white and untidy, and she had a woeful appearance of neglect and hunger. The doctor told Selden that there was no specific disease, but the woman was simply fading out, probably, he thought, from ill-nourishment and drink. As Selden looked into those tortured eyes, he knew from what cause she was dying without being told. He sat by the bed, round which a screen had been drawn. Knowing that Selden had been sent for from Scotland Yard, the authorities guessed that some sort of confession was the reason, and left them alone.

"I sent for you, Mr. Selden," Mrs. James gasped. "I had to tell you the truth, for nothing matters now."

"I think I know most of the story," Selden said gently. "Don't say anything you would rather not."

"I must tell you!" she cried with sudden spirit. "I can't go to my grave without doing that."

"Very well, Mrs. James, if you insist, but I can spare you a lot. I know that Eric was the son of Sir John Harman, for example."

"Was he?" she flared out. "In the ordinary sense he was, and bitterly have I repented, and so did Sir John, but we both thought my husband was dead. We ought to have waited. It's no good going into all that. My husband took his fiendish revenge. He found out when he came back from abroad, though I never told him who was the father, and he injected some horrible fluid into me day after day. . . . I don't know what it was. He had been experimenting for years. It did me no harm, and when Eric was born I was so delighted that he was a normal, healthy baby. There was nothing wrong with him as a child, except that I noticed a tendency to cruelty; he once tortured a cat to death, and maimed a dog with a stone. But I had begun to think that my husband had been wrong in his theories, or that his death had mercifully come in time before he completed his wicked experiment." She paused, panting, and Selden held a glass that stood beside the bed to her lips.

"It was when he was about fourteen that I noticed something really wrong. He developed violent fits of passion, and several times attacked me for no reason. But when these fits were over he did not seem to remember anything. I took him to a doctor, but he could do nothing, only from his manner I judged that he thought he was a mental case, and I was afraid they would try to put him away in some home. From that time, Mr. Selden, his growth stopped."

"At the age of puberty."

"Exactly; he remained to all outward appearance a child, but his mind had been affected by this terrible drug, and he became a fiend. He hated his state, but of course knew nothing of his birth. I can't tell you all, Mr. Selden, I have neither the time nor the heart to do so. His strength became abnormal, and he began to see some advantage in his strange condition. He took to burglary, and was never discovered, for who would suspect this blue-eyed boy of such crimes? My money ran out, and I was ill, and we lived on the proceeds of his stealing. In despair I went to Professor Johnson, as I had no one to consult. I had known him when my husband was alive."

"I begin to see," Selden muttered.

"I ought to have told him the whole story perhaps, but I would not bring in John Harman. Foolishly, I told him of the injections, and he would hear no more. He jumped to a wrong conclusion. He thought somehow that Eric was the result of some diabolical chemical experiment, and drove me from the house. It was many years later that he came to Cold Stairs, and I had altered a great deal. He did not recognize me, and I avoided him as much as possible.

"I can't tell you of those frightful years. I expected something dreadful would happen, for Eric had developed sadistic tendencies.

"At last Sir John came back from Assam, and I met him in London. He had come into the title, and he told me he was married secretly. Of course, seeing Eric as a mere boy, he had no idea that there was any connection between him and our disastrous friendship, and I did not undeceive him. He imagined, I suppose, that I had married again, and lost my husband. Out of pity he took me to Cold Stairs as governess to Sybil. Eric took to strange wanderings in the woods, harmless enough then, but his mind was that of an intelligent man, and he realized the horrible fate in store for him. He could never marry, or follow the normal life of man, for at any moment those fits of passion might come on, when he was unable to control himself. He might perhaps have become reconciled to his lot in time, or possibly he might have grown out of his strange state, but in an evil moment he discovered a diary that Sir John had kept, telling of our old liaison. It was written when he had heard that Dr. Gilkie was alive, and was coming back to England, and we had both been faced with the awful position, knowing that a child of our folly was to be expected. For some reason he had never destroyed it. Eric read the story and taxed me with it, and I was compelled to tell him the truth.

"He made me tell John there had been a son, and that he was alive, but we could not let him know that Eric was that son. I think Eric would have killed himself rather than allow his secret to become known. He was terribly sensitive about it. John then made a will leaving everything to this son, for Eric had forced me to say that if he did not do that he would return and bring the whole matter up.

"From that moment, I am afraid, the idea of murder came into Eric's mind, and I believe he planned the whole thing with diabolical cunning. I could only watch in agony, fearing the worst. He started to create an atmosphere of something dreadful, and, of course, you will have guessed that he never fell down the stairs, but invented the story in order that, as a cripple, he would never be suspected of being a murderer."

"Tell me one thing, Mrs. James," Selden asked. "Did Eric know of the second will, or of the marriage?"

"Never! I think if he had done so, he would have had the whole thing out with John. He would certainly not have murdered him to enable Lady Harman to take possession."

"Why did he teach Anne Jenkins and Sybil that strange ritual of the woods?"

"You know about that? I am afraid I can understand only too well. He wanted power, dominance, and worship. He knew that being immature in a bodily sense, he could only obtain that by mysticism. It gave him a horrible pleasure to pretend to be a supernatural being. I only found out that when we were in Germany, and he revealed all that I am telling you."

"I think that clears up the mystery," Selden said. He felt a sense of loathing creeping over him at the thought of all that had taken place at Cold Stairs and in the dim woods. He could visualize this tortured, deformed mind planning his revenge, and gloating over his victim.

Mrs. James went on feebly: "You will call him a murderer, Mr. Seldon, but the real murderer was my husband. Had he lived, there is no knowing what further devilry he would have done. He held that he could make any type of man or woman by such treatment as he gave me."

Selden saw that the woman could not say much more in her exhausted state, and refrained from more details about the past. He only asked one vital question.

"Did you know about the murder?"

"It is hard for me to say. Looking back now, I suppose I had guessed, for I knew that Eric had left his room, as he frequently had done for years, to wander into the woods at night, and I hoped he had gone there that night. I lied when I said that the children had slept through the night. There was a door, you know, from Eric's room to the passage, as well as that to the play-room where Sybil was."

"I know; I saw it, and that was one of the first things that made me suspicious."

"Of course, Mr. Selden, when we got away to Germany I had no doubt. He as good as told me. He left me there to answer any inquiries, and went by air to Egypt, where he joined the boat for Marseilles. I never saw him again."

Her eyes closed, and Selden rose to summon a doctor. He heard her muttering to herself, and bent low to listen.

"You sent Mrs. Seaton to my room after the murder, and she saw Eric in his disguise going off from the house to his retreat in the woods. She put a supernatural explanation on it, but when she came down to Cold Stairs she got the story of Anne Jenkins from the parents, and then guessed half the truth. She came to see Eric and found him alone, and asked for an explanation.

"It was all too easy when she thought he was a cripple boy, The place was empty, and he strangled her. Then he put her into his bath-chair and wheeled her to that lonely place in a foggy street and left her, wheeling the chair back. He told me the whole story in Germany before he went."

The voice died out in faint, indistinct murmurings that Selden could not catch. He hastily summoned the sister, but before a doctor could arrive Mrs. James was dead. It seemed that she had kept herself alive by an effort of will until the dreadful tale had been told.

THE END

RAMBLE HOUSE's

HARRY STEPHEN KEELER WEBWORK MYSTERIES

(RH) indicates the title is available ONLY in the **RAMBLE HOUSE** edition

The Ace of Spades Murder
The Affair of the Bottled Deuce (RH)
The Amazing Web
The Barking Clock
Behind That Mask
The Book with the Orange Leaves
The Bottle with the Green Wax Seal
The Box from Japan
The Case of the Canny Killer
The Case of the Crazy Corpse (RH)
The Case of the Flying Hands (RH)
The Case of the Ivory Arrow
The Case of the Jeweled Ragpicker
The Case of the Lavender Gripsack
The Case of the Mysterious Moll
The Case of the 16 Beans
The Case of the Transparent Nude (RH)
The Case of the Transposed Legs
The Case of the Two-Headed Idiot (RH)
The Case of the Two Strange Ladies
The Circus Stealers (RH)
Cleopatra's Tears
A Copy of Beowulf (RH)
The Crimson Cube (RH)
The Face of the Man From Saturn
Find the Clock
The Five Silver Buddhas
The 4th King
The Gallows Waits, My Lord! (RH)
The Green Jade Hand
Finger! Finger!
Hangman's Nights (RH)
I, Chameleon (RH)
I Killed Lincoln at 10:13! (RH)
The Iron Ring
The Man Who Changed His Skin (RH)
The Man with the Crimson Box
The Man with the Magic Eardrums
The Man with the Wooden Spectacles
The Marceau Case
The Matilda Hunter Murder
The Monocled Monster

The Murder of London Lew
The Murdered Mathematician
The Mysterious Card (RH)
The Mysterious Ivory Ball of Wong Shing Li (RH)
The Mystery of the Fiddling Cracksman
The Peacock Fan
The Photo of Lady X (RH)
The Portrait of Jirjohn Cobb
Report on Vanessa Hewstone (RH)
Riddle of the Travelling Skull
Riddle of the Wooden Parrakeet (RH)
The Scarlet Mummy (RH)
The Search for X-Y-Z
The Sharkskin Book
Sing Sing Nights
The Six From Nowhere (RH)
The Skull of the Waltzing Clown
The Spectacles of Mr. Cagliostro
Stand By—London Calling!
The Steeltown Strangler
The Stolen Gravestone (RH)
Strange Journey (RH)
The Strange Will
The Straw Hat Murders (RH)
The Street of 1000 Eyes (RH)
Thieves' Nights
Three Novellos (RH)
The Tiger Snake
The Trap (RH)
Vagabond Nights (Defrauded Yeggman)
Vagabond Nights 2 (10 Hours)
The Vanishing Gold Truck
The Voice of the Seven Sparrows
The Washington Square Enigma
When Thief Meets Thief
The White Circle (RH)
The Wonderful Scheme of Mr. Christopher Thorne
X. Jones—of Scotland Yard
Y. Cheung, Business Detective

Keeler Related Works

A To Izzard: A Harry Stephen Keeler Companion by Fender Tucker — Articles and stories about Harry, by Harry, and in his style. Included is a compleat bibliography.

Wild About Harry: Reviews of Keeler Novels — Edited by Richard Polt & Fender Tucker — 22 reviews of works by Harry Stephen Keeler from *Keeler News*. A perfect introduction to the author.

The Keeler Keyhole Collection: Annotated newsletter rants from Harry Stephen Keeler, edited by Francis M. Nevins. Over 400 pages of incredibly personal Keeleriana.

Fakealoo — Pastiches of the style of Harry Stephen Keeler by selected demented members of the HSK Society. Updated every year with the new winner.

RAMBLE HOUSE's OTHER LOONS

The End of It All and Other Stories — Ed Gorman's latest short story collection

Four Dancing Tuatara Press Books — *Beast or Man?* By Sean M'Guire; *The Whistling Ancestors* by Richard E. Goddard; *The Shadow on the House* and *Sorcerer's Chessmen* by Mark Hansom. With introductions by John Pelan

The Dumpling — Political murder from 1907 by Coulson Kernahan

Victims & Villains — Intriguing Sherlockiana from Derham Groves

Evidence in Blue — 1938 mystery by E. Charles Vivian

The Case of the Little Green Men — Mack Reynolds wrote this love song to sci-fi fans back in 1951 and it's now back in print.

Hell Fire — A new hard-boiled novel by Jack Moskovitz about an arsonist, an arson cop and a Nazi hooker. It isn't pretty.

Researching American-Made Toy Soldiers — A 276-page collection of a lifetime of articles by toy soldier expert Richard O'Brien

Strands of the Web: Short Stories of Harry Stephen Keeler — Edited and Introduced by Fred Cleaver

The Sam McCain Novels — Ed Gorman's terrific series includes *The Day the Music Died, Wake Up Little Susie* and *Will You Still Love Me Tomorrow?*

A Shot Rang Out — Three decades of reviews by Jon Breen

Mysterious Martin, the Master of Murder — Two versions of a strange 1912 novel by Tod Robbins about a man who writes books that can kill.

Dago Red — 22 tales of dark suspense by Bill Pronzini

The Night Remembers — A 1991 Jack Walsh mystery from Ed Gorman

Rough Cut & New, Improved Murder — Ed Gorman's first two novels

Hollywood Dreams — A novel of the Depression by Richard O'Brien

Seven Gelett Burgess Novels — *The Master of Mysteries, The White Cat, Two O'Clock Courage, Ladies in Boxes, Find the Woman, The Heart Line, The Picaroons*

The Organ Reader — A huge compilation of just about everything published in the 1971-1972 radical bay-area newspaper, *THE ORGAN*.

A Clear Path to Cross — Sharon Knowles short mystery stories by Ed Lynskey

Old Times' Sake — Short stories by James Reasoner from Mike Shayne Magazine

Freaks and Fantasies — Eerie tales by Tod Robbins, collaborator of Tod Browning on the film FREAKS.

Seven Jim Harmon Double Novels — *Vixen Hollow/Celluloid Scandal, The Man Who Made Maniacs/Silent Siren, Ape Rape/Wanton Witch, Sex Burns Like Fire/Twist Session, Sudden Lust/Passion Strip, Sin Unlimited/Harlot Master, Twilight Girls/Sex Institution*. Written in the early 60s.

Marblehead: A Novel of H.P. Lovecraft — A long-lost masterpiece from Richard A. Lupoff. Published for the first time!

The Compleat Ova Hamlet — Parodies of SF authors by Richard A. Lupoff – A brand new edition with more stories and more illustrations by Trina Robbins.

The Secret Adventures of Sherlock Holmes — Three Sherlockian pastiches by the Brooklyn author/publisher, Gary Lovisi.

The Universal Holmes — Richard A. Lupoff's 2007 collection of five Holmesian pastiches and a recipe for giant rat stew.

Four Joel Townsley Rogers Novels — By the author of *The Red Right Hand: Once In a Red Moon, Lady With the Dice, The Stopped Clock, Never Leave My Bed*

Two Joel Townsley Rogers Story Collections — Night of Horror and Killing Time

Twenty Norman Berrow Novels — *The Bishop's Sword, Ghost House, Don't Go Out After Dark, Claws of the Cougar, The Smokers of Hashish, The Secret Dancer, Don't Jump Mr. Boland!, The Footprints of Satan, Fingers for Ransom, The Three Tiers of Fantasy, The Spaniard's Thumb, The Eleventh Plague, Words Have Wings, One Thrilling Night, The Lady's in Danger, It Howls at Night, The Terror in the Fog, Oil Under the Window, Murder in the Melody, The Singing Room*

The N. R. De Mexico Novels — Robert Bragg presents *Marijuana Girl, Madman on a Drum, Private Chauffeur* in one volume.

Four Chelsea Quinn Yarbro Novels featuring Charlie Moon — *Ogilvie, Tallant and Moon, Music When the Sweet Voice Dies, Poisonous Fruit* and *Dead Mice*

Five Walter S. Masterman Mysteries — *The Green Toad, The Flying Beast, The Yellow Mistletoe, The Wrong Verdict* and *The Perjured Alibi*. Fantastic impossible plots.

Two Hake Talbot Novels — *Rim of the Pit, The Hangman's Handyman*. Classic locked room mysteries.

Two Alexander Laing Novels — *The Motives of Nicholas Holtz* and *Dr. Scarlett*, stories of medical mayhem and intrigue from the 30s.

Four David Hume Novels — *Corpses Never Argue, Cemetery First Stop, Make Way for the Mourners, Eternity Here I Come,* and more to come.

Three Wade Wright Novels — *Echo of Fear, Death At Nostalgia Street* and *It Leads to Murder,* with more to come!

Eight Rupert Penny Novels — *Policeman's Holiday, Policeman's Evidence, Lucky Policeman, Policeman in Armour, Sealed Room Murder, Sweet Poison, The Talkative Policeman, She had to Have Gas* and *Cut and Run* (by Martin Tanner.)

Five Jack Mann Novels — Strange murder in the English countryside. *Gees' First Case, Nightmare Farm, Grey Shapes, The Ninth Life, The Glass Too Many.*

Seven Max Afford Novels — *Owl of Darkness, Death's Mannikins, Blood on His Hands, The Dead Are Blind, The Sheep and the Wolves, Sinners in Paradise* and *Two Locked Room Mysteries and a Ripping Yarn* by one of Australia's finest novelists.

Five Joseph Shallit Novels — *The Case of the Billion Dollar Body, Lady Don't Die on My Doorstep, Kiss the Killer, Yell Bloody Murder, Take Your Last Look.* One of America's best 50's authors.

Two Crimson Clown Novels — By Johnston McCulley, author of the Zorro novels, *The Crimson Clown* and *The Crimson Clown Again.*

The Best of 10-Story Book — edited by Chris Mikul, over 35 stories from the literary magazine Harry Stephen Keeler edited.

A Young Man's Heart — A forgotten early classic by Cornell Woolrich

The Anthony Boucher Chronicles — edited by Francis M. Nevins
Book reviews by Anthony Boucher written for the *San Francisco Chronicle,* 1942 – 1947. Essential and fascinating reading.

Muddled Mind: Complete Works of Ed Wood, Jr. — David Hayes and Hayden Davis deconstruct the life and works of a mad genius.

Gadsby — A lipogram (a novel without the letter E). Ernest Vincent Wright's last work, published in 1939 right before his death.

My First Time: The One Experience You Never Forget — Michael Birchwood — 64 true first-person narratives of how they lost it.

A Roland Daniel Double: The Signal and The Return of Wu Fang — Classic thrillers from the 30s

Murder in Shawnee — Two novels of the Alleghenies by John Douglas: *Shawnee Alley Fire* and *Haunts.*

Deep Space and other Stories — A collection of SF gems by Richard A. Lupoff

Blood Moon — The first of the Robert Payne series by Ed Gorman

The Time Armada — Fox B. Holden's 1953 SF gem.

Black River Falls — Suspense from the master, Ed Gorman

Sideslip — 1968 SF masterpiece by Ted White and Dave Van Arnam

The Triune Man — Mindscrambling science fiction from Richard A. Lupoff

Detective Duff Unravels It — Episodic mysteries by Harvey O'Higgins

Automaton — Brilliant treatise on robotics: 1928-style! By H. Stafford Hatfield

The Incredible Adventures of Rowland Hern — Rousing 1928 impossible crimes by Nicholas Olde.

Slammer Days — Two full-length prison memoirs: *Men into Beasts* (1952) by George Sylvester Viereck and *Home Away From Home* (1962) by Jack Woodford

Murder in Black and White — 1931 classic tennis whodunit by Evelyn Elder

Killer's Caress — Cary Moran's 1936 hardboiled thriller

The Golden Dagger — 1951 Scotland Yard yarn by E. R. Punshon

A Smell of Smoke — 1951 English countryside thriller by Miles Burton

Ruled By Radio — 1925 futuristic novel by Robert L. Hadfield & Frank E. Farncombe

Murder in Silk — A 1937 Yellow Peril novel of the silk trade by Ralph Trevor

The Case of the Withered Hand — 1936 potboiler by John G. Brandon

Finger-prints Never Lie — A 1939 classic detective novel by John G. Brandon

Inclination to Murder — 1966 thriller by New Zealand's Harriet Hunter

Invaders from the Dark — Classic werewolf tale from Greye La Spina

Fatal Accident — Murder by automobile, a 1936 mystery by Cecil M. Wills

The Devil Drives — A prison and lost treasure novel by Virgil Markham

Dr. Odin — Douglas Newton's 1933 potboiler comes back to life.

The Chinese Jar Mystery — Murder in the manor by John Stephen Strange, 1934

The Julius Caesar Murder Case — A classic 1935 re-telling of the assassination by Wallace Irwin that's much more fun than the Shakespeare version

West Texas War and Other Western Stories — by Gary Lovisi

The Contested Earth and Other SF Stories — A never-before published space opera and seven short stories by Jim Harmon.

Tales of the Macabre and Ordinary — Modern twisted horror by Chris Mikul, author of the *Bizarrism* series.

The Gold Star Line — Seaboard adventure from L.T. Reade and Robert Eustace.

The Werewolf vs the Vampire Woman — Hard to believe ultraviolence by either Arthur M. Scarm or Arthur M. Scram.

Black Hogan Strikes Again — Australia's Peter Renwick pens a tale of the outback.

Don Diablo: Book of a Lost Film — Two-volume treatment of a western by Paul Landres, with diagrams. Intro by Francis M. Nevins.

The Charlie Chaplin Murder Mystery — Movie hijinks by Wes D. Gehring

The Koky Comics — A collection of all of the 1978-1981 Sunday and daily comic strips by Richard O'Brien and Mort Gerberg, in two volumes.

Suzy — Another collection of comic strips from Richard O'Brien and Bob Vojtko

Dime Novels: Ramble House's 10-Cent Books — *Knife in the Dark* by Robert Leslie Bellem, *Hot Lead* and *Song of Death* by Ed Earl Repp, *A Hashish House in New York* by H.H. Kane, and five more.

Blood in a Snap — The *Finnegan's Wake* of the 21st century, by Jim Weiler

Stakeout on Millennium Drive — Award-winning Indianapolis Noir — Ian Woollen.

Dope Tales #1 — Two dope-riddled classics; *Dope Runners* by Gerald Grantham and *Death Takes the Joystick* by Phillip Condé.

Dope Tales #2 — Two more narco-classics; *The Invisible Hand* by Rex Dark and *The Smokers of Hashish* by Norman Berrow.

Dope Tales #3 — Two enchanting novels of opium by the master, Sax Rohmer. *Dope* and *The Yellow Claw.*

Tenebrae — Ernest G. Henham's 1898 horror tale brought back.

The Singular Problem of the Stygian House-Boat — Two classic tales by John Kendrick Bangs about the denizens of Hades.

Tiresias — Psychotic modern horror novel by Jonathan M. Sweet.

The One After Snelling — Kickass modern noir from Richard O'Brien.

The Sign of the Scorpion — 1935 Edmund Snell tale of oriental evil.

The House of the Vampire — 1907 poetic thriller by George S. Viereck.

An Angel in the Street — Modern hardboiled noir by Peter Genovese.

The Devil's Mistress — Scottish gothic tale by J. W. Brodie-Innes.

The Lord of Terror — 1925 mystery with master-criminal, Fantômas.

The Lady of the Terraces — 1925 adventure by E. Charles Vivian.

My Deadly Angel — 1955 Cold War drama by John Chelton

Prose Bowl — Futuristic satire — Bill Pronzini & Barry N. Malzberg .

Satan's Den Exposed — True crime in Truth or Consequences New Mexico — Award-winning journalism by the *Desert Journal*.

The Amorous Intrigues & Adventures of Aaron Burr — by Anonymous — Hot historical action.

I Stole $16,000,000 — A true story by cracksman Herbert E. Wilson.

The Black Dark Murders — Vintage 50s college murder yarn by Milt Ozaki, writing as Robert O. Saber.

Sex Slave — Potboiler of lust in the days of Cleopatra — Dion Leclercq.

You'll Die Laughing — Bruce Elliott's 1945 novel of murder at a practical joker's English countryside manor.

The Private Journal & Diary of John H. Surratt — The memoirs of the man who conspired to assassinate President Lincoln.

Dead Man Talks Too Much — Hollywood boozer by Weed Dickenson.

Red Light — History of legal prostitution in Shreveport Louisiana by Eric Brock. Includes wonderful photos of the houses and the ladies.

A Snark Selection — Lewis Carroll's *The Hunting of the Snark* with two Snarkian chapters by Harry Stephen Keeler — Illustrated by Gavin L. O'Keefe.

Ripped from the Headlines! — The Jack the Ripper story as told in the newspaper articles in the *New York* and *London Times.*

Geronimo — S. M. Barrett's 1905 autobiography of a noble American.

The White Peril in the Far East — Sidney Lewis Gulick's 1905 indictment of the West and assurance that Japan would never attack the U.S.

The Compleat Calhoon — All of Fender Tucker's works: Includes *Totah Six-Pack, Weed, Women and Song* and *Tales from the Tower,* plus a CD of all of his songs.

Totah Six-Pack — Just Fender Tucker's six tales about Farmington in one sleek volume.

RAMBLE HOUSE

Fender Tucker, Prop.

www.ramblehouse.com   fender@ramblehouse.com

228-826-1783   10329 Sheephead Drive, Vancleave MS 39565

www.ingramcontent.com/pod-product-compliance
Lightning Source LLC
Chambersburg PA
CBHW030518020726
47494CB00004B/1146